"I get why you're here. Your sister needs you. Your whole family needs you."

Kyle slammed the lid closed on the trash can. "Just don't take your failings out on the rest of us."

Ashleigh stood so quickly her chair nearly tipped over. "My failings?" Such nerve. So he did blame her for the miscarriages. "I'm here, aren't I?"

He shrugged. "Physically."

What did he want from her? Didn't he realize how difficult this was? Coming back to the town where her life had fallen apart.

She stepped to the opposite counter, her back to him. A single tear rolled down her cheek—she'd be damned if she'd give him the satisfaction of seeing her wipe it away.

"I get it." Her voice was hoarse with emotion. "You don't want me here."

"If only that were true."

Before she could spin around and ask what he meant, he had vanished from the kitchen.

LISA DYSON

—

A Perfect Homecoming

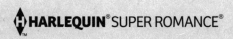
HARLEQUIN® SUPER ROMANCE®

Recycling programs for this product may not exist in your area.

ISBN-13: 978-0-373-60855-3

A PERFECT HOMECOMING

Copyright © 2014 by Lisa Dyson

Printed in U.S.A.

ABOUT THE AUTHOR

Lisa Dyson has wanted to create stories ever since she got an A on a writing prompt in fifth grade. She devoured the Nancy Drew series as much for the mystery as for the relationship between Nancy and Ned. So it came as no surprise to her that her stories revolve around romantic relationships.

Before she stayed home to raise her three sons and volunteer for every sport and activity her children participated in, Lisa worked as a medical assistant and a secretary/administrative assistant. She grew up in a small eastern Pennsylvania town and now lives a short distance from Washington, D.C., with her husband and their rescue dog with a blue tongue, appropriately named Blue. She has three grown sons and a daughter-in-law, as well as three adorable grandchildren. When she's not writing, reading or spending time with family, she enjoys travel, volunteer work and rooting for her favorite sports teams.

To those who ache for a family of their own,
may they discover the way that's right for them.

ACKNOWLEDGMENTS

So many people have supported me, taught me and
believed in me. I will never be able to express my
gratitude sufficiently, but I'll try.

Thank you,

Romance Writers of America and especially the
amazing members of the Washington, D.C.,
Romance Writers chapter for providing workshops,
mentoring and friendships;

My ever-supportive critique partners, Darlene Gardner
and Diane Gaston, for teaching me so much and never
doubting this day would come;

My brilliant editor, Karen Reid,
for her insight and patience;

My family and friends, who knew I would succeed and
made me want to keep reaching for my dream, and,

A special thank you to my husband, Michael,
for his unconditional love and support.

CHAPTER ONE

ASHLEIGH WILSON SWITCHED the phone from one ear to the other and stopped Aunt Viv in midsentence. "Tell me what's going on with Paula. Is the baby okay?" Her pulse accelerated in anticipation of news about her pregnant sister.

"The baby is fine, at least for now," Aunt Viv said. "Paula's blood pressure is high and she just needs to follow doctor's orders."

"What has her doctor suggested?" Getting specifics could take some work. She needed to get Aunt Viv to focus and stop haphazardly jumping from one subject to another.

"Her doctor wants her on bed rest, but that's easier said than done with two boys to take care of."

"Well, she has no choice." Even though she hadn't practiced in over two years, Ashleigh's physician-educated brain reviewed the possible outcomes if Paula's condition worsened. Preeclampsia, preterm labor…a multitude of possibilities. High blood pressure could mean a lot of things. How high was high? Slightly high or very high? "Do you know her actual blood pressure numbers?"

"Paula didn't say." Aunt Viv hesitated a few seconds before adding, "Maybe you should call her and find out."

Ashleigh swallowed the lump in her throat. "I'm not sure that's a good idea." How would she begin a conversation with the sister she hadn't spoken to in almost two years?

Her heart ached for the emotional turmoil her sister must be going through. Pregnancy complications came with unwarranted guilt. Ashleigh knew that firsthand and it took all her willpower to keep her own memories at bay.

"Where's Scott in all this?" Ashleigh asked. "Can't he take leave to care for Ryan and Mark?" Surely Paula's naval officer husband could handle this. Their boys were seven and nine, not quite old enough to fend for themselves but not helpless, either.

"He's in some ocean somewhere in his submarine," her aunt said.

Ashleigh remembered now. Her brother-in-law left about a month ago. Aunt Viv kept her informed about goings-on in their southern Virginia hometown of Grand Oaks, but that didn't mean she retained it all.

"And I'm still recovering from my knee replacement surgery or I'd be at Paula's right now," her aunt said. "My physical therapist would throw a fit if I overdid it."

"Is Mom still in Maryland with Grandma?" Ashleigh headed down the hall to her bedroom. She opened the empty suitcase she'd unpacked barely an hour ago after a business trip to Philly.

"Last I heard," Aunt Viv said, "your mom was real excited about the Alzheimer's facility she found up there." Her aunt sniffled. Grandma hadn't recognized anyone for at least six months.

"Now that Grandma's having other health issues, I'm sure Mom won't want to leave until they're resolved." Ashleigh opened drawers, pulled out clothes and stuffed them in her suitcase.

Without being asked, Aunt Viv reported on other family members, beginning with Scott's twin sisters. "Janie is expecting in a few weeks, so she can't travel from Texas, and Belle is in Germany for her job."

There were five siblings in total on Scott's side. In addition to his twin sisters who were otherwise occupied, his older sister had a special-needs child who required constant supervision, so she was out, too.

"Kyle is always around to help." Aunt Viv spoke cautiously, as if afraid the mere mention of Scott's brother might upset Ashleigh.

A loud bang sounded. She'd unintentionally slammed a drawer shut.

"What was that?" Aunt Viv asked. "Are you okay?"

"It was nothing. I'm fine."

She took a deep breath, blocking the painful memories the man's name elicited.

"Is he still working extra shifts in the emergency room?" Ashleigh reached for the throw pillow on her bedroom chair and collapsed into the seat cushions. She hugged the pillow tightly, as if the inanimate object could take away her deep-seated pain.

"Sure is." Aunt Viv confirmed that he had little time to spare. "The hospital's lucky to have such a dedicated doctor."

Ashleigh swallowed a comeback.

"Would Paula accept hired help?" Ashleigh finally asked, already knowing the answer. "I'd be happy to arrange and pay for it."

Silence. "I already offered. She doesn't want a stranger in her house. She claims she can get by on her own."

That was Paula—always stubborn and never wanting help.

"That's ridiculous!" Ashleigh's heart rate soared as her own blood pressure rose. "How can she be so nonchalant about her pregnancy?"

Probably because, unlike Ashleigh, Paula had experienced two near-perfect pregnancies and didn't have a clue what high-risk felt like.

Until now.

She tossed the pillow aside, stood up and headed to the bathroom to gather her toiletries.

"Maybe it's not as bad as I thought," Aunt Viv said. "Her doctor is probably taking precautions."

Her aunt was successfully baiting her. "That doesn't mean she shouldn't follow her doctor's orders."

"You need to come home, Ashleigh. Make sure Paula does what she's told."

Tears threatened and speaking was difficult. "I'm

already packed." Ashleigh zipped her suitcase and wheeled it to the living room.

"Really?" Aunt Viv didn't sound too surprised. Wasn't that why she'd called Ashleigh? "That's wonderful. I'm sure Paula will appreciate it."

Ashleigh doubted that, but she didn't care how Paula felt about it. The only thing that mattered was making sure her sister didn't do anything stupid to threaten the precious life she carried.

Even if it meant Ashleigh would have to face everyone and everything she had left behind, including Kyle, the ex-husband she'd once loved with every cell of her being.

FIFTEEN MINUTES AFTER hanging up with Aunt Viv, Ashleigh was ready to go. How much gas was in her car? She hadn't paid attention after returning home from the airport. Could she make it out of town before filling up? The drive to Grand Oaks would take about two hours.

Two hours until she came face-to-face with her past.

Maybe she could see about hiring someone to help her sister once she got to town. Paula likely wouldn't want Ashleigh around very long. Their last blowup had been a big one.

She took a final look around her apartment. Lights off, her single plant watered, thermostat set. She'd lived alone for the past two years—no pets, not even a goldfish—because she traveled so much for her job. And because she preferred it that way.

Ashleigh scooped up the pile of unopened mail from the kitchen counter and dumped it into her laptop bag, which also held her work folders. She needed to consider ways to placate both her clients and her boss without taking an actual leave of absence.

She locked her apartment door behind her, thumped her suitcase down the two flights of stairs to the building's entrance and loaded her car.

Ashleigh's cell phone slid out of her purse and lay staring up at her from the passenger seat. Should she call Paula to let her know she was coming? She tossed the phone back into her purse.

She wouldn't give her sister the opportunity to tell her not to come. Ashleigh would never forgive herself if something went horribly wrong with Paula's pregnancy.

Ashleigh shuddered at the thought and turned up the volume on the country music radio station, hoping to blast her own painful memories out of her head.

The April afternoon was overcast and traffic heading south on I-95 was heavy but moved at a steady pace to the I-85 exit. Before she knew it, she'd left the interstates for the country roads she knew so well.

The closer she got to Grand Oaks, the more frequently her painful memories came to the forefront of her mind. Though she and Paula had said such ugly things to each other the last time they'd spoken,

Ashleigh dreaded seeing her ex-husband more. Avoiding him would be difficult enough in a town of three thousand, but he would almost definitely be a frequent visitor at Paula's. Could she endure the inevitable mental and physical tolls?

She consciously relaxed her death grip on the steering wheel.

Aunt Viv had said Paula was renting the Dormans' old house instead of staying in base housing in Norfolk, in order to be closer to family while Scott was at sea. Two blocks from her destination, Ashleigh was again tempted to call her sister. Maybe a phone conversation would make it easier for Paula to accept Ashleigh's help rather than her just barging her way into her sister's life.

Ashleigh pushed the idea aside again. Paula had thought nothing of interfering in Ashleigh's life when she'd had marital problems. Just let Paula try to stop her.

This time it was Ashleigh's turn to butt into her sister's life.

PAULA LAY ON her left side, obeying her doctor's order of bed rest, when there was a rap on the front door of her modest Cape Cod rental home.

The door squeaked as it opened and she heard the voice she'd been dreading. "Paula?" Ashleigh had made record time.

Aunt Vivian had called earlier to say Ashleigh was coming, but Paula hadn't expected her sister to arrive until early evening or later. Paula hadn't wanted her to come at all.

She had several friends in town who'd already stepped up with food and offers of help with errands and watching the boys. She could manage without her sister, but Aunt Viv refused to tell Ashleigh not to come. Why hadn't Paula contacted Ashleigh herself?

"Paula?" Her older sister shouted this time.

Paula took a deep, bracing breath. "In here," she called from her first-floor bedroom.

With each approaching foot-pad, Paula's pulse quickened and her anxiety grew. The last time she and Ashleigh had spoken—correction, screamed at each other—had been right before Ashleigh left Grand Oaks for good more than two years ago.

Her sister stopped at the bedroom doorway, dressed in impeccably fitted jeans and a loose top cinched at her narrow waist. Her thick, blond hair was caught in a casual knot at the back of her head.

In other words, perfect as usual.

"How are you feeling?" The strap of Ashleigh's purse slipped from her shoulder to her elbow and her medical bag hung from her left hand. No "hello" or "hey there." Ashleigh spoke as if Paula were her patient rather than her only sibling.

"I'm fine." Paula wasn't about to list the multiple annoyances she experienced because of her pregnancy. She and Ashleigh might not see eye to eye on certain things, but complaining about her swollen feet, lack of energy and backaches, as well as this stupid bed-rest thing, would just be mean.

Paula soothed her baby bump, imagining what her independent doctor-sister was thinking.

Something in the neighborhood of *How could one person be so needy?*

Ashleigh had always been the perfect one. Voted head cheerleader, always made straight A's, dated and eventually married the star quarterback, went to a great college and then entered medical school. She'd even survived multiple miscarriages and a divorce, only to snap right back to her perfect life.

Then there was Paula, the little sister who'd struggled with acne in high school and could barely do a proper cartwheel—forget perform a respectable cheer. Instead of finishing college, she'd married Scott when she got pregnant with Mark. Now her husband was deployed and she could barely take care of her family because this surprise third pregnancy had her bedridden in torn pajama pants tied under her expanding belly and an old T-shirt of Scott's.

She blinked to clear the moisture building in her eyes. She hadn't even taken a shower today.

"Aunt Vivian called me." Ashleigh's words were clipped.

"I know." Paula wasn't about to act as if nothing had happened between them. "She called me, too."

"She said you're confined to bed because of high blood pressure?"

Paula wished Ashleigh would stop acting like her

doctor, but how to phrase it without sounding petulant? Then they'd fight, her blood pressure would rise even higher and once again she would be at fault.

She inhaled deeply and let the breath out slowly before replying. "My doctor is worried about preeclampsia."

"Rosy Bausch is your doctor?" Ashleigh asked.

Paula nodded.

"How far along are you?"

She didn't have to think about it. "Thirty-two weeks." Her doctor had mentioned it several times at her appointment yesterday afternoon.

"Any blurred vision or headaches?"

"No."

"Abdominal pain?"

"Nope."

"Good." Ashleigh set her purse down and opened her medical bag. "Have you been checking your blood pressure?"

Could their conversation be any cooler? "Dr. Bausch wants me to come in to her office weekly."

"Was your urine protein elevated?"

"No, but she's going to check that weekly, too." Paula nearly addressed her sister as Dr. Wilson but caught herself in time. Ashleigh didn't seem in the mood to appreciate Paula's sarcasm. "You didn't have to come," Paula began.

"Of course I did," Ashleigh shot back. "You're my sister." She paused and leveled her gaze at Paula.

"No matter what." Ashleigh's lip quivered, her vulnerability finally evident.

So Ashleigh wasn't as unaffected as she let on.

Paula's eyes welled up and she swallowed thickly, determined not to cry, even on hormone overload. They should talk—

The front door slammed and the house filled with her seven-year-old's wails.

"Ryan?" Fear for her child had Paula straightening into a sitting position. She cleared her throat when her voice broke. "I'm in my bedroom. Are you okay?"

Ryan cried harder.

"Paula, stay there." Ashleigh moved in Ryan's direction.

"There's something wrong with him." Paula spoke through gritted teeth while swinging her legs over the side of the bed.

Ashleigh narrowed her eyes at Paula. "If you don't lay back down right now, I'm going to call an ambulance and have you admitted to the hospital."

"That's ridiculous!"

"It won't be ridiculous if you go into premature labor," Ashleigh spit. "Trust me, it's not an experience you ever want to have."

RYAN LIMPED INTO the bedroom, right past Ashleigh. He headed directly to the side of the bed in front of Paula, who hadn't lain back down but hadn't rushed to Ryan's side, either. His forehead was scraped and his jeans were torn at the knee, but more significantly, he cradled his left forearm with his right hand.

Except for being two years older and crying, Ryan looked the same to Ashleigh as he had the last time she'd seen him. Spittin' image of his dad, as well as his Uncle Kyle.

The lump in her throat kept her from speaking.

"I fell off my bike, Mommy," he sobbed.

"Tell me where you hurt." Paula looked about to burst into tears herself.

Ashleigh's medical training kicked into high gear. She moved in closer and knelt next to Ryan.

"Hi, Ryan." Ashleigh kept her voice calm. "You might not remember me, but I'm your aunt Ashleigh."

"Mommy has pictures of you." Ryan hiccupped, his deep blue eyes reminiscent of his uncle's.

"How are you feeling?" Ashleigh moved some hair back from his scraped forehead to look closer and felt around the rest of his skull.

"My arm really hurts." Ryan's face scrunched as if in pain.

"I'll bet it does." Ashleigh spoke gently, her attention now on his arm as she carefully probed the limb. Possibly a simple fracture, but an X-ray would tell for sure. "Do you hurt anywhere else, Ry? Like your neck or back? Your legs, belly?"

Ryan shook his head.

"Do you remember if you fell asleep after you fell?"

"No. I was awake. Only babies take naps."

"Good." Ashleigh grinned, then caught Paula's eye while gathering supplies from her medical bag. "Do you have a scarf or maybe a receiving blanket I can use to immobilize his arm until I can get an X-ray?"

Paula pointed to her dresser. "In the middle drawer are scarves."

"Hop up here on the bed next to Mommy," Ashleigh told Ryan. While she cleaned and bandaged Ryan's head and scraped knee, she spoke to Paula. "I'm going to take him into the hospital for an X-ray." So much for avoiding her emergency-room-doctor ex-husband.

"Kyle's not at the hospital today," Paula said, as if reading her mind. "He mentioned at dinner last night that he took today off to do some painting."

Ashleigh stiffened. Kyle had been able to maintain a relationship with both their nephews and her sister, but Ashleigh hadn't even seen a picture of the boys in two years.

She consciously relaxed her neck and shoulders. She shouldn't be surprised at Kyle's involvement. He was probably a big help while Scott was deployed.

Retrieving a scarf from the drawer, she wove it under Ryan's injured arm and tied it behind his neck. "Is Rich Miller still in the building down the street from my old office?"

"As far as I know," Paula said. "We've never needed an orthopedist before."

"Rich is the best, especially for kids," Ashleigh said. "Are you okay with him if he's needed?"

"Yes," Paula agreed.

Ashleigh didn't want to scare Ryan by mentioning his arm could be broken. The orthopedist would take over Ryan's care if the X-ray showed a break.

She turned to her nephew and effortlessly took on her pediatrician persona. "Ryan, you and I are going to go get a special picture taken of your arm so we can see what's going on inside."

Ryan's eyes widened. "Can I see the picture?"

Ashleigh couldn't contain her smile. "Of course. Now why don't you use the bathroom while I make sure your mom has everything she needs. Can you manage without using your hurt arm?"

He bobbed his head rapidly, hopped off the bed and skipped out of the room—definitely not the same sobbing child from a few minutes ago.

Ashleigh turned her attention to Paula. "Does he normally play outside by himself?"

Paula's eyes grew wide at Ashleigh's not-so-subtle implication. "He went bike riding with his friends, not that it's any of your business."

"He's still my nephew and I'm concerned about his welfare."

"You haven't seen him in two years," Paula whispered angrily.

"That was your choice," Ashleigh reminded her.

Paula glared at her. "You left town."

There was so much Ashleigh could say in response, but now was not the time.

"I want to take your blood pressure before I go."

Ashleigh pulled her blood pressure cuff from her bag and attached it to Paula's arm. Having an injured child was bound to raise anyone's blood pressure. "Where's Mark?"

"Playing at a friend's house." Paula stiffened, her words curt. "The mother is supposed to bring him back around six."

They were silent as Ashleigh listened to Paula's rapidly pumping blood with her stethoscope.

"Not bad, but higher than it should be," she told Paula as she removed the cuff. "Just close your eyes and take some deep breaths. I've got everything else covered."

Ashleigh silently packed up her medical bag, afraid to say anything that would inflame Paula and raise her blood pressure.

Like *why couldn't you have been loyal to me when my marriage was falling apart, instead of taking Kyle's side?*

ASHLEIGH HAD NEVER driven a minivan, but Ryan was too young to ride in the front seat of her two-seater sports car, so she'd taken Paula's vehicle. One more reminder that Paula had been blessed with a growing family while Ashleigh had been denied a single offspring.

The mile drive to the hospital provided an abundance of memories. From the quaint shop where she and Kyle had shared a bowl of bubble gum ice cream on their first date in high school, to the tiny apartment they lived in before they bought the historic home that still housed Ashleigh's pediatric practice.

The office where she no longer worked.

Knowing that Kyle wouldn't be at the hospital was a relief. Though it only prolonged the inevitable no more than a day or two.

She'd deal with Kyle and her myriad of emotions when the time came.

Meanwhile, Ryan kept up a constant dialogue during the short drive, forcing Ashleigh's mind away from the memories that haunted her.

"And my friend Jarrod can do a wheelie," Ryan was telling her.

"Wow! That's impressive. Is he the same age as you?"

"He's a year older and doesn't have training wheels anymore."

"Were you trying to do a wheelie when you fell?" Ashleigh's suspicion was confirmed by Ryan's sheepish nod reflected in the rearview mirror.

Rekindling her relationship with her nephew wasn't the time to lecture him on his foolishness. She'd leave that to his mother.

"Here we are," she told Ryan after she maneuvered the minivan into a parking space in the hospital visitor lot. Back in the days when she had privileges here, she'd been able to park in the staff lot, which was closer to the entrance.

Once again, she shoved away those memories and walked Ryan across the parking lot and through the automatic doors leading to the emergency entrance. The sound of a siren got louder as an ambulance pulled up to the hospital.

"Dr. Wilson." The middle-aged receptionist, Kathy something, gave her anything but a warm welcome.

Another convert to the Kyle camp.

The woman's flowery perfume battled with the hospital's unforgettable smell. But the nasty combination of illness, medications and antiseptic made her nostalgic nonetheless.

"How are you, Kathy?" Ashleigh realized how much she'd missed this place, no matter what kind of reception she received. Would this punch in the gut happen every time she ran into someone she once knew?

After exchanging cool pleasantries, Kathy's attention turned to Ryan. "Oh, dear! Let me put this poor boy into the system."

She returned to her computer and took down his information, including the insurance info Paula had sent along. She ushered them right back into a curtained area. "Dr. Phillips should be in to see Ryan shortly," she said before leaving them alone.

Not more than two minutes went by before the curtain was pulled back, but it wasn't Dr. Phillips. Ashleigh's heart leaped into her throat.

Kyle.

Her ex-husband looked even better than she remembered. His thick, dark hair was matted, a product of his longtime habit of moving his protective eyewear to his head when not in use. He had a healthy tan and the corners of his deep blue eyes crinkled ever so slightly. Rather than make him look older, they made him more attractive. Even when those gorgeous eyes barely glanced at her before landing on Ryan.

She blanched at Kyle's insolence. Not that she blamed him. She'd been out of his life long enough for him to go on without her.

He did his customary tug at the neck of the T-shirt he wore under his blue scrubs and cleared his throat. Kyle was the only man she'd ever known who looked hot in scrubs.

"Hey, buddy." Kyle bypassed Ashleigh and spoke directly to his nephew, who sat cross-legged on the gurney. "What happened?" He gently removed the scarf from the boy's arm and handed it to Ashleigh without taking his eyes from Ryan.

As their nephew related the tale, Ashleigh took a mental inventory of Kyle, searching for battle scars, perhaps, that matched her own. She saw none.

Hers weren't visible on the outside, either.

CHAPTER TWO

IF ASHLEIGH HAD THRIVED without him, Kyle didn't want to know. He purposely kept his eyes and attention averted, unprepared for his inevitable physical reaction whenever she was near. Instead, he concentrated on Ryan as the boy explained how he got injured.

"I thought we talked about that wheelie stuff," Kyle admonished gently.

Ryan hung his head, the expression on his face reminiscent of his father back when Scott and Kyle had been young and adventurous.

"At least wait until your training wheels are off before you try any of those tricks," Kyle reminded him.

Ashleigh drew in an audible breath, probably upset that he would approve what she would consider dangerous behavior. He turned his head partway in her direction. "Better a wheelie than something worse." He paused and made the mistake of catching her eye. She'd always been a stickler for safety and rules, even though she used to flip backward off someone's shoulders onto a hardwood floor as a high school cheerleader.

"I was told you weren't working today." Ashleigh's comment was more of an accusation than a question.

"Multicar accident on Hamilton." He'd been about to go home when Paula called him about Ryan. Thankfully, she'd given him a heads-up that Ashleigh was in town and was bringing the boy in.

Ashleigh turned back to Ryan. "*Maybe* you should wait until there's an adult with you before you try a wheelie."

Ryan looked to Kyle for confirmation, but the emergency room doctor on duty interrupted them.

"Hey, Hank." Kyle turned from the gurney and greeted him, shaking the older man's hand when he came through the curtain before making the proper introductions. "Dr. Ashleigh Wilson, this is Dr. Hank Phillips. He joined the staff about a year ago."

While the two shook hands, Hank ran his other hand through his thinning gray hair. "Are you Paula's sister? The resemblance is remarkable."

Kyle should have mentioned Ashleigh was Ryan's aunt. Even if she hadn't kept in contact with the boy.

"You've met my sister?" Ashleigh's eyebrows rose.

"Oh, yes." Hank chuckled. "She's included me in several of their holiday gatherings since my kids all live a few time zones away."

The color drained from Ashleigh's face.

Kyle wondered how she liked hearing that this stranger played a bigger role in her family's lives than she had.

Ashleigh changed the subject back to Ryan. "From

the way Ryan's holding his arm and the radial pain on contact, I'm pretty sure it's a simple break."

Hank turned to examine Ryan. "How you doin', buddy?"

Meanwhile, Kyle went against his better judgment and scrutinized a preoccupied Ashleigh.

Dr. Ashleigh Wilson. He'd never minded that she'd kept her maiden name when they'd married. An homage to her father, Dr. Clayton Wilson—a man Kyle had been proud to know.

Ashleigh was a little thinner since the last time he'd seen her, pounds she couldn't afford to lose. Other than that, she looked even more beautiful than he remembered. His fingers itched to touch the loose tendril that escaped from her casually knotted hair. He longed to place his lips on the skin beneath it, to taste the sensitive spot on her neck that never failed to make her suck in her breath....

"Kyle?" From Hank's tone, it wasn't the first time the man had addressed him. All three of them stared at him.

He blinked twice. "Yes?"

"Do you want to go to Radiology with Ryan?" Hank narrowed his gaze and cocked his head in puzzlement.

"Of course." Kyle then said to Ryan, "Let's get you a wheelchair to ride in. Dr. Hank wants to take a picture of your arm." Ryan's eyes lit up as expected.

"Can we do a wheelie in it?" Ryan asked.

"We'll see." Kyle avoided Ashleigh's gaze.

"But you and Aunt Ashleigh will both be there," Ryan said. "Didn't she say I needed an adult? Now I have two."

"Aunt Ashleigh is going to wait for you here." Kyle needed a break from her after that barely controlled fantasy.

"No," Ashleigh countered. "I'm going with you."

Kyle shrugged. "You'll have to wait in the Radiology waiting room."

Ashleigh's cheek muscles tensed and she narrowed her eyes at Kyle. The daggers were locked and loaded.

"Hospital regulations," he said pleasantly before she could argue. "You no longer have privileges at this hospital." Her choice, but he didn't say it aloud.

"You're a pediatrician, as I recall." Hank appeared oblivious to the tension in the room. "Where are you practicing now?"

Ashleigh's color heightened. "I'm no longer practicing medicine. I work out of Richmond as a hospital fund-raiser."

The reality of Ashleigh's words hit Kyle in the pit of his stomach. Ashleigh had given up the career she adored because she could no longer bear to be around children.

ASHLEIGH FUMED AS she sat on the thinly padded vinyl chair in the radiology department waiting room. How dare Kyle exclude her? She was every bit the doctor he was, even if she hadn't cared for patients since she left town.

She was perfectly happy working as a hospital fund-raiser. Turned out, she was pretty darn good at coming up with unique ways to get people to part with their money.

Which didn't mean she never regretted giving up medicine—specifically working with children. She loved being in an office full of laughing and crying little ones, the noise and confusion never more than she could bear.

Until her last miscarriage.

That was the child she was supposed to finally carry to term. She'd made it into her second trimester and had begun telling people she was pregnant.

She crossed her arms over her abdomen and bent forward in pain at the vivid memory of that first wave of cramps that had ended her dream of giving Kyle the child he deserved.

"Are you okay?"

Ashleigh straightened at the young woman's voice. "Yes, I'm fine." Ryan sat in his wheelchair in front of a woman in purple scrubs. Her name tag read "Molly," but she didn't look familiar. She didn't appear to recognize Ashleigh, either.

"Ryan's all done." Molly had a perky lilt that matched her smile. "Dr. Jennings and Dr. Phillips asked for him to wait with you while they consult with the radiologist."

Ashleigh's jaw clenched. She was being shut out

again. She'd known the radiologist, Jim Gorman, since preschool. Under other circumstances she'd barge into his office, but she decided not to push the issue. In the short time she'd been at the hospital, several old acquaintances had given her a wide berth. They obviously weren't fans of hers since the divorce.

Molly turned and left them alone in the waiting area.

"How's your arm feeling?" Ashleigh asked Ryan.

"Okay, I guess. They let me see the picture of my arm bone. It was cool!" He busied himself locating hidden pictures in a kids' magazine someone had given him, so Ashleigh didn't say anything more.

She leaned back in her seat and closed her eyes for a moment before realizing the voices around the corner were speaking about Kyle.

"It's a shame about Dr. Jennings," one female voice said.

"I know, he's so nice. And cute, too." The other female let out a quiet moan.

Ashleigh listened carefully, assuming they were discussing how she'd divorced poor Dr. Jennings, when two other people deep in conversation entered the waiting room. As they walked past her to the reception desk, Ashleigh could no longer hear the women.

So she rose from her seat and pretended to search for a magazine on the vertical acrylic rack bolted to the wall, while tuning her ears to the conversation around the corner.

She could only pick up certain words, but they were important words.

Accident, lawsuit, brain injury.

PAULA ROLLED FROM her side to her back and stared at the bedroom ceiling until she was ready to scream. Or at least until she found herself out of breath, forcing her to roll back onto her left side.

A few minutes ago, Mark had slammed the front door to announce his arrival and now she heard him rooting through kitchen cupboards searching for a snack.

"Don't spoil your dinner," she yelled.

"I won't," he promised, and she believed him. He'd been going through a growth spurt and he consumed food and outgrew clothing before the money left the checking account.

Paula struggled to a sitting position. Propping herself up with pillows against the headboard, she took her laptop from the drawer next to her bed and turned it on.

She needed to let Scott know what was going on. Kyle had confirmed Ryan's arm was broken when he called about a half hour ago, but she didn't want her husband to know the doctor had put her on bed rest. He had enough stress with his job and he didn't need to have to worry about her, too.

"This is all my fault." She spoke quietly to the empty room, choking up. "All my fault."

As she typed an email to Scott, her fingers kept

hitting the wrong keys because her eyes had blurred from gathering tears. She blinked and they rolled down her cheeks and onto the overstretched but clean shirt she'd put on after her shower.

She should be out of tears—she'd spent her entire shower sobbing. Bed rest. They sounded like the cruelest words ever. *She* should have taken her son to the emergency room.

She wiped the moisture from her cheeks and concentrated on the email.

Hey, Scott, I miss you so much. I hope you're safe in whatever ocean you're navigating.

Mark is doing well. He got an A on his spelling test this week and you know how much trouble he's had in the past. He also had an assist in his soccer game. They lost three to one, but he was happy anyway.

Unfortunately, Ryan had a bike accident this afternoon and his arm is broken. Before you panic, it's a simple break, no surgery needed. He'll be in a cast for four to six weeks. Kyle is making sure he's well taken care of. In fact, Kyle has been a huge help with the boys while you've been away. We should do something nice for him when you get back.

I saw the doctor today and my blood pressure is a little higher than it should be. Again, no need to worry. I'm doing exactly what she says.

Believe it or not, my sister arrived this afternoon.

Aunt Viv called her and blew my situation all out of proportion. Ashleigh got here right before Ryan got hurt, so she was able to take him to the E.R. I have no idea how it went with her and Kyle, but she should be home with Ryan any time now.

I think that brings you up to speed. Always remember, I love you bunches and can't wait until you're back in my arms.

Paula hit Send and closed her laptop. She leaned her head back, missing the top of the pillow and hitting the headboard instead. Scooting to a more comfortable position would take too much energy. She simply shut her eyes and breathed deeply...until the next interruption came.

Her friends, Rhonda and Jean, had both brought over casseroles earlier and now apparently word was out that she was bedridden because she'd gotten several phone calls with offers of help.

Unsure if she drifted off or not, her eyes popped open at the tinkling sound of a text message on her cell phone. She reached over to the nightstand to pick it up.

Scott. He must have read her email already because he wanted to video chat.

She pulled her computer onto her lap again and opened the program that would bring his face into their bedroom.

"Hey, Paula," Scott said when they connected. "How are you?" His usually laughing blue eyes were filled with concern and she couldn't help but feel his love.

"Okay." She tried to keep her tone light, but her voice cracked. She put a hand to her mouth.

"Everything will be fine, P."

His soothing tone allowed her to take a few calming breaths.

"Do you need me to come home?" he asked. "I can talk to the chaplain and apply for hardship if this blood pressure thing is serious."

"No, no, that's okay. Everyone's been so nice, offering help and bringing meals so I can take it easy. And I told you Ashleigh's here."

He chuckled. "Yeah, how's that going?"

"Kind of chilly," she admitted. "But we haven't spent much time together yet. Ryan's injury interrupted us."

"Maybe her visit is what the two of you need to work things out."

"Yeah. Exactly what I need right now to keep my blood pressure down," she joked.

"Just follow doctor's orders."

"I know." She tried to sound upbeat but failed.

"Talk to me," he coaxed.

She gulped, unprepared to delve into her emotions. "You know how unhappy I was when I found out I was pregnant," she began in little more than a whisper. It was supposed to be her time now that the boys were in school all day. She could finish her degree and then get her master's in physical therapy. She'd finally have something to be proud of, an accomplishment of her own.

"This isn't your fault, Paula," Scott pointed out. "You accepted this pregnancy a long time ago, unless you changed your mind?"

"Oh, no!" she cried. "Of course not! I already love this baby more than I ever expected to." She swallowed.

"Stop thinking you're to blame." Scott's tone was firm. "For both you and the baby."

Easier said than done.

She deliberately changed the subject because he'd never convince her that she wasn't responsible and then they'd only get into an argument. So they discussed Ryan's injury until voices carried from the front door.

Ashleigh and Ryan had returned.

"They're back from the orthopedist," Paula told Scott. "Do you want to say 'hi' to the boys?"

"Sure." He put his index finger up and Paula did the same, getting closer to the screen until it appeared as if the tips of their fingers touched. "I love you, P." This time *his* voice broke slightly.

"I love you, too, Scotty." Tears spilled down her cheeks. "Let me call the boys."

"I'll be home soon."

She tried her best to smile and then turned her head in the direction of her bedroom door to call the boys.

Was that Kyle's voice, too?

What she wouldn't have given to be a fly on that hospital wall when he and her sister saw each other again after two years.

ASHLEIGH WAS SURE there must be steam coming out of her ears as she parked Paula's minivan in the driveway. Ryan had chosen to ride in Kyle's truck—not that she could fault the boy—and now Kyle walked right into her sister's home as if he lived there.

Ashleigh couldn't imagine feeling less connected to any of them.

She took a minute to gather herself, refusing to give in to hurt feelings. They'd all successfully gone on with their lives without her.

So what?

So had she. In fact, she needed to check in with a few clients. She walked to her car and retrieved her suitcase from her trunk. She wheeled it up the walkway, along with her briefcase and medical bag. Her purse hung over her shoulder and she made it to the front door before it slipped down her arm.

Debating whether to knock or walk in, she straightened her back and entered her sister's home.

Voices came from Paula's bedroom, but Ashleigh chose to avoid Kyle. Instead, she parked her things off to the side of the front door and went into the kitchen to brew a cup of tea.

While waiting for the water to boil, she considered Paula's house. Aunt Viv had mentioned that the older couple who'd owned the house for longer than

Ashleigh had been alive had passed away within weeks of each other. Rather than putting the house up for sale in the depressed real estate market, their children had chosen to update and rent out the home. Ashleigh hadn't been upstairs yet, but more than likely, the Cape Cod contained a full bath and two bedrooms on the second floor, one for each of the boys. Paula's bedroom appeared to be the only bedroom on this floor. Where did that leave Ashleigh?

She sighed. Looked like she'd have to make do with the living room sofa for who knew how long. The one decent hotel was fifteen minutes out of town and that would make school mornings more hectic than necessary. Plus, if Ashleigh didn't sleep in the house, then Paula would have to get up with the boys if they needed something during the night.

The teakettle whistled. Since there were several tea flavors to choose from in Paula's cabinet, Ashleigh decided to ask if she'd like a cup. Not like in the past when they could practically read each other's minds. Or at least not complain if the wrong kind of tea was brewed for them.

Ashleigh started back down the hall as Kyle exited Paula's bedroom.

"I'm giving them some time alone," he told Ashleigh, implying she shouldn't interrupt Paula and her boys.

"Asking Paula if she wants tea will only take a second."

"She never passes up a cup of tea," Kyle said. "Any flavor that's decaf."

Ashleigh hated when he answered a question before she could ask it. Or maybe she hated the fact that he knew her sister better than she did.

She turned on her heel, annoyed when he followed her to the kitchen.

He pulled out a cup of his own from the cupboard when she didn't offer him one and brewed himself a single cup of coffee.

"You're pretty comfortable here," she said before she could stop herself.

"I come over a few times a week," he said. "Dinner, helping with Mark's homework, yard work. You know."

She nodded, even though she didn't know. The last few months of their marriage, he'd put in so many hours at the hospital that she'd barely seen him. Eating one meal a week together, maybe two if she was lucky, had been the extent of their interaction. Much less time than he'd been giving her sister and nephews.

There were countless comebacks on the tip of her tongue, but she held them in, unwilling to begin a fruitless argument.

Kyle took lemon juice from the fridge and held it out. "For Paula's tea."

Ashleigh's fingers shook as she took the bottle and added a splash to the tea. How could she have forgotten how her sister preferred her tea? Had two years turned them into strangers?

Kyle sipped his coffee, set the cup on the counter and pulled out a spoon, efficiently swirling the liquids in Paula's cup together. When he picked up the cup to take it to her sister, Ashleigh realized she'd been mesmerized, remembering how those fingers used to manipulate her until she lost complete control of both body and soul.

Kyle left with Paula's tea. Ashleigh didn't argue, needing a minute to slow her breathing. She sat at the kitchen table and dunked her tea bag up and down, staring at it until her eyes blurred.

"Hi, Aunt Ashleigh!" Mark's sudden appearance in the kitchen doorway startled her.

"Mark! You've grown so much!" Ashleigh stood to hug the grinning nine-year-old who came almost to her collarbone even in her three-inch wedge heels. She was about to ask how school was going, but he ran off when Ryan called him.

Mark was no sooner gone than Kyle appeared in the kitchen doorway. "I'll help the boys move Ryan into Mark's room before I go."

"I don't want to kick him out of his room." She stared at the swirls in her tea.

"He's fine with it," Kyle said. "Mark has bunk beds."

Of course he'd already finalized details. He practically lived here.

"Scott doesn't mind you spending so much time

with his family?" The snotty question flew from her mouth before she could stop it.

Two years ago she'd have done anything to get him to show a little emotion. She'd gone so far as to divorce him, but even that hadn't produced a reaction. Now he was silent until she turned to look at him and realized with alarm that she'd made him angry. Narrowed eyes and pursed lips were his tell.

Yep, definitely angry.

She wasn't sure if she'd been trying for that reaction or not. Maybe she'd wanted some kind of response from him. Anger, joy, resentment, pleasure. Anything but steely control.

Whatever his emotion, Kyle's words were deliberate. "Before he was deployed, Scott asked me to look after his family. If you have a problem with it, then maybe you should go back to your life in Richmond."

A slap in the face would have been less painful than his contempt.

Ashleigh kept a tight rein on her own emotions. *Act cool.* "Whatever."

"No, not 'whatever.'" His voice rose in volume as he set his coffee down too fast. It sloshed over the top and onto the table. He turned to the sink for a paper towel, jerking the roll so hard that the sheets unraveled. He tore off a single sheet and cleaned up the mess in one infuriated swipe.

He held the used towel over the trash can and glared at Ashleigh. "I get why you're here. Your sister needs you. Your whole family needs you." He slammed the lid closed on the trash can. "Just don't take *your* failings out on the rest of us."

Ashleigh stood so quickly her chair nearly tipped over. "*My* failings?" Such nerve. So he *did* blame her for the miscarriages. "I'm here, aren't I?"

He shrugged. "Physically."

What did he want from her? Didn't he realize how difficult this was? Coming back to the town where her life had fallen apart?

She stepped to the opposite counter, her back to him. A single tear rolled down her cheek—she'd be damned if she'd give him the satisfaction of seeing her wipe it away.

"I get it." Her voice was hoarse with emotion. "You don't want me here."

"If only that were true."

Before she could spin around and ask what he meant, he and his coffee had vanished from the kitchen.

CHAPTER THREE

"THIS IS PURR-FECT," Paula said on a sigh to Kyle, and took another sip of her tea. "Thank you."

"Ashleigh's idea." He spoke more harshly than he intended. No need to take his frustration out on his sister-in-law. "Hungry?"

She narrowed her eyes and tipped her head. "I could eat. The kids are probably hungry, too."

"Anything in particular?"

"A couple of friends stopped by with casseroles, but I'm not sure what's there. I told them to stick the food in the fridge." Paula set her cup on the bedside table and straightened herself up against the pillows. "Amazing how quickly news gets around this town."

"Tell me about it. I'll go check it out and let you know what's there." He was about to leave but stopped at Paula's next words.

"You're staying for dinner, aren't you?" Paula's expectant look told him she didn't want to be the only adult in the house with Ashleigh.

"Sure." He couldn't hold back his grin. He gave her a wink and chuckled. "As long as you promise not to let your sister get to you."

She sighed. "I'm trying." Then she groaned and threw her head back. "Believe me, I'm trying."

"I know this has been a stressful day, but everything's fine now." He stepped closer, touched her shoulder to comfort her as he would his sisters. That was what he'd always considered Paula—whether or not he was married to her sister or she was married to his brother. "Just close your eyes for a few minutes and breathe."

"Yes, Doctor." She giggled, did as she was told, but then opened one eye to a squint. "That's not the first time today I've been told to do that. Maybe you and Ashleigh have more in common than you think." She shut her eye again and leaned back as if cutting off any retort he might have.

"Maybe." They just weren't the things that allowed them to be in the same room together without friction.

Paula may have taken his side in the divorce, but he was acutely aware that she'd never given up hope that he and Ashleigh would reunite.

He turned to leave but not before her lips turned up slightly in amusement.

Kyle didn't know what else to say, so he went directly to the kitchen. No sign of Ashleigh or her tea. He opened the fridge to discover three casseroles, as well as a salad.

He removed the food and set it on the counter for a better look. Lasagna, chicken enchiladas and some kind of mystery pasta casserole labeled with cooking directions. Not caring which they ate, he decided to leave it up to Paula. He strode out of the kitchen and turned right to go down the hall, nearly knocking Ashleigh down in the process. Instinctively, he grabbed her upper arms to keep her from falling.

"Sorry." They both spoke at the same time.

Kyle hadn't been this close to Ashleigh in years. He hadn't touched her bare arms, inhaled her distinctive scent or seen those blue eyes up close in so long. Their azure color always reminded him of the island paradise where they'd honeymooned.

As brand-new doctors, they couldn't afford an expensive vacation. At the time, he had just been hired by the Grand Oaks Community Hospital as an E.R. doctor and Ashleigh's dream of becoming a partner in her father's pediatric practice was about to come to fruition.

Both had agreed they wouldn't spend money they didn't have. So when they discovered their siblings had pooled their money to give them a honeymoon as a wedding present, they were ecstatic.

The trip had been idyllic. No work, no worries, only each other. Swimming and snorkeling during the day, dinner alfresco on their private balcony in the evening and making love whenever the mood struck.

If only they had been able to avoid the devastation and heartbreak that followed.

"Kyle?" Ashleigh's whisper interrupted his reverie.

He immediately released her, dropping his hands to his sides as if burned.

"Sorry." He stepped back and searched for something more to say. He rubbed his palms against the outside of his thighs to erase the tactile memory of her. "I was going to ask Paula which casserole she'd like for dinner. Maybe you should see if there's one you prefer."

Ashleigh replied by bobbing her head as she walked past him into the kitchen.

Fool! How could he have allowed her to see him so vulnerable?

He strode to Paula's room and rapped louder than he should have on the doorjamb.

Paula's head jerked in his direction. "Is everything okay?" She set aside the magazine she'd been flipping through.

"Yes." He paused. "No." Another pause. "I don't want to talk about it."

"Ah." Paula's eyebrows rose. "Ashleigh strikes again."

"I said I don't want to talk about it." He racked his brain to remember the choices for dinner and finally recited the list. "Do you have a preference?"

"Enchiladas sound good." She patted her abdomen and referred to her baby. "Bam-Bam likes spicy food. Too bad I can't have a margarita with it, but Jean said she made some corn bread. I think it's in a pan on the counter and there should be a salad in the fridge, too."

"Sounds good."

Kyle returned to the kitchen where Ashleigh was turning on the oven.

"I was just preheating to three-fifty," she said. "I didn't know which one we were cooking."

He took the enchilada casserole from the counter and put it into the oven, setting a timer according to the written instructions. He found the corn bread and pulled out the salad. A noise behind him was a reminder that Ashleigh was still in the kitchen.

She'd gotten out plates, silverware and napkins, butter for the corn bread and dressing for the salad. Now she sat at the table, hands folded.

"Kyle?" Her tone was soft.

He gave her his attention, saying nothing.

"At the hospital today," she began, visibly swallowing. "I heard some talk about a lawsuit. Are you in trouble?"

His jaw clenched so tight he was in danger of cracking a tooth. "I'd rather not discuss it." He turned his back to her.

ASHLEIGH KNEW WHAT that meant. He didn't want to discuss the lawsuit with *her*.

After a moment of staring at his back in disbelief, she straightened her spine and rose slowly. She carefully pushed her chair in and left the kitchen, gathering every ounce of self-respect she could muster. She needed a moment alone to pull herself together—just one moment.

She headed to the powder room located off the living room. She entered, closed the door and leaned her forehead against the natural finish of the oak door. Slow, deep breaths finally calmed her.

What kind of trouble was Kyle in? Was it bad?

Maybe she could help him. She didn't know how, but he could have at least told her what was going on. They'd been married for three years, together since high school. Fifteen years total. Didn't that count for something?

They'd been through so much together.

Hadn't she been the one he'd come to when he didn't get accepted into his first choice of college? And she'd gone directly to him when her father was diagnosed with prostate cancer the spring of their sophomore year in college.

He'd dropped everything, including studying for a major exam, to come to her when she'd called in tears. He'd held her through the night, breaking the dorm curfew rules and not caring when her roommate came in. She'd woken in his arms, both of them fully clothed, and she'd realized for the first time how much he truly meant it when he told her he loved her.

When had they stopped coming to each other? Had it been after the miscarriages? Or had it begun before that?

They'd led busy lives as physicians, but they always made time to catch up with each other—an occasional lunch, a late-night glass of wine in bed.

Kyle couldn't have been more supportive during

her first miscarriage. By the third, he'd made several contacts around the world with infertility experts.

At the same time, Ashleigh couldn't handle the pressure. She was failing to produce a child and didn't know how to deal with it. Kyle had always been the one she turned to, but now he spent all of his free time looking for answers.

Ashleigh washed her hands, taking extra time to run her wrists under the cool water. She dried off and braced herself to face whatever came next. Then she slipped out of the bathroom and went directly to her briefcase near the front door.

She took refuge in the living room, using the Mission oak coffee table to spread out her files.

From the sounds of it, Kyle was upstairs—likely helping the boys move some of Ryan's things into Mark's room. Several minutes later, Mark came down to retrieve Ashleigh's suitcase, insisting he could get it upstairs himself.

"Ugh," Mark grunted. Her suitcase probably weighed as much as he did.

Ashleigh grimaced as her luggage hit the wall halfway up the stairs.

"Let me give you a hand." Kyle came to his aid before Ashleigh could rise from the sofa.

"I got it," Mark insisted, breathless.

Shortly after, the house became quiet as Ashleigh stared blindly at her client folders, unable to make sense of her notes.

She leaned her head back on the tweed sofa and

closed her eyes. The sound of voices carried from Paula's room. It sounded like Kyle and Paula were talking.

"She's going to find out," Paula was saying. "Whether you tell her or she hears it from someone else, there are no secrets in this town."

"She just arrived today." Kyle was clearly frustrated. "I thought there'd be more time."

At first Ashleigh assumed they were talking about the lawsuit he refused to discuss, but then she wondered if there was something else. Was he involved with someone?

She was suddenly light-headed. Was someone sharing his life, his bed? Maybe even his heart? Her throat closed and her breath nearly choked her.

"Why don't you tell her?" Paula was saying. "Then it's all out in the open."

Ashleigh strained to listen. She never eavesdropped and now she'd done it twice in the same day.

"I don't want her in the middle of it." His words made Ashleigh's heart clench. "She made her choices and they didn't include me. She has her own life and so do I."

He had no clue about her solitary life back in Richmond. Her clients, mostly hospital boards and large nonprofit corporations, were her main providers of interpersonal communication. She didn't date, didn't *want* to date since that could result in a relationship and she couldn't do a relationship.

What would she lead with? *This can't go anywhere*

because I'm unable to bear children. Where did that piece of information fit? Right before dessert on the first date seemed a little presumptuous. After the third date? The eighth?

There was way too much to consider.

It wasn't as if she didn't have a social life. She had a few casual friends she hiked with and this past winter they'd skied a few times. She'd even gone to dinner with a former medical school classmate when she was in San Francisco last fall on business. Unfortunately, he'd gotten the wrong idea, leaving her to explain how she wasn't looking for a relationship, not even a one-night stand.

When he took offense to her noncommittal explanation, she finally spilled her real reason and left the restaurant in tears.

That was when she made the decision to never date again. Period.

The oven buzzer went off and Kyle's hurried footsteps sounded as he came down the hallway from Paula's room and into the kitchen to turn it off.

He stepped out of the kitchen to call up the stairs to the boys, "Dinner in five." He glanced over at Ashleigh a mere second, then called to the boys again, "Get washed up." Laughter and scuffling accompanied their nephews as the water flowed through the pipes until Mark and Ryan came bounding down the stairs.

After she put her files away and washed her hands in the powder room, Ashleigh entered the kitchen to find Paula sitting at the table, her boys on either side of her.

"What are you doing out of bed?" The words had sounded much less accusatory in Ashleigh's head.

"I invited her to sit at the table to eat," Kyle said, taking sides against her. Not surprising but painful, nonetheless. "Much less stressful than having the boys eat in the bedroom with her."

"We enjoy eating meals together," Paula explained as if Ashleigh was some clueless twit when it came to family dynamics. "Especially with Scott gone."

Ashleigh pinched her lips shut to keep from saying something snarky in front of the boys. Kyle and Paula had made their positions clear. It was the two of them against her.

Well, game on.

IF NOT FOR HAVING the boys at the table, dinner could have been a disaster.

Mark and Ryan took over the conversation, eager to tell how Ryan could climb up to the top bunk in Mark's room with just one good arm.

"We took the sheets off Ryan's bed," Mark said. "And Uncle Kyle helped us put clean ones on. He said we made the bed perfectly. Like Dad does on his sub."

"You guys are going to a lot of trouble for me," Ashleigh told them. "I'm supposed to be here to help out, not make more work."

"That's okay, Aunt Ashleigh," Ryan said. "We had fun with Uncle Kyle."

"Yeah," Mark agreed. "We always have fun with him."

Ashleigh blinked several times, her demeanor projecting sadness if you knew her well enough to read it. Which Kyle did.

After dinner, Paula returned to her bedroom, herding the boys with her to finish their homework.

Ashleigh worked alongside Kyle as they cleaned up the dinner dishes and put away the leftovers. There was no need for conversation. They worked silently, diligently avoiding any possibility of physical contact. Nevertheless, his fingers itched to touch her while they were in such close proximity, causing him to be extra wary. The adage "if you can't stand the heat, get out of the kitchen" repeated over and over in his head.

Relieved to be done without incident, Kyle was about to make his escape when Ashleigh spoke up.

"Kyle?"

He turned to her.

"Can I talk to you a minute?" she asked.

The subject could be anything and he wasn't up to getting into a battle with her.

He opened his mouth to say just that when Ryan and Mark came running down the hall.

"Mom asked if you'd start the shower for us," Mark said.

"Sure," Kyle agreed, thankful for Paula's timing.

"I'll be right up. Let me grab a plastic bag to wrap Ryan's cast." As the boys ran up the stairs, Kyle turned to Ashleigh. "Our discussion will have to wait."

He didn't stick around for a reply and left the kitchen with the plastic bag and no remorse. He stayed upstairs while the boys took turns showering so he wouldn't have to deal with Ashleigh again.

"This is ridiculous," he mumbled to himself, and slowly descended to the first floor to find her.

She was on the phone in the living room. From the little he could make out on her side, it sounded like a personal call.

Not that he cared. She could have a hundred boy-friends. It was none of his business.

Yeah, that's why the sudden weight on his chest made breathing a chore.

With Ashleigh on the phone it was the perfect opportunity to get the boys tucked into bed and va-moose. So he did just that.

He took a minute to check on Paula and nearly made it to his truck.

"Kyle!"

He could have easily ignored Ashleigh, but he'd never been a coward.

Although he'd also never claimed to be brave, ei-ther, especially when it came to his ex-wife.

He reluctantly turned to Ashleigh, allowing her to catch up to where he stood next to his truck.

He turned his car keys over and over in his hand

while he waited for Ashleigh to speak her mind. Because if he stopped twirling them, he knew he'd clench his fist so hard it would set off his vehicle alarm.

ASHLEIGH'S HEART BEAT wildly as she struggled for the words that might allow the two of them to peacefully coexist. They'd never return to the days when they were a couple, but she couldn't stand feeling like an outsider. Her relationship with her sister didn't have a prayer of improving until she could convince Kyle she wasn't the enemy. He was the first step toward family harmony.

"Thanks for waiting." Her words came out weak and raspy. She coughed to clear her throat. If not for her boss refusing to end their phone conversation until he was satisfied that she would follow up with her clients, then she wouldn't have had to run after Kyle and get so out of breath.

Kyle leaned back against his truck. "You wanted to talk?" The jingling of his keys rattled her nerves.

She swallowed with difficulty. "I wanted to apologize."

Silence.

"For things I said earlier," she continued. "Like about spending so much time with Paula and the boys."

He opened his mouth to speak, but she raised a hand to stop him.

"I know it's been hard on my sister, not having

Scott around to help out. Especially since she's pregnant." She brushed an errant hair off her face. "Thank you for being there for them. You're a busy person with a demanding job and I appreciate how much you've given to my family."

"They're my family, too." His monotone fairly oozed disdain.

"Of course they are. And I know it's difficult for you to have me around." Her heart beat faster. "Difficult for everyone."

The slight twitch in his right eye indicated a chink in his self-control. "If you expect me to forget the past and act like everything's fine, then you're going to be disappointed."

She shook her head and took a step toward him. "No, no. I understand that, but I'd like us to call a truce while I'm here." She paused. "For Paula's and the boys' sakes."

And because I can't stand being considered an outcast, especially by my own family.

She took his silence as agreement and went on. "I came here to help Paula get through her pregnancy and it's imperative we not upset her. If we can be civil until after she delivers, I promise I'll do my best to keep our contact to a minimum." She took a quick breath. "I've only ever wanted the best for everyone." She paused. "Most of all, for you."

Ashleigh reached across the few feet that separated them to touch his arm. He jerked away.

"What the hell do you think you're doing?" His eyes blazed.

"I don't know what you mean. Please lower your voice." She swung around to see if anyone had overheard them.

The late-April sun had set an hour ago. The currently deserted neighborhood was shadowed by the bluish white of the mercury-vapor streetlights and the occasional porch light, but the neighbors would come wandering out if they heard raised voices.

"You're playing me," he accused.

"What?" This time *her* voice was too loud. She lowered the volume. "I have never 'played' you."

"Sure you have," he said stiffly. "You do it to everyone. You soften people up to get them to do what you want them to. I have to give you credit. You're successful ninety-nine percent of the time."

Ashleigh's hackles rose because he was right—she went on the offense. "What is it you think I want you to do, Kyle?" If he'd figured out that she wanted to know about his lawsuit, then she'd kick herself for being transparent.

"You tell me," he spit. "Tell me exactly what you want from me."

Angry tears clouded her vision at his uncharacteristic harshness, but she refused to show weakness. "I don't want anything from you except some civility while I'm here." She crossed her arms over her chest, rubbing at the goose bumps on her upper arms caused by her blatant lie.

"Done."

"Good. Now what do you want from me?" she asked. "What can I do to make things easier?"

He barely paused long enough to consider his answer. "Go home. Go back to your precious new life." His words slashed at her. "There are enough people around to take care of things here."

She could barely speak over the lump in her throat. She should fight him, except she was tired of arguing. And anyway, wasn't that what she wanted? To return to her life in Richmond and not look back?

"You'd love that, wouldn't you?" She straightened her spine, surprised by her own words. "Well, think again. You can't tell me what to do. This is *my* family and I'm not going anywhere."

"You'd rather risk Paula's health by sticking around?"

Ashleigh couldn't believe he'd said that. "That's not what I'm doing. I'm taking care of her boys so she can rest like she's supposed to."

Kyle didn't say anything, simply turned to his truck.

She didn't want to leave the conversation unfinished. "Wait." This time she did touch his sleeve. His bicep flexed at the contact.

He clicked his truck locks open as his head spun around. In the low light, she could see he wasn't immune to her. His breathing accelerated and the heat coming off his body intensified.

She drew her hand back when she realized the same was true for herself.

He grabbed her hand and jerked her close, his eyes fixed on hers. She couldn't pull her gaze away, no matter how much she tried.

His body was solid and unyielding, as was his expression. He was furious. She placed a hand on his chest and he swore. His mouth was hot and rough when it captured hers. Her eyes closed and her world tilted.

Their issues were put on hold. No hurt, no betrayal, no misunderstandings.

Only lust. Pure, unadulterated lust.

She'd spent the past two years avoiding thoughts of them together like this and now the heat was spreading through her body like a spark to kindling.

If she stopped to dwell on all she'd lost, there would have been pain. Indescribable agony. Now here she was, rediscovering the magic between them, reviving the sexual claim they had on each other with no thought about where this was headed or what the consequences might be.

No thought whatsoever.

Her arms encircled his waist and her splayed hands moved upward, recognizing his solid back muscles by touch alone. Her fingers moved then, to the deep ridge in his lower back where his firm backside began. All the while, his mouth was doing delicious things to hers, as if the past few years hadn't happened.

Perhaps they had a chance at civility after all.

Kyle drew away abruptly, taking a step backward. They stood a foot or more apart. A sudden chill enveloped her.

"Sorry." His tone was gruff as he ran a hand through his hair. "That shouldn't have happened."

He turned his back to her, missing her hand fly up to cover her silent, openmouthed gasp.

He retrieved his keys from the curb where they must have fallen when he grabbed her. Then he continued with purpose around the truck to the driver's side.

His door was halfway open when she said, "Kyle?"

He stopped, his expression unreadable in the darkness.

Her heart sank. Not only had she gotten the wrong message from his kiss, but now things between them had definitely gotten more complicated.

If that was even possible.

"Never mind," she whispered.

CHAPTER FOUR

PAULA HAD BEEN in and out of bed all night. Why couldn't OBs understand that complete bed rest was virtually impossible when your pregnancy bladder acted like an alarm clock? Of course, every time she got out of bed and moved around it woke Bam-Bam, who was instantly ready to shake, rattle and roll.

Nothing like a kick in the ribs to keep you awake.

She finally gave up and decided to read for a while, but she must have fallen asleep because a knock on her bedroom door startled her awake.

"Come in." Daylight peeked through the front window where the curtains met and the book she'd been reading lay across her chest. She searched the covers for her bookmark and set the book next to her.

Ashleigh entered, carrying a tray that, from the delicious smell, must be breakfast.

"Good morning." Ashleigh's words sounded more cheerful than her expression conveyed. "I hope you still like eggs on a raft. I came to ask you before I started cooking, but you were asleep."

"I haven't had that in years!" Paula's ho-hum attitude changed slightly for the better. "The boys like scrambled eggs, so that's what I usually fix."

Ashleigh set the tray down. Along with the poached eggs on toast were hot tea, orange juice and blueberry yogurt. Perfect, just like Ashleigh.

"You didn't have to go to so much trouble." Paula pushed aside her mental insults because she couldn't wait to dig in. "Thank you."

"You're welcome." Ashleigh helped Paula get the tray settled and glanced around the bedroom. "Is there anything else you need? The boys are finishing breakfast and I started a load of laundry."

Paula swallowed her first mouthful of food and shook her head. "No, this is wonderful." She cut off another bite of toast and ran it through the perfectly done yolk. "Grandma used to make this for us."

Ashleigh's eyebrows rose. "I remember."

She probably hadn't expected Paula to solicit a conversation, but what the heck. They needed to start somewhere. This pregnancy still had several weeks to go.

"Remember that day she spent so much time teaching us how to crack eggs without breaking the yolk?" Ashleigh's hint of a smile at the memory seemed genuine.

"And the number of eggs we wasted!" Paula took a sip of tea and it sloshed close to the edge of the mug when she unexpectedly chuckled. "We must have gone through close to two dozen and there was more shell than egg in the bowl."

"Then Grandpa came into the kitchen, asking what all the racket was about." Ashleigh's lips curved into a smile. "And we were astonished when he demonstrated his perfect, one-handed crack of an egg. That day he became my hero."

Paula sobered, recalling her deceased grandparents' loving relationship. "I remember the way he always looked at Grandma and I used to think, 'That's how I want my husband to look at me.' I was about eight or nine at the time."

"That's exactly what you've got," Ashleigh reminded her in a quiet voice.

"I know. We both have men like that." The words escaped Paula's mouth before she realized what she was saying. "I didn't mean—"

Ashleigh stiffened, crossed her arms over her chest and turned toward the bedroom door. She did an immediate one-eighty. "I need to say something."

Paula had an apology ready on her lips, but instead she waited for Ashleigh to continue before making things worse.

"I know it's awkward having me around but I'm not leaving." Ashleigh kept her eyes averted. "I'm here for the duration."

That was the last thing Paula expected Ashleigh to say. "Where did that come from?"

Ashleigh's lips quivered as she spoke. "Kyle and I—" She cleared her throat. "We talked last night. He wants me to go back to Richmond. That way there would be less stress on you."

Paula couldn't believe her ears. She hadn't wanted Ashleigh here in the first place, but she'd known it was for the best. Not because she and the boys needed someone they could count on, but because she and Ashleigh needed to work things out.

"Kyle said that?" Paula's words came out harsher than she'd intended. "You know, I'm getting pretty sick and tired of everyone making decisions for me without even consulting me."

"He just wants what's best for you—we both do," Ashleigh said.

"We?" Paula spoke sharply, her temper flaring. "Since when are you and Kyle *we?*" She could feel herself becoming irrational, but it ticked her off that everyone was ganging up on her.

"Paula—"

"I don't want to hear any more." She'd lost her appetite and shoved the food tray to the other side of the bed.

Paula didn't want anyone's help. She wanted to manage on her own like she always did.

The mix of emotions flowing through her was enough to make her want to bawl her eyes out. But she'd be damned if she'd give Ashleigh the satisfaction of knowing she'd upset her.

"You really should eat."

Paula stared at Ashleigh until she silently picked up the tray and stood at the end of the bed as if waiting for Paula to say more.

Instead, Paula got her oversize, pregnant self out of bed and walked into the bathroom with her head held high. She slammed the door, essentially ending the conversation with the stranger who had never felt less like a sister than right at that moment.

KYLE TOOK A healthy swig of coffee in the nearly empty hospital cafeteria. His cell phone rang. The caller ID read "Paula" so he answered immediately.

"Is everything okay?" His heart rate accelerated. Paula rarely called, preferring to text instead.

"No," Paula barked into his ear. "Everything is *not* okay."

Was she in labor? He didn't have a chance to ask before she continued. "What right do you have telling Ashleigh to go home?"

This was not good. How much did Paula know about last night? "So you're okay? Physically?"

"Yes, I'm fine. Still pregnant, still on bed rest, and now I'm ticked off. What did you say to Ashleigh?"

"I thought you didn't want her here." Kyle remembered to moderate his voice in the public cafeteria.

"I don't," she shot back. "But she's my sister, in case you've forgotten."

"No, I haven't forgotten," he said gently. "Do you want me to ask her to stay?" *Please say no.* After he'd kissed Ashleigh last night, he'd wanted to kick himself.

He'd also wanted to kiss her again, and again, if truth be told. He'd always been physically attracted to her, no matter what was going on emotionally.

"It doesn't matter." Paula's voice caught. "She told me she's here for the duration. Even if I asked her to

go, she wouldn't. Not that she's ever listened to me."
A sound like a sob came from Paula.

"Are you crying?" He couldn't tell if she was angry or sad, but he knew better than to point out her irrationality.

Another sob. "No, I'm not crying," she said before succumbing to actual crying.

"Listen, would it help if I talked to her and apologized?"

"I don't care. I'm tired of people plotting behind my back."

"You know that's not what we're doing."

"Really?"

"We're trying to do our best for you and your baby."

Paula sniffled. "I know. I'm sorry." She sobbed, a choking sound that nearly broke Kyle's heart. "I just want to be back in charge of my life."

Kyle grasped for something to say. "This will all be over soon and you'll forget about the bad stuff when you hold your baby."

"Promise?"

"Promise."

Paula ended the call and Kyle wasn't sure if he was supposed to talk to Ashleigh or not.

LATER THAT MORNING, after Ashleigh got the boys off to school and knew Paula would be okay until lunchtime, she headed out to run some errands. Paula's stress level would be lower without Ashleigh hanging around. Besides, she had her cell phone with her if an emergency arose.

First off was her pediatric practice to see how things were going.

"Good morning, Dr. Wilson." Cammie Varrone, the fortysomething office manager, greeted her with a welcoming smile. "I didn't realize you were in town."

Ashleigh returned her smile. "I'm helping out my sister. She's having some pregnancy complications." That sounded like a reasonable answer, as long as no one asked about her relationship with her sister.

"Tell her we're wishing her well and let us know if we can do anything."

"That's very kind of you," Ashleigh said. "Is Dr. Mitchell in?"

"He's returning calls in his office. His first patient isn't due for another fifteen minutes."

Ashleigh pointed to the closed door that led to her father's office when he'd owned the practice. "I'll peek in for just a minute."

She knocked quietly on the door and heard, "Come in." She slowly opened the door and stuck her head in the room.

Stan Mitchell's eyes widened and he smiled. He held up one finger and ended his phone call. "Let me know if the fever continues with the new antibiotic." He hung up the phone, rose slowly from his chair and came around the desk. "Come in, come in! It's so good to see you!" He hugged Ashleigh and it crossed her mind that this man she didn't know that well was giving her such a warm welcome, while others she'd known for years had barely acknowledged her presence.

He held her at arm's length and looked at her. "So how are you? What brings you here?"

She quickly updated him on her life and explained in minimal terms why she was in town. Yet, during their conversation, she got the distinct feeling that there was something wrong with Stan.

"Are you feeling all right?"

"Busy as usual," he said. "You know how it is."

When Ashleigh moved to Richmond, Stan had taken over the pediatric practice she'd inherited from her father upon his death. Stan had grown up in Grand Oaks but had spent his medical career at a children's hospital on the West Coast. The high stress level had worn him down, so he'd gratefully accepted the position in Grand Oaks.

"Well, just make sure you're taking care of yourself." Ashleigh wasn't convinced he was simply overworked. "I can help out while I'm in town, you know. Come in a few hours a day to give you a break."

"What about your sister? I thought you were here for her." At least Stan didn't give her a flat-out no.

"She doesn't need me twenty-four seven—in fact she'd probably like the break. The boys are in school during the day, so I can come in the morning, go home to get Paula lunch and then come back for an hour or two until the boys get home."

Stan lowered himself onto the corner of the desk. "If you think you can do it all, then I'd be grateful. I am feeling kind of worn-out these days. My wife's been complaining that I barely have enough energy to eat dinner." He laughed, but Ashleigh's concern heightened. "I probably need some B vitamins to perk me up."

They set up a schedule for the rest of the week and Ashleigh went on her way. Other than forcing him into a doctor's office for a physical, she wasn't sure what else she could have done. Next time she saw him, though, she'd push the physical idea. One step at a time.

AFTER A QUIET MORNING in the E.R., there had been a sudden rush of patients when Kyle was about to take an early lunch break. Now it was nearly one and his starvation was finally appeased after finishing a turkey sub and two apples.

"There you are." The young female voice behind Kyle startled him. "You didn't answer your page so they sent me to look for you."

He turned to answer the young student nurse. "What's up, Katelyn?" He checked the beeper at his waist, wondering why he hadn't felt it. He must have been really hungry not to notice.

"Dr. Mitchell was brought into the E.R. with an apparent heart attack. Ms. Snyder thought you'd like to know," she said, referring to the E.R. ward clerk.

"Stan Mitchell?" The guy was in his mid-fifties.

At the girl's timid bob of her head, Kyle rose from his chair, nearly knocking it over in the process. "Thanks," he said over his shoulder, and hurried through the busy hallways to the E.R.

"What's Dr. Mitchell's status?" he asked breathlessly of the E.R. ward clerk.

"He's in curtain three," she said. "His wife is over there." She pointed toward the waiting room where a petite blonde was wringing her hands.

Kyle turned on his heel to speak to Stan's wife, unable to recall her first name. He pulled a metal chair closer to the youthful-looking woman probably in her mid-forties and sat. "I'm Kyle Jennings, Mrs. Mitchell. Stan took over my ex-wife's pediatric practice." The term "ex-wife" would never flow smoothly off his tongue.

She nodded her head. "Yes, I remember you. We met at that hospital fund-raiser." Her eyes were red and puffy. "Is Stan going to be okay? One minute he was talking to me at lunch and the next—"

"I'm going to see how he's doing and I'll let you know." Kyle stood and put a hand on her shoulder. He squeezed it gently before hurrying off to curtain three.

The E.R. doctor on duty exited from Stan's curtained area. "How is he?" Kyle asked.

"Lucky," Chuck Borden answered. "His wife was with him and was able to get the first responders there quickly. She did chest compressions until they took over. They almost lost him in the ambulance."

Unbelievable. The cardiologist on duty would order tests to find out how much damage Stan's heart had endured. At least now he had a good chance of recovery.

"I'll let his wife know he's stable and that she can come sit with him."

Chuck nodded and made a notation on Stan's chart.

As Kyle walked back to the waiting room, a thought occurred to him. Ashleigh would have to deal with Stan's health issues and necessary absence since she still owned the practice.

Kyle wasn't sure why she hadn't sold it. Beyond family, it was her last tie to the town.

Now he needed to figure out how to get someone else to make the call to Ashleigh to let her know Stan's condition.

He dialed her pediatric practice from memory and the office manager answered. Cammie was the perfect choice to pass on the news about Stan to Ashleigh.

AFTER LEAVING HER pediatric office, Ashleigh spent the morning stopping at a few of her favorite places in town. There were some things she couldn't get in Richmond that she'd grown accustomed to in Grand Oaks. Like the homemade bread from Mama's Bakery on Market Street and a fresh supply of dry red wine from Mossy Oak Vineyard.

She'd barely pulled into the parking lot of the vineyard, located about two miles out of town, when her cell phone rang.

Why would someone from her pediatric practice be calling? "Hello?"

"Dr. Wilson?"

"Yes?" Ashleigh answered.

"This is Cammie, um, Cammie Varrone, the office manager at Dr. Mitchell's—I mean your—pediatric office."

"Yes, Cammie, what is it?"

"Well, I'm afraid Dr. Mitchell is in the hospital—"

"Oh, no! What happened? Is he all right?" Ashleigh's heart was in her throat as she waited for details. She'd barely left him a few hours ago.

"He apparently had a heart attack," she said with a trembling voice.

A heart attack? He was too young for that, she thought, even though the doctor in her knew he wasn't. "How bad?"

"They're not sure how much damage his heart sustained."

"Thank you for letting me know. I'll call the hospital and see if they have an update."

"Um, Dr. Wilson?"

"Yes?" Was there more?

"We have no one to take over Dr. Mitchell's caseload."

Cammie didn't know about Ashleigh and Stan's schedule, so Ashleigh filled her in. "What about Dr. Charles?" Livvy Charles had a pediatric office in the next town over and served as Stan Mitchell's backup.

Ashleigh couldn't handle the practice full-time and take care of her sister and nephews, too.

Silence. "She's on maternity leave," Cammie finally said. "Her baby was born a few days ago and Dr. Mitchell has been seeing her patients."

Of course he was.

"Okay." Ashleigh sighed. "Let me figure out what to do and I'll get back to you."

"I've canceled all the well-baby and physical appointments for today, but I don't know what to do about the rest."

Ashleigh considered her options. The pediatric practice was still her responsibility—she should have sold it before moving to Richmond.

"You did good, Cammie. Give me half an hour and I'll be over to figure out how to handle this."

They disconnected and Ashleigh remained in the vineyard parking lot to make some phone calls. Unfortunately, no one was available to step in and no one knew anyone they could recommend.

After nearly fifteen minutes, she finally hit upon Samantha Collins—an old medical school colleague who could fill in temporarily. The only problem was that Samantha couldn't come for a few days due to teaching obligations. But Ashleigh could deal with that.

Ashleigh let out a relieved sigh. "Thanks so much, Sam."

"This will be fun," she told Ashleigh. "I don't get

to practice nearly as much since I took this teaching job at the medical school."

They spoke for a few more minutes before Ashleigh ended the call. There was no way around it. She would have to take over the practice until Sam got here.

Now she—and Paula—had no other choice. Ashleigh would have to find someone to help out at her sister's, at least part-time.

Ashleigh made a few more phone calls and ended her search for household help successfully.

She called Paula. "How's it going?"

"Fine." Paula's lack of enthusiasm wasn't a surprise.

"Stan Mitchell had a heart attack." Ashleigh hadn't meant to blurt it out, but she'd lost the ability to converse normally with her sister.

Paula gasped. "Is he okay?" Ashleigh related what she knew about Stan and then told her about the young woman who would be helping out.

"Mrs. Baxter, next door to you, has a twenty-two-year-old granddaughter who's looking for work. She says the two of you met last Christmas. Emma graduated from college in December and is willing to help out until she finds a full-time teaching job. Her degree is in elementary education." Ashleigh paused a second. "She can get the boys off to school, do laundry and grocery shop. Then I can take over when I get home."

Paula was quiet for an uncomfortably long time.

Ashleigh was about to speak when Paula finally said, "I guess that will work."

"Then I'll see you after I get things straightened out in the office. Emma will come over right away."

Ashleigh put the car into Reverse and backed out of the space.

So much for the wine.

Not long after that, Ashleigh pulled up in front of Paula's. "I'm here," she called out cheerfully when she entered the house.

"I'm still in bed," Paula groused, her tone of voice cool.

Her sister was sitting up in bed, paperwork spread out around her that appeared to be bills. Her hair was damp and secured with combs away from her face. Her creamy complexion was flushed. She looked at Ashleigh, apparently waiting for her to speak first.

"Did it work out with Emma?" Ashleigh asked.

Paula shrugged unenthusiastically. "I guess so." She wasn't about to make this easy, was she? "She just left."

"What did she make you for lunch?" Ashleigh asked.

"I told her I wasn't hungry."

Unacceptable. Lunchtime had come and gone a few hours ago. Keeping her censure to herself, she went to fix Paula some lunch, whether she wanted it or not.

LESS THAN AN hour later, Ashleigh was entrenched in her former office at the pediatric practice her father opened in the late sixties. She drummed her fingers on the desk as she waited to see her first patient in two years.

She took in the strangely unfamiliar surroundings. This was Stan's domain now, with his diplomas and awards displayed on the walls. Pictures of his wife and two grown daughters were arranged on the credenza, along with a photo of a black lab with a stick in its mouth.

Stan initially told her he wanted to work part-time after putting in so many grueling hours at his last job. Ashleigh expected to have her work cut out convincing him to return to his hometown, but it hadn't taken much coaxing after he realized he'd be able to play golf and tennis at the refurbished country club. As soon as they'd settled into their newly renovated farmhouse on ten acres outside of town, his wife had jumped right into the Grand Oaks Garden Club.

How was Linda doing now? Ashleigh could only imagine how worried she must be.

She was reaching for the phone on the desk to call her when a knock sounded at the door. Cammie must be coming to tell her that her first patient was in exam room one. "Come in," she called out. "I'll be right—"

It wasn't Cammie at the door, but Kyle. Her mouth stopped functioning.

He yanked at the collar of his button-down shirt. His sleeves were rolled up to the elbows, and her gaze was drawn to his forearms. The instantaneous memory of running her hands down his arms to entwine her fingers with his had her blood heating to a rapid boil.

"I saw your car parked outside and figured you'd heard about Stan." His voice was both solemn and sexy.

She nodded hesitantly and recovered her voice. "How is he?"

Kyle filled her in on Stan's condition, ending with, "He's scheduled for a triple bypass tomorrow."

Ashleigh did the recovery calculation in her head. "So he won't be able to come back to work anytime soon."

"That's if everything goes smoothly."

There was an uncomfortable silence until Kyle finally spoke. "Stan put his own stamp on this office, didn't he?" He gestured to the mementos spread around the space.

"I remember coming here as a little girl when it was my dad's office." Her throat thickened with emotion. "He had that huge oak desk that had been passed down from his grandfather. The one I used to use." She'd put it in storage when she moved away from Grand Oaks.

"He would set me right here." She motioned to the area on the desk in front of her. "And he would point his finger at me and say, 'You can be anything you want to be. Just because I chose medicine doesn't mean you have to.' Then he'd wink and say, 'But it sure would be nice to work next to you.'" Then he would pull a lollipop from the desk drawer and hand it to her.

"He was a great guy," Kyle said with a sad smile. "It's too bad the two of you didn't get to live out his dream for longer than that one year."

A cloud of melancholy blanketed her as the memories of her now-deceased father bombarded her. "He used to tell me how, back when he first opened the practice, people would pay him in chickens and vegetables or even cigarettes when money was scarce. Especially the families who had someone serving in Vietnam, leaving the women to deal with everyday life at home, including their sick children."

"Those must have been tough times," Kyle said.

Ashleigh nodded. "My dad would make house calls back then. Not only to those with sick children, but he regularly visited homes where food was scarce. He'd bring them the food other patients had paid him in, saying he couldn't use all of it before it would spoil."

Kyle spoke gently. "I always considered him as much a mentor as a father-in-law."

Ashleigh missed her father so much, but he would have been extremely disappointed in her. He wouldn't have liked knowing she'd left town when her marriage failed, abandoning the practice he'd built.

Kyle walked over to the credenza under the window to look at Stan's framed photos. He finally broke the silence with a change of subject. "Stan won't be able to work for a while. Do you have anyone to help out with the practice?"

Ashleigh related her plan to fill in until Samantha arrived.

"What about Paula? You can't be two places at once."

"I've got someone coming in to help while I'm here. Paula's not happy about it, but I've given her no choice." Paula's compassion for Stan was the only reason she gave in about hiring help.

"She understands, though, right?"

Ashleigh met his dark blue questioning gaze. "I guess so. Not that she's pleased about it." She stood and shoved the wheeled desk chair back into the bookshelves. Blood rushed in her ears. "Can't blame her, though. First, she didn't want me here, and I tell her that I'm here whether she likes it or not. Then I say I'm sorry but I have to help out somewhere else and, oh, by the way, here's a stranger I hired to take care of you."

She knew her voice was getting louder and louder, but she couldn't help herself.

"It's not like you're responsible for Stan's heart attack."

Ashleigh turned away, crossing her arms over her chest. "I'm not sure that's a true statement."

"Ashleigh?"

She didn't say anything. The guilt was eating her up. Stan wasn't well this morning. Why hadn't she suggested he see a doctor right then and there?

She spun in Kyle's direction, changing the subject before she blurted out the truth.

"Anyway, Kyle, I'm not sure why you care so much about what's happening with me and this practice. You're the one who told me to go home last night!" Ashleigh came around the desk until she was a few feet from him. She lowered her voice to an angry whisper. "'You're not needed here,' you said. Well, if I took your advice, then I'd never have a chance of repairing my relationship with my sister. Or maybe that's what you're hoping. As long as Paula and I are estranged, then I won't be back to visit and you won't have to risk running into me."

His jaw dropped open and he quickly snapped it shut.

A knock sounded on the door and Cammie stuck her head in. "Your first patient is waiting in exam room one." She was gone as quickly as she'd appeared.

Kyle didn't say a word. Said nothing to contradict Ashleigh's statement. He merely left the office and never looked back to see the hurt that had to have been apparent on Ashleigh's face.

CHAPTER FIVE

PAULA GLOWERED AT KYLE as he removed the blood pressure cuff from her arm a little while later. She waited until after the distinctive ripping sound of Velcro to hiss, "Of course my blood pressure is going to be high. It's not like I'm living a stress-free life here."

"Get over it," he mumbled. He was sick of having his mettle sorely tested. His patience was growing thin. "You love the attention." He spoke more gently, knowing Paula wasn't to blame for either her predicament or his own. "You know we're all concerned about you." He returned the equipment to his medical bag. Keeping his gaze averted, he confessed, "That's not the only reason I stopped by."

"Go on," she said.

"I wanted to apologize again for interfering last night. For asking Ashleigh to leave."

"I understand why you did it."

"You do?" He snapped his bag shut and met her eyes.

Her smile was devious. "She scares you."

Kyle laughed at the idea. "That's crazy."

As crazy as Paula's mood swings. One minute she was angry, the next sweet. Treating him as if he was the enemy was quickly followed by acting like his therapist. Who knew where her hormones would lead next. Not that he was about to verbalize his thoughts.

"Is it crazy?" She quirked an eyebrow exactly like her sister.

"Of course it is. Why would I be afraid of Ashleigh?"

"Maybe because you've never stopped loving her and now you're afraid with her in town that she's going to figure it out?"

"That's *definitely* crazy," he repeated, but then he paused to consider the notion. "Maybe I still care about her, but that's as far as it goes. We were involved for half our lives. Feelings don't have switches, you know."

She tilted her head and narrowed her eyes. "Maybe you're afraid she doesn't feel the same way about you?"

"That's ridiculous." This whole conversation was ridiculous.

Paula's skepticism was written all over her face. "Whatever you say." Her eyes danced. Whether at his discomfort or her absolute confidence that she was right, he didn't know. Possibly both.

"No, not whatever I say," he argued. "Ashleigh left. Period. She feels nothing for me and I'm definitely over her."

Paula's eyebrows rose.

"That's the truth!" He didn't know how to convince her. "Just because of that one ki—"

He shut his mouth when her eyes widened and her lower jaw dropped. So she *didn't* know about the kiss. *Damn.*

Paula slowly closed her mouth and stared at him. "You two? You kissed? When? Last night? I can't believe it. Then why did you tell her to go home?"

He inhaled slowly, not sure how much to admit. "Yes, last night, but it meant nothing." At least nothing to Ashleigh.

"You idiot!" Paula slapped her hand on the blanket next to her.

"Hey!" He already knew he was an idiot. He didn't need Paula reminding him. "Look, we're divorced and we've both moved on. I'm even pretty sure she's seeing someone."

Paula scowled at him.

"You know you look like Mrs. Buffington when you make that face," he told her, referring to the strictest teacher they'd all endured back in their elementary school days.

She glared at Kyle. "Stop trying to change the subject."

He cleared his throat. "I need to get back to the hospital."

She waved a hand at him. "Go ahead. Ignore the truth."

"Did you ever think that maybe you're wrong?"

She shook her head vigorously. "Nope." She raised a finger. "Oh! And don't forget to come back for dinner tonight."

"I didn't know I was invited."

She narrowed her eyes. "It's the least you owe me for the latest trouble you've caused between Ashleigh and me. You'll be our buffer."

Kyle considered it. "All right." He turned to leave. "I'll see you later then." Over his shoulder, he added, "Behave yourself."

"No fun in that!" she yelled with a laugh as he went out the front door shaking his head.

If only Paula weren't so close to being right about so many things. Even when he and Ashleigh were in the middle of splitting up, it was Paula who kept telling him their divorce was too civil. No fighting, no screaming, no knock-down-drag-outs.

Not until their divorce became final and Ashleigh had run away had Kyle realized how right Paula had been. Maybe if he and Ashleigh had gotten out some of their anger two years ago, they wouldn't be as combative now.

He started his truck and shoved the gearshift into Drive. Paula couldn't be right. No way did he have feelings for Ashleigh after all this time. She'd practically crushed the life out of him when she left him to grieve alone for the babies they'd lost.

ASHLEIGH STEPPED OFF the elevator on the hospital's fifth floor. Thanks to Cammie's efficiency, Ashleigh already had temporary privileges at the hospital, enabling her to park in the staff parking lot.

She headed down the hall to the newborn nursery, her palms damp. According to Cammie, the patient she was here to see was male, born late yesterday afternoon, vaginal delivery with no complications. He was a few weeks premature, but his birth weight was five pounds, fifteen ounces, and his vitals were strong enough to keep him out of the Neonatal Intensive Care Unit.

As much as she had braced herself, the sight of several healthy newborns swaddled in plaid blankets in their bassinets was staggering. She'd hoped most of them would be off in their mothers' rooms, but the infants were having their vitals checked in the nursery.

She stopped a moment and took a deep breath to stave off her light-headedness before approaching the R.N. at the desk.

Ashleigh held out her badge, attached to a lanyard around her neck. "I'm Dr. Wilson." She cleared her throat when she realized her words were barely audible. "I'm here to do a physical on Baby Boy—" She checked the paper Cammie had written the name on. "Baby Boy Stanton."

The nurse retrieved the baby's chart and motioned for Ashleigh to follow her to the patient. Ashleigh had difficulty concentrating on the update the R.N. was giving her as every tiny squeak and wail around her caused the vise on her heart to squeeze tighter.

She'd long ago accepted that she'd never have a child in this or any other newborn nursery. It wasn't meant to be.

That didn't make being in this atmosphere any less painful.

She pushed the ache aside and concentrated on the physical examination. The boy was a pretty newborn and she couldn't say that about all of them. His skin was pink and clear, his hair was dark and there was quite a bit of it. He closed his hand around Ashleigh's index finger and her cheek itched when a tear escaped.

She swiped it away angrily and gingerly turned the boy over onto his tummy. It had been too long since she'd examined a newborn and she wasn't as adept as she used to be.

"He's strong and healthy," she told the nurse when she finished making notes in his chart. "Let me know if anything changes or if he has trouble passing the car seat assessment, although I don't expect a problem." The test entailed spending time in his car seat in the nursery while his vitals were monitored. If there was any sign of distress, he would be reevaluated. "Otherwise, I'm writing the order for discharge. He can go home when his mother does, as long as the infant visits my office within forty-eight hours to check his bilirubin."

Ashleigh stepped over to the tiny office to record the physical report, which would be transcribed by someone in the medical records department. Then she hurriedly left the area and found the nearest ladies' room. Her hands were shaking and her skin was pale and clammy.

This embarrassing emotional reaction to being around infants and children was exactly why she'd given up pediatric medicine.

KYLE PARKED HIS TRUCK in the staff lot at the hospital and made his way to the second floor where he was meeting the hospital lawyer about his lawsuit.

"Hey, Tom." Kyle and his longtime friend shook hands. "Please tell me you've made this lawsuit go away."

Tom Patterson grimaced. "Afraid not." He gestured for Kyle to take a seat at the conference table and sat down across from him.

"But I did everything according to standard procedures," Kyle insisted. "There was no way for me to know the guy was a recovering drug addict." Blood pounded at his temples. This whole thing was ridiculous—a waste of time and money. "He had a freaking compound fracture. His femur was sticking through his skin at a right angle. All the guy did was yell for pain meds."

Tom made a face at the explicit details and raised a hand, while his other hand tapped his pen on the table next to an open folder. "He claims differently. He says he never would have asked for drugs when he'd been clean and sober for nearly three years."

"How was I supposed to know that?"

"He swears he was wearing a medical-alert bracelet. And he has documentation that shows he's had it since he left rehab."

"Impossible!" Kyle couldn't believe this. "We were at the scene of a horrific car accident. It's one of the first things I checked when I pulled him out of the car. Could it have come off in the accident?"

Tom shrugged. "That's possible, I guess, but it never showed up. He also says he carries a card in his wallet."

"There was definitely no wallet on him and his car was on fire. I was lucky to get him and his passenger out before the car exploded." Kyle ran his hands through his hair. He'd been the only other person on the road when he came across the one-car accident. "What's the status of his passenger? Is she still in a medically induced coma?" The woman had been airlifted to Shock Trauma in Richmond, so Kyle hadn't been able to monitor her condition.

"Last I heard," Tom verified. "Which means we can't count on her testifying whether or not he was even wearing the alert."

"But it *is* possible he wasn't wearing it, right?" That had to be it. The scenario made more sense than if it had fallen off during the accident.

Tom hesitated before answering. "It's been known to happen." He consulted his notes. "My investigator says this was a first date for the pair. They'd met through an online dating service." He looked up at Kyle. "It's possible the guy didn't want questions about his addiction. A medical-alert bracelet or even a necklace would have brought up obvious questions."

"But we can't prove that."

"Exactly."

"I'm positive he had no medical-alert jewelry on his person." Kyle ran his fingers through his hair.

"That's exactly what you should say in the deposition next week. No more, no less."

Kyle considered the advice. "Will this actually go to trial?" He'd never been involved in a malpractice suit before.

"That depends on whether or not we can get any information from the passenger. You know I'll do whatever I can to make this go away." He paused and stared at Kyle. "I owe you."

"Not true."

Back in high school, Tom and Kyle became friends through football. Kyle was the school's starting quarterback and Tom was the best receiver Grand Oaks High had seen in two decades. He caught balls that most players didn't even try for.

Which was how Tom's football career ended. He'd been scouted by several top football colleges and finally decided to go to the University of Southern California. Unfortunately, he tore up his knee in the second game of his freshman season while stretching full out for a pass, ending his football career.

Kyle had been there for him, flying to California to see him and later suggesting he transfer to a Virginia school so they could all support him.

Tom never let Kyle forget how much that meant to him.

"I'll let you know if there's any change in the woman's condition," Tom said.

They spent a few more minutes discussing the deposition before they ended the meeting and went their separate ways.

Kyle had stepped into the elevator to go to the fourth floor to check on Stan when Ashleigh's familiar voice called out, "Hold the elevator!"

Kyle was close enough to the doors to hold them open with his hand as Ashleigh came rushing down the hall.

"Thanks," she said breathlessly.

Did the blood really need to drain from his brain to his crotch because he had a déjà vu moment at the sound of her voice? Okay, not *just* her voice—that had been her sexy bedroom whisper. The tone she took when she seduced him.

He inhaled deeply and took control of his body. "How did it go with your patients?"

"Pretty routine." She focused on her hands as she folded and unfolded them.

"What brings you to the hospital?" For some reason he couldn't be silent on the short elevator ride. "Are you visiting Stan?"

She shook her head.

Fine, she didn't want to talk to him.

The elevator doors opened on four and Kyle stepped into the hallway. He turned to say goodbye and realized how pale she was. "Are you okay, Ashleigh?" he asked.

She shrugged, still concentrating on her hands.

He was about to walk away but instead stepped back into the elevator.

"What are you doing?" she asked.

This time their gazes collided and he realized how upset she was.

"Trying to be considerate." His words were clipped. "Although you definitely make it difficult."

Her eyes widened. "How am I doing that?"

"By denying that practicing medicine again is one of the most difficult things you've done in a long time. That's how."

Her shoulders straightened and she shot back. "What business is it of yours anyway?" The elevator reached her floor and she stepped out before the doors were completely open.

He gritted his teeth. "You're right, it's none of my business. You made it none of my business when you took off for Richmond." He punched the number for his floor again and the close doors button, but she was already gone.

"DR. WILSON!"

Ashleigh turned at the male voice calling to her from down the hallway and couldn't help but smile. She'd just checked on her teenage patient, which had given her a chance to cool down after her run-in with Kyle. Now, seeing her old friend, her mood lightened considerably.

"Dr. Wilson?" she teased Tom. "Is that how child-hood friends greet each other, Attorney Patterson?"

They hugged and he kissed her cheek. "Good to see you, Ashleigh," he said. "It's been too long." He paused a moment and winked when he added, "And I prefer Thomas Patterson, Esquire."

They shared a chuckle and Tom asked, "What brings you back to town? Not enough happening in Richmond?"

She smiled, surprisingly relaxed as she told him about Paula's condition. "And now I'm also filling in for Stan Mitchell until he's ready to come back to work after his heart surgery."

"What?" Tom's eyes widened. "I met with Kyle earlier and he never mentioned any of that." He checked the time on his watch.

Ashleigh wasn't surprised that Kyle hadn't talked about her being in town. After all, he didn't want her here in the first place.

"You had a meeting with him?" she asked. Tom was the hospital lawyer. Could their meeting have been about Kyle's lawsuit?

Tom checked his watch again, as if he'd forgot-ten what time it was a few seconds ago. "I did." He sounded rushed all of a sudden. "Ashleigh, I have a meeting in ten minutes that I'm probably going to be late for." He cocked his head. "How about lunch tomorrow?"

Ashleigh didn't hesitate. "Name the time and place." Tomorrow was Saturday, which meant drop-in morning hours at her office, but then she was free. She'd discharged both of her hospital patients, so as of right now she had no hospital rounds to perform. "Maybe a late lunch since I have to work in the morning?" She recalled times when her waiting room was filled with sick children and she hadn't finished seeing them until midafternoon. Hopefully tomorrow wouldn't be one of those days.

"One o'clock at The Tavern?" he suggested.

"Perfect." She smiled, then gave him a quick hug. "Thank you," she whispered close to his ear.

Puzzlement clouded his eyes when he asked, "What for?"

She shrugged, a little embarrassed. "I haven't gotten what you'd call a warm reception since I've been back, so I appreciate that you actually want to spend time with me."

"Of course I do." He rubbed her upper arms in a friendly gesture of support. "I could never take sides between you and Kyle. You know that."

She did know that. She'd been friends with Tom since they were kids, neighbors on the same street.

"I can't imagine not being friends with either of you," Tom added. "In fact, I'd love to get your opinion on something at lunch tomorrow."

Ashleigh's throat tightened at his sincerity. "Of course. You know our friendship goes both ways." She'd worried about him after Theresa broke their engagement. Hopefully, enough time had passed and he'd gone on with his life.

"I know." He glanced at his watch a third time. "Gotta run." He took a few hurried steps away from her and waved. "See you tomorrow."

"Looking forward to it." She spoke loudly enough for him to hear it down the hallway.

She slowly followed in his path as she made her way down to the first floor and her car. Getting to her sister's for more bickering wasn't appealing in the least, so why rush the inevitable?

"Paula's napping," Emma told Ashleigh when she got home. "The boys are in the basement playing video games. I thought it would be okay since there's no school tomorrow," she added quickly as she gathered her long brown hair into a ponytail.

"I'm sure that's fine." Ashleigh smiled. "I'll take the blame if there's a problem."

"I'm also supposed to tell you that Dr. Jennings will be here for dinner."

Ashleigh's eyebrows rose. Had Paula invited him? Before or after they ran into each other at the hospital? He never mentioned it, not that they'd had an in-depth conversation.

After Emma left, Ashleigh inventoried the food and checked on the boys so they knew she was there.

"What should I heat up for dinner, guys?" She recited the list and one wanted spaghetti and the other wanted hot dogs, which she'd never even mentioned. "Tell you what. I'll ask your mom and Uncle Kyle what they want and we'll see which meal gets the most votes."

They both cheered. What was it with boys always making things a competition?

She returned to the kitchen, preheated the oven and put together a salad before checking on Paula again.

"You're awake." Ashleigh felt ridiculous after voicing the obvious.

Paula looked up from the magazine she was thumbing through.

When Paula simply stared at her, Ashleigh continued. "I told the boys I'd take a vote on dinner, but I'll make whatever sounds good to you." Again she recited the growing list of food Paula's neighbors and friends had been bringing by, and she realized how well-liked her sister was in the community. "I already made a salad to go with whatever you choose."

"Spaghetti sounds good," Paula said. "There should be a frozen loaf of garlic bread in the freezer that we can throw in the oven, too."

Ashleigh turned to leave.

"Ashleigh?"

She faced Paula.

"I invited Kyle to come for dinner." Paula's complexion deepened.

"I know, Emma told me." Ashleigh couldn't stop from asking, "When did you invite him?"

"Right after lunch. He came to take my blood pressure. Why?"

"Because he didn't say anything when I ran into him at the hospital."

Paula scratched her head. "I wonder why."

Ashleigh shrugged. "My theory is he's trying not to cause problems between any of us."

"Yeah, that's probably it." Paula essentially dismissed her by turning her attention back to her magazine and muttering, "But so far he hasn't done a very good job of it."

"WHY DON'T YOU invite your friend over, Uncle Kyle?" Ryan asked in the middle of dinner. "She was a lot of fun when she came to my game."

Kyle nearly choked on his mouthful of spaghetti. He must mean Theresa. Dinner had been civil so far, with the conversation centered on his nephews—he intended to keep it that way.

Kyle held up one finger, swallowing his food before speaking, which gave him a moment to think. How could he explain why the woman who used to be engaged to his best friend was now pretending to spend time with him?

He glanced at Ashleigh before answering. She appeared to be patiently awaiting his reply. "I don't know. Maybe we can call Theresa and see if she wants to do something with us."

What the *hell!* Why had he said that?

"Yay!" Ryan cheered, while Paula's eyebrows rose in surprise and Ashleigh turned pale.

He caught Paula's eye over the table and winced. She didn't approve of what he was doing—heck, he didn't even have a reasonable explanation to satisfy himself.

"Excuse me." Ashleigh rose, her skin still pale.

"Ashleigh?" Kyle stood without thinking, ready to do whatever necessary to make her feel better, including confessing that there was nothing going on between Theresa and him. They'd innocently met several times about the charitable organization he was forming, but it instantly revved the rumor mill into a frenzy. Theresa then decided she might as well use the situation to make Tom jealous.

Personally, Kyle thought it was a dumb plan.

Ashleigh barely whispered, "I need some water." She went directly to the cupboard for a glass and filled it with ice and water from the fridge dispenser. He lowered himself back into his seat. He'd explain to Ashleigh at the first opportunity.

Meanwhile, Ryan continued the conversation about Theresa. "Do you think she'd like to go roller-skating, Uncle Kyle?"

"What?" The question caught Kyle off guard. "Why don't we talk about it later."

He steered the conversation away from Theresa and the rest of the meal went reasonably well.

In fact, the remainder of the evening continued fairly comfortably until he was ready to leave. He hesitated. He needed to come clean to Ashleigh about Theresa.

"Ashleigh, do you have a minute?" He'd tucked the

boys in and said good-night to Paula before finding Ashleigh sitting alone in the living room with a book.

She set the book aside. "Sure."

"About what Ryan said at dinner tonight," he began. "About Theresa?" As if there was any question what he was referring to.

Before he could say more, Ashleigh raised a hand. "There's no need to explain. If you want to date your best friend's ex-fiancée, it's none of my business."

"But—"

"Really, Kyle. We're divorced. There's no reason why you shouldn't be seeing anyone you want."

He thought she grimaced as she spoke, but he must have been mistaken because it disappeared as quickly as it appeared.

"It's not like I haven't had my share of dates." Her admission cut through him.

His chest constricted. The mere thought of another man touching her, let alone doing anything more intimate with her, made him want to throw up. Followed closely by the urge to punch the guy's lights out.

What had he expected? That she'd stay celibate the rest of her life?

Wasn't that pretty much what he'd been doing?

"I'm sure there are plenty of eligible men in Richmond." He cleared his throat because he'd barely been able to choke out the words.

"If you're seeing Theresa or whoever, it's not a problem for me." She rose, turning her back to him while she moved her book unnecessarily. She swiped a hand across her cheek so quickly before turning back that he nearly missed the action. "I'm happy you're moving on. Because that's exactly what I'm doing."

"Oh." He clenched his hands so he didn't reach out to pull her to him. To erase the memory of any man who'd ever caught her eye. "That was the impression I had when I overheard a little of your phone conversation last night," he said.

Her brow furrowed. "Last night?"

He tried for nonchalant. "You were talking to someone in the living—"

"Oh! Sure. I didn't realize you—" She stumbled over her words. "He's—"

"It's okay, we're clear. No need for explanations." His heart was heavy in his chest. "We've both moved on."

He turned to the front door and walked out to his truck on legs that didn't want to work.

CHAPTER SIX

AFTER A GRUELING Saturday morning of walk-in patients suffering from everything from colic to strep throat to an allergic rash, Ashleigh was relieved to be pulling into the parking lot of The Tavern. The good news was that she'd been so busy all morning that her anxiety in relation to being around children—and sundry other things—had barely surfaced. Her hands had even been steady while examining a ten-day-old infant.

That didn't mean her apprehension wasn't there, waiting for the right opportunity to slap her upside the head.

She checked the time on her dashboard clock. She was a few minutes late for her lunch with Tom. Grabbing her purse from the passenger seat, she slid out of the car as gracefully as possible in her navy pencil skirt and matching spectator pumps with their four-inch heels.

Not the clothes she would have chosen for a day with patients—especially young children with sticky fingers and runny noses. Dress pants and fitted blouses were preferable under a lab coat, but the only clothes beyond denim she'd brought with her were suits for out-of-town work meetings that she might schedule. *So much for that.* She'd barely given her clients a thought since Stan's heart attack.

Ashleigh stepped carefully across the parking lot with its broken macadam. The sun shone bright on this spring day. If not for the blowing wind that lowered the air temperature, Ashleigh wouldn't have needed her matching tailored jacket.

Unbidden, she recalled the many times she and Kyle had met here for lunch or dinner back in happier days.

She swallowed thickly, slightly nauseous. There it was. Her omnipresent angst—front and center.

Straightening her spine, she opened the outer door to step into the restaurant's vestibule and then reached for the second door handle. Tom's sweet, smiling face was visible through the glass and her entire being relaxed. Tom was a good friend and lunch should prove to be fun and stress-free, whether or not she could finagle information about Kyle's lawsuit out of him.

"Sorry I'm late," she told him when they hugged and he kissed her cheek.

"I just got here myself." He turned to the hostess. "We're ready to be seated now."

The hostess retrieved two menus. "Right this way." She led them to a deep red upholstered booth near the back of the richly decorated restaurant with its dark walnut wainscoting and framed historic maps.

After they sat, she placed a menu in front of each of them. "Carla will be your server. Enjoy your meal."

"Thank you." Then Tom looked at Ashleigh, his smile broad.

"What?" She felt her head. "Is my hair sticking up or something?"

He laughed. "No, no, I'm just glad you're back in town. Even if it's only for the time being."

She grimaced.

"You don't seem pleased." He raised one blond eyebrow. His boyish good looks had barely matured over the years, the minuscule laugh lines at the corners of his hazel eyes the single visible sign that he'd aged right along with her.

"It's complicated," she said.

His eyebrows rose and he pointed to the wine list on the back of the menu. "Too early?"

She chuckled. "Under other circumstances, I would say no, but I'm on call."

"On call?" he repeated. "Isn't there some other pediatrician to do that?"

She waited until after their server took their drink orders to explain the situation, omitting her difficulties with Kyle and Paula. Tom was friends with all of them—she wouldn't want him to feel he had to take sides.

After the server brought their iced teas and took their lunch orders, Ashleigh asked, "What's new with you?" She folded her hands on the table and leaned in conspiratorially.

He shrugged, but she knew there was more to it.

"Didn't you say you wanted to talk to me about something?" She grinned at him. "Come on, we're like family. You're the brother my parents never gave me."

He laughed, saying, "Yeah, I was always the 'brother' and Kyle was the love of your life."

He'd poked an open wound; she forced herself to get past the pain. She lowered her voice to a whisper. "Believe me, I'd love to hear about someone else's life rather than my own."

He frowned. "It's nothing. I shouldn't have said anything." He focused on his hands, folded on the table.

She was about to oblige him and change the subject when he continued.

"I can't get over Theresa." He smiled a little nervously and pretended to wipe the sweat from his brow. "There, I said it out loud."

Ashleigh reached across the table to touch his arm. "You two were together for quite a while."

Did he know Theresa and Kyle were seeing each other?

She cocked her head and waited patiently for him to continue.

"I've tried dating other women, but all I do is compare them to Theresa. One laughs too loud, one has no sense of humor. One is a picky eater, one is a horrible cook."

"Sounds like you've been doing a lot of dating."

"Not really. I always notice something that either annoys me or convinces me that they don't measure up to Theresa—and then I don't ask the woman out again." Their food arrived and Tom waited until they were alone again before continuing. "What am I going to do, Ash? I keep finding flaws in women. I'm never going to get over Theresa at this rate."

"You know that no one's perfect." Ashleigh took a bite of her chicken Caesar salad.

"Of course." He was silent for a few minutes, chewing a bite of his Reuben thoughtfully before speaking. "But Theresa is as close to perfect as I've ever come."

He poured a pool of ketchup on the side of his plate and dipped a French fry into it.

She understood completely. When she tried dating after her divorce, no one was as good as Kyle. Lucky for her, she'd had the excuse of infertility to make her decision about never dating a bit easier. If you could call infertility a good excuse.

She reached over to steal a fry and plopped it into her mouth before he could slap her hand away. "So what's your plan?"

"My plan?" He pushed his plate closer to her so she could take more fries. She declined with a shake of her head.

"What's your plan to get Theresa back?"

"I guess I don't have a plan."

"Maybe you *should* have one."

He grinned and began eating with gusto. "Maybe I should."

Ashleigh didn't want to mention Kyle's part in all this. Tom had issues that needed fixing if he wanted Theresa to consider taking him back, without worrying about his best friend's role in all this. There would be time enough to give him the bad news later.

Too bad her own problems were way beyond any plan that she might come up with.

TOM TOOK ANOTHER BITE of his sandwich, slowly chewing it and swallowing while he pondered Ashleigh's analysis of his situation.

He needed a plan.

"Hey, you guys!"

"Theresa! Hi. So nice to see you!" Ashleigh greeted his ex-fiancée warmly while Tom tried not to choke on his iced tea.

He hadn't talked to her in nearly six months. Although he'd seen her around town from a distance several times, this was the first she'd spoken to him since she called off their engagement right after the Halloween party they'd hosted.

On second thought, Theresa wasn't technically speaking to *him*. She had turned her back on him and was talking directly to Ashleigh.

This was not a good way to begin his plan to win her back. Not that he had the vaguest idea what that plan might entail.

"I heard you were back in town for a while." Theresa's bouncy chin-length blond haircut was new. He decided it matched her personality, although today she exuded nervous energy rather than perkiness. "We should get together."

"That would be great," Ashleigh agreed, giving Tom a quick look.

"Hi, Theresa," Tom finally said when she was about to leave without even acknowledging his presence.

"Oh, hi, Tom." Her tone was flippant, but there was something in her eyes. Maybe pain? Regret?

He was fooling himself. She'd made it perfectly clear months ago that she wanted nothing to do with him. Only his imagination remained unconvinced.

"Listen, I have to go." Theresa pointed to the exit. "Someone's expecting me." She glanced at him, probably gauging his reaction.

No. Just his delusional imagination at work.

"I'll give you a call, Ashleigh." She hurried away and exited the restaurant without glancing at him again or even saying goodbye.

"Well, that was uncomfortable," Ashleigh noted. "I can't believe she showed up right after we were talking about her."

"I know. Freaky."

Ashleigh scrunched up her face as if hesitant to speak. "Do you think she's seeing anyone?"

"If she is, it's news to me." Tom squeezed the napkin balled in his hand while trying to sound nonchalant.

"You still want her back even if she's involved with someone?" Ashleigh asked in her blunt fashion.

"Do you really think she's dating someone?"

"Don't answer my question with a question, Mr. Lawyer."

They both relaxed at her teasing, but he couldn't reply to her question because he didn't know the answer. "She hurt me pretty bad, Ash, but I want her back." A sharp pain in his midsection hinted that he couldn't stand the thought of Theresa being with anyone else.

"I know she hurt you." Ashleigh squeezed his hand and gave him a sympathetic look with pursed lips and a slight tilt of her head. "Let's change the subject." At his nod, she continued. "So…what can you tell me about Kyle's lawsuit?"

Tom was taken aback. He took a long drink of his iced tea to give him time to think. "You know that's confidential. Even if you were still married to Kyle," he added.

"I know, I know." She bobbed her head rapidly. "It's just frustrating that I can't get anyone to tell me anything." She sipped from the straw in her iced tea. "Just give me some idea of how much trouble Kyle's in."

"I can only tell you what's public knowledge." Tom explained about the crash and how Kyle pulled both occupants out of the burning car. "Now the guy is suing because he was given pain meds. He claims he was wearing a medical-alert bracelet that said he was a former drug abuser." That part had been reported in the local newspaper—what he couldn't tell her was anything his investigator had dug up.

"I can't believe Kyle wouldn't have checked," Ashleigh said. "It doesn't sound like him."

"That's what Kyle claims, too. I'm sorry, that's all I can tell you, Ash," Tom said. "You can check out the library for the old newspaper articles on it. I'm not sure how long they keep back issues on their website."

"I understand. Thanks for filling me in. The library's a good idea." She looked directly into his eyes and asked. "What are his chances to beat this?"

"I'm doing everything I can," Tom told her confidently. "Right now our best bet is the other passenger who's in a medically induced coma in Richmond."

Ashleigh digested the information and they spent the next few minutes eating in silence.

ASHLEIGH CHEWED HER FOOD thoughtfully, unable to come up with a suitable change of subject until the people from the neighboring booth got up to leave.

"Mrs. Thornton!" Ashleigh exclaimed when the older woman stopped at their table. "How have you been?"

"Very well, thank you." Mrs. Thornton patted her freshly dyed ash-blond hair while keeping the other hand on her walker for balance. "I just came from Betty Lou's to meet my friend, Estelle, for lunch."

She gestured to the other woman who'd walked ahead to the exit.

"Betty Lou did an excellent job," Tom told her. "Your hair looks especially lovely today."

Mrs. Thornton blushed, adding more color to her overly rouged cheeks. "And you're every bit the flirt you've always been, Thomas Patterson." She fiddled with the pearls at her neck that matched the buttons on her two-piece lilac sweater set.

They exchanged a few pleasantries, including the predictable question of why Ashleigh was in town, before Mrs. Thornton asked the inevitable. "How is that husband of yours?" Her eyes narrowed as if Ashleigh were on the witness stand.

"He's doing well," Ashleigh answered, deciding not to correct the "husband" part of the question.

"What a gift he is," Mrs. Thornton exclaimed. "So helpful and generous."

"Yes, sometimes too helpful, I suppose." Not everyone would have stopped to help a stranger along the side of the road.

"Why, whatever do you mean, too helpful? I didn't know there was such a thing."

Ashleigh smiled. "I just meant not everyone appreciates his helpfulness. Like that man whose life he saved—some show of gratitude, suing him for malpractice now." Tom kicked her under the table. "Ouch!" She glared at him and leaned down to rub her sore shin.

"Suing him?" Mrs. Thornton was oblivious to anything but Ashleigh's words. "I hadn't heard that."

Tom spoke up then, his look daring Ashleigh to say another word. "It's not a big deal, Mrs. Thornton. A misunderstanding is all. I'm sure we'll get it settled soon."

"Well, this is news to me." The woman harrumphed and turned her walker to make an exit. "This is news to me." She shook her head and mumbled to herself all the way to the restaurant's entrance.

"Why did you kick me?" Ashleigh asked, her shin still smarting.

"Because you brought up the lawsuit—we're trying to keep it low-key."

"Oh, crap. I'm sorry. I just assumed people knew.... That was dumb of me. I haven't seen her in years and I just started gabbing. Sorry."

"It's okay. In ten minutes she'll have hopefully found a more sordid piece of gossip to indulge in," Tom said.

Ashleigh figured she should change the topic. "How long has she had the walker?"

Tom's brow furrowed. "At least several months. She broke her hip a while ago, but I guess at eighty-five it's hard to recover completely."

"Must make it difficult for her to get to all her charitable organization meetings," Ashleigh noted.

"Agreed. Although with her money, I'm sure she's

able to have someone accompany her whenever she likes."

"True." Mrs. Thornton had been a widow for several years. Even before her husband died, she'd generously spent most of her time and money on bettering the lives of the less fortunate in Grand Oaks and the surrounding communities, concentrating mainly on the children. "Did she seem a little intense when she asked how Kyle was doing?"

"Maybe a little," Tom agreed. "She's definitely a product of her generation. Maybe she has a problem with your divorce."

Ashleigh considered it. "That's probably it. She did make it a point to call Kyle my 'husband' rather than 'ex.'"

After paying their check, Ashleigh and Tom left the restaurant. "It was great to see you again," she told Tom as she hugged him goodbye.

"You, too." He gave her an extra squeeze before releasing her. "Let's do it again soon."

She smiled and waved, walking to her car while digging in her purse for her keys.

The time on her dashboard clock read 2:35 p.m., which meant she'd have plenty of time to get to the library, as well as play with her nephews before making dinner.

Maybe if she was lucky, her sister would be napping when Ashleigh arrived and there would be no need for conversation.

KYLE SPENT THE entire day painting the bedroom he was turning into his home office. Pleased with the results of his neutral color choice called mocha, he wiped an errant spot of paint from the hardwood floor. Then he cleaned his roller and tray before showering. Hopefully he'd get the second coat on tomorrow.

He'd moved into the two-bedroom apartment not long after Ashleigh left their small apartment over the pediatric practice. He couldn't bear to stay there without her. Too many memories flooded his brain every time he crossed the threshold.

Their first night there.

The intimate dinners they'd shared, sometimes not making it through the meal before their sexual appetites for each other became more important than sustenance.

The lazy Sunday mornings they stayed in bed, made love, did the crossword puzzle together, made love again, and then showered together. Blissfully whittling away the day.

Then there was the first positive pregnancy test, followed shortly thereafter by a miscarriage. They'd been devastated. But soon afterward they had another positive pregnancy test. They had no doubts about the second pregnancy because they both understood that spontaneously aborted first pregnancies were common.

They turned out to be overwhelmingly wrong in that assumption.

He never saw it coming. One day he'd been in the E.R. when the head of the department came in to relieve him so he could go be with his wife. He refused to acknowledge the loss of another baby until he saw the distraught look on Ashleigh's face in the OB's office. Her tearstained cheeks and red-rimmed eyes, now devoid of emotion, made it real for him.

That pattern continued until they'd closed themselves off from both the world and each other. Cocoons of pain, grief and loneliness. He spent every free moment researching new cures and procedures for miscarriages, with no success.

Kyle took a deep breath and pulled himself from the past. He turned off the shower and yanked his towel from the rack.

He'd barely stepped out of the shower when the phone rang. He wasn't on call, so he stood in the doorway leading from the bathroom to his bedroom, listening for a message on the answering machine which sat on his bedside table.

"Kyle, this is Edna Thornton. Please call me as soon as possible."

"What in the world could she want?" he said aloud when she ended the message.

He hurried to towel off and dress in jeans and a T-shirt before returning her call.

"Hello, Mrs. Thornton, this is Kyle Jennings," he said when she answered the phone. "How are you?"

She skipped the pleasantries. "I saw your wife

today. Ex-wife, I guess you would call her." She sounded perturbed and Kyle didn't know why.

"Yes, Ashleigh's in town for a few weeks," he confirmed.

What Edna Thornton told him next made him want to throw something against the wall.

CHAPTER SEVEN

ASHLEIGH GOT INTO her car in the Grand Oaks library parking lot and started the engine. The newspaper articles hadn't provided any more information about the car crash and subsequent injuries of the driver and passenger. The one thing she'd learned were the ages of those involved. The driver was thirty, his passenger currently in a coma was a mere twenty-two.

Tom had pretty much given Ashleigh the lowdown on the situation. The one thing missing in the follow-up articles was a mention of the lawsuit. She still didn't understand why the driver was suing Kyle— he would have absolutely checked for medical-alert jewelry before giving him anything. She knew that with all certainty.

How tragic for everyone involved.

With the engine still idling, she retrieved her cell phone to search for the Richmond hospital's number. She entered it into her phone, hit Call, and the operator answered on the first ring.

"I'd like the condition of—" Ashleigh glanced at the paper where she'd written the young woman's name. "The condition of Miranda Green."

"One moment, please."

Silence would have been preferable to the interminable recorded message over an eighties song blaring in her ear.

"Fourth floor," the young-sounding woman on the other end finally answered.

Ashleigh repeated her request.

"Ms. Green's condition is stable but critical," Ashleigh was told. "Are you a relative?"

She could have lied or at least mentioned she was a doctor so she'd be transferred to the R.N. assigned to the patient, but that wasn't how she operated. "No, I'm not."

"Visitors are limited to immediate family," the hospital employee said. "I'm sorry, but that's all I can say."

"I understand," Ashleigh said. "Thank you very much," and ended the call.

She tossed her phone into her bag and put her car in Reverse to back out of the parking space. What a horrible situation for both the patient and her family, losing valuable time while she remained in a coma… with no idea if she'd be the same person when and if she regained consciousness.

So much for trying to help Kyle. He probably wouldn't appreciate her help anyway from the way he'd been treating her. She just couldn't stand seeing him wrongfully accused of something.

Maybe there was some sort of public record that she could look up to see what the guy was claiming.

If only she knew where to begin… Oh, well, she'd run out of ideas for the time being.

She arrived at Paula's to find the boys had finished their homework and were now playing their daily allotment of video games.

She went downstairs into the basement to check on her nephews. "Can I play?" She'd never been good at video games. Her focus had been on schooling as a kid and young adult, but she was hoping for a good bonding experience with her nephews.

Both boys stared slack-jawed at her, their unabashed shock at her request a little insulting.

"Do you know how to play?" Ryan asked.

"Not the game you're playing," she said. "But I'm sure you guys are good teachers."

The boys glanced at each other. "Sure. Okay," Mark said.

Ashleigh grinned at them, glad they didn't mind including her in their fun. "Good. I'll go change and be back in a flash."

Thirty minutes later Ashleigh was comfortable in jeans and a fitted tee, still trying to remember which buttons did what on the game controller. Her hesitation made the boys laugh hysterically each time she made a mistake.

Another fifteen minutes and she was begging for mercy.

When the game was over and she'd lost both in score and integrity, Mark said, "Uncle Kyle is way better than you."

"Yeah," Ryan chimed in. "You should have him give you some lessons."

"Thanks for the bruise to my ego, guys." Ashleigh's words were lighter than her heart at the mention of Kyle.

Mark narrowed his eyes. "Aunt Ashleigh, why aren't you and Uncle Kyle still married?"

Ashleigh's breath left her lungs in a whoosh. She hadn't seen that question coming. "Well, what has your mom told you?"

As good a place as any to start.

"Mom said you and Uncle Kyle didn't get along even more than Ryan and me," Mark said.

"And that's why you got a 'vorce," Ryan added.

"De-vorce," Mark corrected with overdone enunciation.

Ashleigh's cell phone erupted into song and she couldn't help thinking she'd been figuratively "saved by the bell."

"I should get this," she told them, even though she didn't recognize the number. She struggled to get up from the floor, her legs stiff. "I'll be right back, guys."

She hobbled upstairs to the kitchen where it was quieter. "Hello?"

"Hi, Ashleigh, this is Theresa Banks."

"Hi, Theresa." She was surprised to hear from her so soon after talking to her at the restaurant earlier that day. "What's up?"

There was a slight hesitation before Theresa spoke.

"I was serious about getting together and I wondered if you might want to meet up for a drink tonight."

"Tonight?" Ashleigh repeated, feeling a little stupid for sounding like an echo simply because she didn't want to hear Theresa confirm that she was involved with Kyle.

"Yeah, I'd like to get your advice on something."

Something or *someone?* Had Ashleigh suddenly become the Dear Abby of Grand Oaks? First Tom, now Theresa.

Ashleigh couldn't help cringing at the idea that Theresa might want Ashleigh to give her blessing for her to date Kyle.

"Listen, Theresa," Ashleigh began.

"Please don't say no," Theresa begged, not allowing Ashleigh to finish.

She was struck by the raw emotion in Theresa's plea. Ashleigh had nothing else going on after the boys were tucked into bed. Her sister would probably go to sleep early and Ashleigh would have her cell phone in case she was needed.

She was a *relatively* free woman on a Saturday night.

"All right. But I'll have to wait until after the boys are in bed," Ashleigh said.

"Agreed." Theresa named a quiet bar on the road to Millersville. "Nine-thirty work for you?"

"Sounds good, see you then." Ashleigh disconnected, thinking at least she'd have a drink in her hand to provide a crutch when she gave Theresa the okay to see Kyle—not like her previous conversation with him when she claimed she didn't care if he dated or not. She could have used a whole bottle of whiskey during and after that.

She went back downstairs and turned her concentration back to the boys.

"Next time we'll play a game of my choice," Ashleigh told them after another fifteen minutes of video game hell where they constantly laughed at her ineptitude. "I better start dinner."

"Can we have pizza?" Mark asked over his shoulder.

"Yeah!" Ryan added his vote.

"Hmm." Ashleigh considered it. "Let me talk to your mom and see what she wants."

"She loves pizza," Ryan said. "Especially with yucky vegetables on it."

Mark made a gagging sound.

"Okay, okay." Ashleigh laughed. "If we do pizza, then what do you want on it besides vegetables?"

The boys' noses turned up and their tongues came out.

"We like cheese." Mark spoke emphatically and added a beguiling smile.

"Yeah, just cheese," Ryan echoed. "And sauce and crust, too."

"Deal. I'll talk to your mom."

Ashleigh checked with Paula before calling in the order to their favorite pizza place. "Pizza will be here in a few minutes," she told the boys. "Finish that game and put everything away before washing up."

"Okay," they chorused.

Ten minutes later there was a loud knock on the door. Thinking it was pretty quick for the pizza delivery, Ashleigh took a step toward the door only to have it fly open before she got there.

"Kyle?"

His expression was unreadable.

"We've ordered pizza," she told him. "There's enough if you haven't eaten yet."

His narrowed eyes burned through her. "We need to talk." His jaw muscles clenched.

Not good. Not good at all.

Mark clunked down the steps from upstairs in untied basketball shoes, Ryan right behind him. "Hey, Uncle Kyle," Mark said.

"Hey, guys." Kyle's tone was almost friendly. Then he looked at Ashleigh and repeated gruffly, "We need to talk."

She squinted at him. "O...kay," she said slowly.

"Privately."

KYLE RELAXED HIS fisted hands. The short drive from his apartment to Paula's house hadn't helped cool his temper.

"Pizza will be here soon," Ashleigh said. "Will this take long?"

"I don't know." Kyle hesitated. "I'll go say hello to Paula. And once the pizza arrives, I'll get the boys settled with dinner and then we'll talk." The privacy of his truck was probably the best place for this discussion in case their voices rose, which he fully expected. No need to draw an audience.

Ashleigh's eyes were wary. She must have sensed his anger, because she was much too agreeable.

Kyle was headed down the hallway to see Paula when the doorbell rang. It wouldn't be long now before Ashleigh would have to explain herself.

Paula's bedroom door was open and he knocked lightly on the doorjamb. She looked up from her laptop and he said, "Hey."

"Hey yourself," she said. "What's wrong?"

He took a deep breath. He was lousy at hiding his anger. "Your sister. Don't want to get into it."

"Ah!" Paula nodded knowingly, specifics unnecessary.

He half listened while Paula shared news about his brother. Scott's ship would be returning to port in Newport News within the next few weeks.

"Which means he'll hopefully be here when the baby arrives." Paula was almost giddy.

Paula's excitement should have lessened his anger, but for some absurd reason he couldn't help contemplating what it would be like to have someone—namely Ashleigh—overjoyed at the prospect of spending time with him.

Would he ever find that again? Was he even actively looking? Ashleigh was under the impression he was seeing Theresa. He still had to correct that misunderstanding, but first things first.

Ashleigh interrupted when she brought Paula her pizza loaded with onions, peppers and mushrooms. "Would you like some?" Ashleigh asked him.

"No, thanks." His appetite had deserted him.

She turned to Paula. "The boys are eating and they've promised to bring you more pizza before they get seconds for themselves." She glanced at Kyle. "I trust that whatever Kyle needs to discuss with me won't take too long."

Kyle kept his anger in check. "I'll meet you at my truck." He turned to leave and said over his shoulder, "Bye, Paula. See you later."

He waited in his vehicle for what seemed like a long time, but his truck's dashboard clock said it was only five minutes. The sun had set and the road was illuminated by street lanterns and porch lights.

The passenger door opened suddenly and Ashleigh slid into the leather seat.

She half turned toward him. "What's all this about?"

His hand gripped the steering wheel so tight he wouldn't be surprised if he'd left finger indentations. It took all his might to loosen his grip and relax enough to speak.

"I hear you were at The Tavern today with Tom," Kyle began.

"Yes. You know Tom and I are friends." She

cocked her head. "If you have a problem with me hanging out with—"

"Stop." Kyle held up his hand and ground out, "I told you before, I don't care who you're seeing or not seeing. And while we're on the subject, I am not dating Theresa and I never have."

"Oh." Ashleigh's confusion was revealed in her eyes. "Then what is your problem?"

Unintentionally, his voice rose. "My problem is what you discussed with Mrs. Thornton."

She stiffened. "If you mean the lawsuit, then I have nothing to apologize for. You wouldn't tell me anything," she spit. "So I went to Tom." She took a quick breath and he could see her own anger igniting. "He didn't tell me anything that wasn't public knowledge."

He gritted his teeth, shut his eyes a second. He opened them and kept his voice even. "I don't have a problem with you talking to Tom about it. I trust him to keep things confidential. What I have a problem with is you discussing it with Mrs. Thornton."

Her brows furrowed. "What do you mean? I didn't discuss anything. I just mentioned it… I thought it was common knowledge…."

"I got a call from her today."

"Why did she call you? Did I say something to offend her?" She continued without waiting for his answer or even taking a breath. "I thought I was polite, and what does it matter anyway since we're divorced?"

He pounded his fist on the steering wheel. Ashleigh flinched so he deliberately lowered his voice. "She pulled her funding from my nonprofit."

"Nonprofit?"

He ignored her interruption. "She didn't think I was 'the proper role model for the charity because of the lawsuit.'" The words alone made his blood boil. The lawsuit was a frivolous waste of everyone's time and now his reputation was being tarnished because of it. "She didn't know anything about the malpractice suit until you *mentioned* it."

"But isn't that public knowledge?" she asked.

"The accident was reported in the paper, but not the lawsuit," he said. "Yes, she could have accessed that information, but until today she had no reason to suspect she'd have to."

"I'm so sorry." Ashleigh was reverent. "I had no idea. I didn't know—"

"There are a lot of things you don't *know* about since you ran away."

Her tone became churlish. "I didn't run away, Kyle. I needed to refocus on something other than my failures."

"And I needed to focus on something other than my grief," he said.

She paused as if digesting his words. "What does your charity do?"

No sense in holding back now. There was no way he'd be able to move forward until he found another benefactor. If she wanted to know what she'd ruined, he'd be happy to fill her in. He took a deep breath. "I've been working on setting up a fund for children in need of nonemergency medical care. Things insurance won't cover. With so many people on unemployment, there are elective procedures people can't provide for their children. Orthodontics, cranial remolding, elective plastic surgery."

The diagnosis of his older sister's son, Jeremy, with a debilitating syndrome requiring exhaustive therapy had been the defining moment when Kyle realized not everyone could afford proper medical care for their children. His sister, Maddie, was one of the lucky ones.

"Mrs. Thornton's hundred k would have made a lot of children's lives better."

Ashleigh swiped at her cheek. Darkness was closing in when she said softly, "You're following through on the idea my dad always talked about."

ASHLEIGH COULDN'T BELIEVE Kyle had taken her dad's idea and run with it. She should have been the one to carry on her dad's brainchild. But she'd barely been able to function after she left Grand Oaks, while Kyle had put his energy into doing good for others—exactly what *she* should have done to honor her father.

Her dad and his older sister had been raised by an elderly aunt after they lost their parents at a young age, so there had been no money for the multiple surgeries his sister should have had to correct a congenital facial deformity. She drowned accidentally as a teenager, but Ashleigh's father always thought it had been his sister's way of freeing herself from the looks and ridicule she'd constantly received.

And now Kyle was following up on her father's dream.

"I'll call Mrs. Thornton and see what I can do," she said. "I've gotten pretty good at talking people out of their money."

"No!" Kyle thundered. "Stay out of it."

She was taken aback. "But I can help—"

"There's nothing you can do. You've done enough damage. Don't say or do anything more."

"But it was what my dad always hoped for," she said. "He always talked about how so many children were in need of our help." Ashleigh's voice caught. "He just didn't live long enough to put it into action."

"I know."

They were silent a few minutes before Ashleigh finally spoke. "I'm really very sorry, Kyle. I didn't mean to jeopardize your funding. If there's anything, and I mean anything, I can do to make it right, I'll be happy to help."

He didn't answer as he looked straight out over the steering wheel into the near darkness.

He didn't appear to have anything more to say. Ashleigh reached for the door handle and exited the vehicle. When she reached Paula's front door, she turned to look at Kyle's truck and whispered, "Good night, Kyle."

He had taken on a huge task by starting the charity. Her heart squeezed and a lump formed in her throat.

An unexpected emotional reaction caused by her ex-husband.

She didn't know whether to be happy, sad or downright confused.

No doubt about it. Definitely confused.

By NINE-THIRTY, the out-of-the-way piano bar was beginning to get crowded and Ashleigh had to park behind the building.

Theresa was already there, perched at a pub-height table near the far wall. She raised a hand to wave at Ashleigh, who smiled and made her way through the modern industrial furnishings. The place had received quite an overhaul since the last time she'd been there.

The sleek and modern glossy black bar took up most of the right side of the room with its U shape and smoky gray leather bar stools with stainless steel legs. Top-shelf liquor bottles were arranged prominently on a glass shelving unit in the center of the bar, while wineglasses, martini glasses and various other shapes and sizes of drinkware were displayed above them.

"I'm so glad you agreed to come tonight." Theresa pulled a surprised Ashleigh in for a hug. "I've missed you."

Theresa raised a hand to the person Ashleigh

presumed was their server and soon Ashleigh was ordering a dirty martini.

"I like your new haircut," Ashleigh told her, not knowing exactly what to talk about. She'd never really known Theresa until she'd begun dating Tom. Even then, they hadn't been close friends. In fact, Ashleigh couldn't remember the last time she and Theresa had even spoken. Certainly not since Ashleigh moved away.

Theresa touched a hand to her head and smiled over her glass before taking a sip of the green liquid she'd said was an appletini. "Thanks. After, well, you know…" Theresa's broken engagement to Tom was old news. "Anyway, I needed a change after that."

Ashleigh briefly touched on the parts of her own life that were different since her divorce and she realized she'd changed everything around her, but physically she had remained the same. She wasn't sure what that said about her, but maybe the dirty martini the server set in front of her would provide answers.

She took a sip and nearly sighed aloud. She set the glass aside.

At least Kyle had come clean about not being in a relationship with Theresa and she didn't have to worry about that discussion….

To hell with it. She'd taken a verbal lashing from Kyle tonight. She picked up her glass and gulped down a mouthful. Ashleigh wasn't technically on call until the morning since she'd arranged with the hospital emergency room to care for any of her patients who called her answering service. "So tell me what you've been up to."

She half listened while Theresa told her about teaching third grade and her new apartment, but completely avoided a mention of her social life. Ashleigh could understand why Tom couldn't get over Theresa, with her blond hair now cut in a perky bob and those big round sapphire blue eyes and long lashes. Tonight she was dressed in a bright pink V-neck top that fit snuggly over her shapely figure and was paired with black skinny jeans and plat-form heels.

With half a drink in her, Ashleigh blurted, "What's with you and Kyle? I've heard mixed stories."

Theresa immediately choked on a bite-size cheese cracker from the snack bowl on their table.

Ashleigh rose to help her but Theresa raised a hand. "I'm fine," she said hoarsely. "Give me a sec."

"I'll get you some water." Ashleigh got their serv-er's attention, miming a drink. As soon as she saw Theresa coughing, the server raised a finger before hotfooting it to the bar.

A glass of water appeared in front of Theresa as if by magic. "Thanks so much," Ashleigh told the server.

Theresa finally settled down and was able to speak. "I'm sorry about that. Um…the cracker went down the wrong way."

Ashleigh waited in silence for Theresa to reply to her question.

"It's not what you think." Theresa spoke quickly, reaching out for Ashleigh's forearm. "Kyle's a friend, that's all. I've been helping him set up his nonprofit. Someone saw us together and made the assumption. The story grew from there. You know small-town gossips." She laughed then. "It's kind of great that even you were fooled into thinking there's something going on between us."

"I shouldn't have said anything," Ashleigh told her. "It's none of my business. Whatever's going on with you and Kyle has nothing to do with me." Although her story *did* match up with Kyle's.

Theresa sighed. "But you don't understand. I'm not interested in Kyle as more than a friend. A platonic friend," she added. "I'm still in love with Tom. That's why I haven't been correcting the rumor, hoping to make Tom jealous."

Ashleigh furrowed her brow. "You're still in love with Tom?" At Theresa's nod, Ashleigh continued, "Weren't you the one who called off the wedding?"

"Yes," Theresa said. "I didn't know what else to do. No matter how many times I talked to him about how he took me for granted, he never got it. He gave me no choice but to break off our engagement."

"Go on."

"Well, at the beginning, I was convinced Tom would miss me and would work harder at fixing our relationship."

"But that didn't happen." Ashleigh realized from her conversation with Tom earlier in the day that he didn't know *how* to fix their relationship—or even how to get back into one with his ex-fiancée.

That wasn't for her to tell Theresa, though. If Tom wanted her to know, he would have to do it himself.

"So you and Kyle are just friends and working on the nonprofit?"

Theresa chuckled. "Yes, but if Tom thinks otherwise, then I'm okay with it. A little taste of the green-eyed monster never hurt anyone."

"And how's that working out for you?" Ashleigh already knew the answer.

Theresa's hangdog look spoke volumes. "It's not. I'm pretty sure Tom doesn't even care." Her eyes became bright with tears and Ashleigh was at a loss for words. "I don't know what to do to get him back."

"Would you like me to talk to him?" Ashleigh couldn't stop meddling.

"Oh, no, I didn't ask you here to get you to help me. I wanted to make sure you knew there's nothing going on between Kyle and me." Theresa raised her eyebrows and added, "You know there's no one for Kyle but you."

"Not true," Ashleigh said, although her statement wasn't as heartfelt as she'd expected.

"Yes, true. Kyle would never settle for anyone he thinks doesn't live up to your perfection."

"Perfection?" Is that what people thought of her? "I'm far from perfect."

Theresa smiled. "You don't see what the rest of us see."

Just then their server interrupted their conversation. "Excuse me, ladies, but these are from the gentlemen at that table." She set down two fresh drinks on their table and pointed to two men a few tables over who waved.

Ashleigh and Theresa waved back and mouthed, *Thank you.*

The two women looked at each other and grinned. "This hasn't happened to me since medical school." Ashleigh laughed.

"It's *never* happened to me," Theresa said, then added under her breath, "probably because I don't hang around in bars." She grimaced. "What should we do?"

Ashleigh's phone vibrated. She held up a finger to Theresa and she checked the caller ID. Kyle. He could leave a message. She'd been yelled at enough tonight.

"What do you want to do?" Ashleigh asked.

Theresa's eyes widened. "I don't know!"

Ashleigh laughed. "Let's let them make the first move." She didn't feel like explaining to strange men why she no longer dated, even if they weren't bad looking.

The men rose from their seats in tandem and were walking toward the women when Ashleigh's phone vibrated again. "Now what?" She checked the caller ID. Paula's home number. "I've got to take this," she told Theresa. "Hello?" She headed to the front door, gesturing to her phone when she passed the men who'd bought the drinks.

"Where the hell are you?" Kyle barked into her ear. "And why aren't you listening to your messages?"

Ashleigh pulled the phone away from her ear to check the screen. Three messages. "I'm sorry, I didn't hear my phone. What's wrong?"

"Paula's in labor. I'm taking her to the hospital."

"Labor?" Her stomach cramped and she could barely breathe. "Did her water break?"

"No."

"What about the boys?" she asked.

"Spending the night with a neighbor," he said, "I couldn't reach you."

She stopped before she apologized. Now wasn't the time to bicker with Kyle.

She should have stayed home with Paula tonight. Ashleigh's stomach acid made itself known. "I'll meet you at the hospital."

CHAPTER EIGHT

KYLE HAD CALLED ahead to let the hospital know he was bringing Paula in, so they were met with a wheelchair when he pulled up to the emergency room entrance.

"Thanks, Tim," he said to the orderly who'd opened the passenger-side door and helped Paula transfer to the wheelchair by the time Kyle came around the vehicle. "I can take her from here. Would you mind pulling my truck into the staff lot for me?"

"No problem, Doc." The tall, wiry young man with dreadlocks smiled when Kyle tossed him the keys.

"Great, thanks. Give my keys to whoever's manning the E.R. desk." Kyle turned his attention to Paula, struggling with her relaxation breaths. "Can you talk through it?" he asked. He glanced at his watch. Five minutes since her last contraction.

"Barely," she gasped, then inhaled deeply and blew out slowly when she reached the end of the contraction.

"Hang in there. Dr. Bausch is on her way. She'll meet us up on five," he said, referring to the labor and delivery floor. He wheeled her into the hospital, through the emergency room to the elevator.

Paula simply nodded, conserving her energy.

A few minutes later, after Paula's care had been transferred to a labor and delivery nurse, Kyle found himself pacing the hallway outside of Paula's labor room.

Much like the times he had been here to verify Ashleigh had suffered a miscarriage. Or the one incomplete miscarriage that had required a D and C. He wrung his hands and cracked his knuckles. What a nightmare those times had been.

Why wasn't his brother here? And why the hell was this happening when Paula wasn't even thirty-three weeks along?

Should he try to contact Scott? Probably not until they knew what was going on for sure. His brother wouldn't make it home in time anyway.

How big was the baby? Were his or her lungs developed enough to survive? Would there be lasting medical consequences after such an early birth?

His heart raced at every new worry that came into his head.

"How is she?" A breathless Dr. Rosalinda Bausch came up behind him, as if she'd taken the stairs rather than wait for the elevator. She wore jeans and sneakers, barely a hint of makeup on her olive complexion, and her always meticulously styled dark hair was pulled back into a ponytail. "I was at my son's soccer game," she explained.

"Sorry about that, Rosy. Paula's in there." He pointed to the closed door. "We got here a few minutes ago." He gave her the scoop on Paula's contractions. "That's all I know." He could only hope they'd be able to stop her labor before Paula reached the point of no return.

"Okay." Rosy spoke over her shoulder with one hand raised to knock on Paula's door, the other on the doorknob. "I'll let you know what's going on as soon as I can."

She no sooner disappeared into Paula's room than Ashleigh came rushing down the hall. "How's Paula?" She impatiently brushed a strand of hair from her face.

He gestured to the seating area a short way down the hall and repeated what he knew, staring at the carpeting while he spoke.

They were silent for several minutes, each sitting several feet away from each other in straight-backed blue vinyl-and-metal chairs in the small alcove that served as the labor and delivery waiting room. A flat-screen TV mounted high on the wall was tuned to an all-news station with a lively woman talking incessantly while stock prices and headlines streamed across the bottom of the screen.

He recalled the many other times he'd waited here. The world around you went on, no matter how much pain you were in at the time.

A sniffle from Ashleigh's direction caught Kyle's attention. She sniffed again, leaning over to dig through her purse for something. Her hair was loose and hung down over her face. She finally hefted her purse onto her lap and continued searching, pulling things out to get a better look.

Tears streamed down her face.

"Paula's going to be fine." *Damn.* He never could resist comforting her when she was upset.

She didn't look at him while she continued her search.

Before he could stop himself, he changed seats to sit next to her. He put a gentle hand on her back, relieved when she didn't shrug him off. "She's getting the best care." He spoke quietly, trying to reassure both of them.

She stared straight ahead and whispered, as if to herself, "Sometimes that's not enough."

ASHLEIGH'S MIND WAS going a mile a minute and she couldn't put the brakes on.

Yes, she was extremely worried about her sister and her baby, but that didn't block out the memories of every time Ashleigh had been on this floor. She wrapped her arms around her shoulder bag and squeezed it to her middle like a pillow, reliving the associated pain and heartache she'd suffered.

How many times had she come to this floor? Not only when she miscarried, one of those times requiring a D and C, but multiple times for testing, too. The specialists always started out with encouraging phrases like "eighty percent success rates" before eventually crushing her hopes with "nothing more we can do."

She glanced at Kyle. This seating area was where he had waited for news about her on several occasions, but he couldn't possibly have experienced the same emptiness she had when she'd miscarried. The distress in the pit of her stomach when she'd spotted, knowing it signified the end of another pregnancy. The end of her hopes for the child she carried. The end of her dreams for having a family. The harsh reality that she'd failed to give Kyle the children he had anticipated.

The children he deserved.

A tear dripped onto her forearm and she swiped at the stream running down her cheeks, hoping Kyle didn't notice. She blotted her runny nose with the balled-up tissue she'd dug from her purse a few minutes ago.

"I'm sure your sister will be fine." Kyle repeated his prediction, misinterpreting her tears.

Ashleigh didn't correct him.

"In all probability," he continued, "Paula's already been given steroids to protect the baby's lungs and antibiotics to prevent infection. If her membrane hasn't ruptured, then Rosy will probably prescribe a calcium-channel blocker to stop labor."

Didn't he think she knew that? Ashleigh stood so quickly that her purse fell to the floor. She faced Kyle with her hands on her hips. "I'm a doctor, too, or have you forgotten?"

He stared at her, his mouth pinched shut after her sudden outburst.

"I've also been where she is," Ashleigh continued. "Or is that something else you've conveniently put out of your mind?" When he remained mute, she added, "I may not have been as far along as Paula, but the worry and fear are the same." She frowned at him. "But you wouldn't understand."

She stepped away from him and looked down the hall in the direction of Paula's room. "Why is Rosy taking so long?" She didn't expect an answer. "Shouldn't Rosy have come out by now to let us know what was going on?"

Ashleigh settled in a seat far away from where Kyle sat silently, his head now in his hands. Several more minutes went by before he finally spoke.

"For months...after that last miscarriage—" His voice sounded ready to break. "For months," he repeated, "I avoided this floor. I couldn't bear the pain, the memories, the awful feeling of helplessness."

Ashleigh turned her head in his direction. He spoke to the floor. "These hallways bring all that back," he said. "The sounds, the smells, the decor. Everywhere you look on this floor you're reminded that this is where babies are born."

"And the realization that I'd failed you," Ashleigh added.

"What?" His head came up and he stared, wide-eyed and incredulous, at her. "Why would you think you'd failed me?"

The acid in Ashleigh's stomach churned. "You know very well why. I couldn't give you children."

Now Kyle stood, his hands balled into fists. "You wanted children as much as I did. Why the hell would I blame you for the miscarriages?"

"Because that's what you did," she said bluntly.

"How?"

"You kept insisting we see doctor after doctor, specialist after specialist. When nothing could be done, the blame lay directly on me. You were perfect, enough healthy sperm to fertilize a small nation. I was the one who couldn't carry a baby to term."

"I never once blamed you, Ashleigh, and you know it." He rubbed at the strain in his temples.

"Maybe you didn't say those exact words," she said, "but I know that's how you felt."

"How could you know how I felt?" His tone was seeped in frustration. "We never even discussed it."

He'd avoided her, that's why they never talked.

"If you're going to hold yourself responsible, then I have to do the same for myself," he said when she remained silent.

His statement sounded utterly ridiculous to Ashleigh. "How do you figure that?"

"Because it takes two to have a baby and if it becomes impossible, then it's the result of both parties."

"Then why—"

"Excuse me." Rosy had come down the hall without either of them hearing her. They looked at her expectantly. "Paula's one centimeter dilated and fifty-percent effaced. Even though her contractions were strong, they weren't efficient."

"Were?" Ashleigh let out the breath she didn't even know she'd been holding. "Did you stop her labor?"

"Not quite," Rosy said. "But I've started nifedipine and her contractions have already slowed."

"How's her blood pressure?" Ashleigh asked. "Are there any signs of preeclampsia?"

Rosy shook her head. "Her blood pressure is a little high, but not as high as it was at my office a few days ago. I'm more concerned right now about stopping her labor."

"Are you going to let her go home?" Kyle asked.

"No, I think it best we keep her in the hospital for the rest of her pregnancy to monitor her, even if we're able to completely stop her labor."

Kyle nodded. "I agree." He turned to Ashleigh, who had taken it all in. There was a buzzing in her ears. "Ashleigh?"

She looked at him because that's what seemed to be called for. Her breathing became normal again.

Relief can do that to a person.

At the same time, she selfishly wondered why Paula was always the lucky one.

KYLE HADN'T MOVED after Rosy's update and subsequent departure. Knowing Paula was being well taken care of, his thoughts returned to his conversation with Ashleigh.

How could she have believed he blamed her for

miscarrying? Had he been so blind to her emotional needs that he never recognized the guilt she carried?

It made perfect sense now, but when it was all happening neither one of them was thinking rationally.

He and Ashleigh walked down the hall to visit with Paula for a few minutes. They'd promised Rosy they'd only stay long enough to see if she wanted anything, because Paula needed to rest.

"I hear you have an obedient child," Kyle kidded when they entered Paula's room, trying to keep the atmosphere light.

She gave him a tired smile. "Bam-Bam must have heard me yelling at the boys and decided I don't take guff from my children."

"Smart for someone who can only hear."

"Bam-Bam?" Ashleigh had remained unobtrusive at the end of the bed until now.

Kyle explained, "That's what she nicknamed this one."

"We decided not to find out if it's a boy or a girl," Paula added. "Either way it's got quite a kick. Hence, Bam-Bam."

Ashleigh blinked rapidly several times.

Kyle tugged at the neck of his shirt, useless to diminish the lump in his throat. They'd never gotten far enough along in their pregnancies to nickname the fetus, let alone settle on actual names.

"We don't want to stay long—you need your rest,"

Kyle said. "Is there anything you want us to bring you tonight?"

Paula pursed her lips as if considering. "I'm good for now. If you can get me a pencil and some paper I can start making a list for tomorrow. I'm not sure how long I'll be in here."

Kyle didn't want to be the one to tell her she'd be in for the duration—let her doctor be the one to break the news.

"What about Scott?" Kyle asked.

Paula's head jerked up. "What about him?"

"Don't you want to let him know what's going on?" Ashleigh asked.

"What is this, gang-up-on-Paula time?" Her voice rose and her eyes narrowed as she included both of them in her query. "When and if I tell Scott about me being in the hospital is up to me. Is that understood?" She waited until they both nodded in acknowledgment before she relaxed back into the pillow, running her hands through her hair.

Turning away, Ashleigh dug through her shoulder bag for writing materials and passed them to Paula.

"Thank you," Paula said politely.

"You're welcome," Ashleigh answered in a matching tone.

Kyle kept his mouth shut, even though it was difficult to see the sisters be so awkwardly civil to each other. "Are you ready to go?" he asked Ashleigh.

She gave him a puzzled look. "I have my own car."

"I'll walk you out." When she continued to stare at him, he added, "I want to finish our earlier conversation."

"Oh."

Paula's unconcealed attention was on Kyle during his exchange with Ashleigh. He prayed she wouldn't ask what they were talking about, because he wanted to keep her out of it for now.

After promising to bring the boys and her laptop back in the morning, they said goodbye and left together.

When the elevator doors closed, Kyle asked, "What were you about to ask when Rosy interrupted us?"

Ashleigh furrowed her brow. "What do you mean?"

"You said, 'Then why—' right before Rosy appeared with news about Paula."

"Oh, it was nothing."

Kyle caught her arm and gently turned her to face him. "It wasn't nothing. What were you going to ask me?"

She held up a finger when the elevator doors opened on the first floor. "Wait till we get outside."

They walked down the hallway and through the emergency room, stopping along the way to pick up his truck keys. They were going to be grist for the rumor mill from some of the glances they received.

They walked to the staff lot. "It's almost midnight," Ashleigh said.

"Yeah, what a way to spend a Saturday night. Sorry I messed up your plans."

"Oh, no. I'm glad you got in touch with me. Thank you."

They reached Ashleigh's car and she had her keys ready. An awkward silence ensued. "I guess I'll see you in the morning?" she finally said.

He cocked his head. "You promised to tell me—"

"I know." She met his eyes. "I'm not sure what I was going to say. Maybe I wanted to know why…" She stopped as if trying to decide how to phrase it.

"Why I was such a jerk?" he suggested.

She smiled somberly and her features relaxed. She stepped closer, less than a foot from him. "No, you were never a jerk. You…you were a doctor."

He was puzzled. "But I *am* a doctor."

"I know. I guess what I mean is I needed you to be my husband and best friend during that time more than I needed you to be a doctor."

He thought for a moment, surprised at her revelation. "I guess I fell back on what I know best. I'm trained as a doctor…and I've definitely proven to stink at being a husband."

"Not true." She laid a hand flat on his chest. "Not true at all. It's taken me two years to figure things out. Don't beat yourself up for not figuring them out before I did."

He covered her hand with his own and the warmth and softness of her instantly penetrated the hard shell he'd erected to protect himself.

Their eyes met before her gaze traveled to his mouth. He moved a fraction of an inch toward her and she jerked back a step, just out of his reach.

"I'm sorry." She lowered her head and spoke to the ground. Her hair hung down over her face. "I didn't mean—"

He lifted her chin and stopped her words with his mouth, taking care to give her the freedom to end the contact.

Instead, she kissed him back, moving forward into his arms until their bodies met in their old familiar way.

His hands cupped her face and he deepened the kiss. He'd never expected to kiss her again.

She moaned in the back of her throat. He'd missed that sound, and the urgency of her mouth, as she gave as much as she took.

He finally forced himself to regain control of the situation. "We're in the parking lot." He leaned his forehead against hers and she bobbed her head ever so slightly.

"I should go," she whispered.

Exactly the opposite of the words he'd been hoping to hear.

He cleared his throat and tugged on the neck of his T-shirt. He spoke to the asphalt and kicked at a loose rock like a five-year-old. "That's a good idea."

Worst idea ever.

Ashleigh unlocked her car and opened the driver-side door. With a little wave, she slid into the seat and shut the door.

Kyle took a few steps back to allow her room to back out of the parking space.

Click.

Click. The engine wasn't turning over.

Click.

Even through the dark car windows, he could see Ashleigh leaning her forehead against the steering wheel. Then she sat up, moved the gearshift and tried the key again.

Click.

Kyle walked around to her door—he had to believe there was a greater power looking out for his interests.

He opened her door.

"I think I left the overhead reading light on." She sighed. "Stupid!"

He checked his watch. "It's only been on for about two hours. How old is your battery?"

She grimaced. "As old as the car?" Automotive maintenance had always been his responsibility.

He chuckled.

"It's not funny!" Though she sounded only slightly offended.

"I wasn't laughing at you," he assured her. "But you have to admit the situation is slightly ironic."

"Ironic?"

He chuckled again. "You're trying to make a quick getaway and your car doesn't cooperate?"

She smiled and tucked a lock of hair behind her ear. "I wasn't trying to get away." She paused, probably searching for another reason for leaving. "It's late. I just want to get home and go to bed."

"Right." Going to bed had been his intention, too, he realized with a start. Except his goal was slightly different and there was no resting involved.

"It's true, Kyle!" Even she was laughing when she got out of her car. She swiped at him, but he edged away in time. "Stop laughing at me."

"You're laughing, too," he pointed out.

She sobered. "I guess I am."

He shut her car door. "Lock your car and we'll worry about it in the morning."

"But—"

"I'll give you a ride home since I don't have any jumper cables in my truck. It's late and I know you'd rather go to bed than wait here for the auto club."

She opened her mouth as if to protest.

"Don't argue." He took her elbow to lead her to find his truck. "I'll take you to Paula's. No funny business. If you want, I won't even stop. I'll just slow down in front of the house and you can jump out." He looked at her and winked. "Just remember to roll away from the moving truck."

Now he had her laughing so hard she nearly stumbled, if not for his hold on her arm.

How long had it been since they'd laughed together? Several years at least. He couldn't remember the last time.

Before he could check himself, he swung his arm over her shoulders and pulled her closer while they continued to walk. "You know, I'm not even sure where my truck's parked." Her head jerked in his direction and she stared at him until he explained that an orderly had parked it.

"There it is." He pointed to one row over, suddenly wondering how he would feel with her in the passenger seat of the same truck he'd driven while they were married.

He pulled out of the parking lot and they waved to the security guard in his patrol vehicle like the old days. Kyle decided it was easier than he expected to have her next to him. Much more natural.

After a few minutes of comfortable silence, Ashleigh said, "I'm glad Paula and the baby are okay."

"Me, too," he said.

"Where did you say the boys are?"

He gave her the details and, until they reached Paula's house, they chatted companionably about the boys teaching her how to play video games.

"Thanks for the ride." She reached for the door handle, then turned back to say, "And thanks for not making me jump out." She gave him a genuine smile, making his heart yearn for the way things used to be.

"My pleasure." He grinned. "I'll even walk you to the door."

"No, no, that's not necessary," she said.

Before he knew what was happening, she leaned

over to him and pressed her lips to his. "Good night," she whispered. Her breath was warm on his mouth.

She was already unlocking Paula's front door before he could think straight since the blood had drained from his brain to his crotch, naturally expecting it was needed there. Little did his circulatory system know how wrong that assumption would turn out to be.

He kept the truck in Park, watching Ashleigh go from room to room. Lights went on, then off, while he imagined her making her way upstairs.

His hand on the gearshift, he finally shifted into drive and slowly pulled away from the curb. There was no sense staying on the street any longer.

Had he expected Ashleigh would change her mind and wave to him from the window to come in?

Of course not. They were divorced. They'd been divorced for over two years. They'd both gone on with their lives.

At least Ashleigh had.

For most of that first year, he couldn't sleep at night and could barely function during the day. If not for his intensive medical training, his intrinsic ability to treat patients, and a stellar grief counselor, he would most likely be unemployed and homeless by now.

He found himself going around the block and stopping in front of Paula's house again. What the hell was he doing? He should be at home in bed. Alone. By himself.

Not panting for a female like a teenage boy.

The house was dark except for a dim light he supposed was the upstairs bathroom. The light in Ryan's bedroom went on and Kyle pulled away from the curb again.

What would she think if she saw him outside? That he was nuts, that's what.

He turned right at the end of the block for the third time and once again he took two more right turns to end up in front of Paula's.

The house was dark. She'd gone to bed. He continued to drive.

She'd always looked fresh and sexy when she'd come to bed at night. Her face would be washed and moisturized, her teeth brushed, and her hair soft and flowing over shoulders that were usually bare. The combination of floral and mint had become an aphrodisiac.

Right now was no exception.

He drove around the block and this time when he reached Paula's house, he pulled into the driveway and put the vehicle in Park.

He turned off the engine and got out of the truck, pocketing the keys before he changed his mind.

The walk to the front door was heady, not knowing what kind of reception he'd get.

How could it be any worse than when they divorced?

He raised his hand to knock on the door, surprised when it opened before he made contact. Ashleigh stood like a vision before him in a bubblegum-pink tank top and matching plaid pajama pants. "I wondered how many times you were going to drive around the block."

CHAPTER NINE

ASHLEIGH STOOD BACK from the door to let Kyle in. Her palms were sweating and her knees were literally knocking. What the hell was she doing?

When he was clear of the door, she shut and locked it, ignoring the warnings blaring in her head.

She shoved everything from her mind and smiled at Kyle. Neither spoke, at least verbally, when she took his hand. He entwined their fingers and gave them a reassuring squeeze before he followed her to the second floor in the dark.

She kept the lights off but lifted the shade on the rear window to allow the moonlight to stream in. She turned to him and their gazes locked. He had always had such intense blue eyes, framed by thick dark lashes that any woman would kill for.

She disengaged their fingers and slowly ran her hands over his chest and across his shoulders, down over his biceps and forearms to again entwine her fingers with his.

How was it that the act of hand-holding could feel so seductively intimate?

Her body melted against his and with their hands still joined, he put his arms around her back and held her close. The top of her head came to his chin and the warmth of his mouth when he pressed his lips to her hair had her eyelids closing. With her cheek against his chest, she listened to the pounding of his rapid heartbeat as it matched her own.

"Are you sure about this?" His voice was so quiet that she wondered if she'd imagined it.

She tilted her head up to look at him, pulling away slightly. He kept a firm grip on her so she couldn't escape and he repeated the question.

"No," she answered in amazement. "I'm not sure at all."

He dislodged her fingers from his and she was able to reach up and slide her arms around his neck, helping ease the sudden tension she'd noticed in his body.

"I'm not sure at all about what we're doing," she repeated. "But right now I'm trying very hard not to listen to the voices in my head."

He exhaled audibly, then framed her face with his palms and, putting on his oh-so-sexy smile, he asked, "You hear voices?"

She chuckled, unable to answer because he'd covered her lips with his. She curved into his body, enjoying the power of knowing that the erection pressing into her midsection was all because of her.

Just as the blazing heat inside her was the product of her undeniable need for him.

"You hear voices." He'd stopped kissing her, his voice low, close to her ear and definitely amused. "Why did I never know that about you?"

She turned her head to give him a peck on the cheek and then his mouth. "I try to ignore them." Their kiss deepened and she slid her hands under his T-shirt, caressing his bare back. Such a comfort to fall into their old rhythms, their familiar touches. Even their shared sense of humor was alive and well.

He pulled her hair away from her neck and tasted the skin below her ear. Delicious chills ran up and down her spine, fanning out to the far reaches of her extremities.

"Can I tell you how glad I am—" he moved to her bare shoulder and lightly nipped her skin when he snapped her thin strap with his teeth "—that you've chosen—" His mouth slid lower to her collarbone and the exposed area of her breast right above her tank top. "That you've chosen right now to ignore those voices." He licked at her hardened nipple through her clothes.

She groaned and Kyle stopped abruptly.

"What's wrong?" She was breathless. *Don't stop now,* her brain screamed, slightly panicked that he may have changed his mind.

She couldn't see his expression clearly in the moonlight, but when he finally spoke his voice was raspy. "Do you have any idea how much that sound you make turns me on?" He made quick work of her clothes before bending down to sweep her off the ground and into his arms.

She ran her hand around to the back of his neck, her fingers recalling the feel of his short, silky hair.

She fulfilled her insistent need for his mouth by drawing him to her. The cool bed comforter was her single clue that he'd lowered her to the bed. Even though he stripped his clothes off in record time, his body couldn't move fast enough before finally covering her naked body with his own.

KYLE DIDN'T KNOW how much later it was when he awoke, one arm over Ashleigh's bare midsection and the other asleep because it was curled uncomfortably under the pillow they were sharing while they spooned.

Twin beds were not made for more than one person to sleep in.

Or two people to make love on.

His body came to life at the memory and he breathed in the citrusy smell of Ashleigh's hair that tickled his nose. Not the same shampoo she used to use but arousing all the same.

His fingers itched to touch her skin again, to cup her breasts, tease her nipples until she cried out.

He wanted to taste her, tempt her, desire her until she made him her conquest with her blazing climax. Making love with Ashleigh had been natural, as if they'd come home again. Home to their private, safe world where nothing could touch them.

No need to wake her and make his lascivious thoughts a reality, because she abruptly wiggled her bottom seductively against his hardened erection and her chuckle vibrated deep in her chest.

"Again?" she whispered over her shoulder.

"Again," he echoed before raining kisses from the side of her neck around to her mouth.

He would make love to her all night if he could. Who knew where their time together would lead? This could be their second chance.

Or merely a reaction to the stress Paula's early labor had produced.

He couldn't endure another heartbreaking desertion. Keeping his guard up would be the only way he could survive this time with Ashleigh. Chances were excellent that she would bolt at her first opportunity.

PAULA HATED HOSPITALS. All the noise, the beeping, the footsteps back and forth through the hallway.

Her grandmother had once told her that back in her day a woman could stay in the hospital for up to ten days when she gave birth. So that's exactly what her grandmother did in order to get some rest.

Apparently hospitals were more like spa vacations in Grandma's day.

During the night, there had been a steady stream of people in and out of her room every few hours to check on her. How was she supposed to get the rest everyone kept telling her she needed if someone was always taking her pulse and checking her blood pressure?

How many times had staff members asked if she was experiencing any labor pains or other discomforts? Her answer had consistently been a solid "no."

Wouldn't she hit the call button for help if her labor had started again? Come on, people, use your heads.

Paula rested a hand on her abdomen, relieved beyond belief that her child had changed its mind about staying inside her a little longer. The heartbreaking possibilities had been present in her mind from the moment she experienced that first contraction—she'd never been more scared in her life.

The time on her cell phone was 5:39 a.m. Too early to call and check on the boys.

She scooted around until she found a somewhat comfortable position. With an IV in her arm and catheterized so she wouldn't have to get out of bed to urinate, she had no choice but to lie on her left side or on her back with the head of the bed raised.

She ought to call the nurses' station to ask for another pillow or two to put between her knees. Her right hip and back had begun to ache, missing the usual support she used at home.

A quiet knock sounded on her doorjamb and the outline of a backlit woman materialized. "Sorry to disturb you," the woman said in a soothing voice as she neared Paula's bed. Her name tag read Harriet Cummings, Licensed Practical Nurse, and she appeared to be close to retirement age from her short, pale gray hairstyle.

"That's okay," Paula told her. "I was already awake."

Harriet took Paula's vitals and then recorded the

stats by the light of a small penlight. "Was that Dr. Wilson I saw with you last night?"

"Yes, she's my sister."

"Really? I didn't know she had a sister." Harriet checked the IV bag hanging next to the bed and continued speaking. "Is Dr. Wilson moving back?"

"I doubt it," Paula answered. "She's here to help me out with my two boys while my husband's deployed at sea. She's working in Richmond now."

"How nice for her. I'm sure Richmond is glad to have such a fine pediatrician." Harriet continued before Paula could correct her assumption. "My daughter brought all three of her children to Dr. Wilson and my Sonja raved about how good your sister was with them. Always patient, soft-spoken—never rushing them out the door."

"Uh-huh." Perfect Ashleigh strikes again. As always, everything was all about Ashleigh.

"Poor girl had such a difficult time a few years ago," Harriet said. "It was heartbreaking to watch everything she and that handsome doctor husband of hers went through to have a baby."

Paula swallowed thickly. What could she say to that? Of course it had been bad, but now Paula was the patient. Couldn't she get a little sympathy, too?

Harriet continued with her sympathetic discourse. "The miscarriages, the testing, the surgery. She went through it all." Harriet slowly shook her head. "And all for nothing."

Paula listened halfheartedly. Even though she

hadn't been there physically for the majority of Ashleigh's medical procedures because Scott's assignment back then had been clear across the country, Paula had supported her as much as possible.

Ashleigh had been rightly devastated, but she refused to talk to anyone about other options for achieving motherhood. She became inexplicably angry whenever adoption was mentioned, and Paula to this day couldn't figure out what that was all about.

"I'm all done here," Harriet said. "You tell Dr. Wilson that Harriet Cummings asked about her. She's one brave little girl."

"I'll do that," Paula promised. Brave? Paula wouldn't have used that word to describe Ashleigh, but now she could see it kind of fit.

Paula's vision blurred when her eyes filled to overflowing. Knowing how scared she'd been last night about delivering early, she could only imagine what Ashleigh had gone through when she had her miscarriages. Then there had been all those other procedures. She must have felt like a lab rat the way they kept searching for new research initiatives.

"Is there anything you need?" Harriet finally stopped talking about Ashleigh to focus on Paula.

"Another pillow maybe?"

"Why, of course!" Harriet tsked. "I don't know why they didn't offer you one when you were brought in." With that, she disappeared out the door and down the hallway.

Paula's baby moved inside her as if to comfort her with its presence. She wiped an errant tear from her cheek and ran a loving hand over her abdomen.

Things would be all right as long as Bam-Bam stayed right where he or she was until the time was right.

She reached to turn on the light, squinting until her eyes adjusted. Then she retrieved the list she'd started last night— pajamas, underwear, bathrobe, sundry toiletries, makeup (not that she'd bother with it much).

She added thank-you notes to the list—she might as well make use of her time in the hospital. She flipped to the next page in the notebook. Her growing list of helpers was getting longer by the minute.

There was nothing like a medical emergency to make it clear who your friends were. Some of the people who'd brought meals and offered rides to the boys were barely acquaintances. And she hadn't had contact with others since before she and Scott moved around the country with the Navy.

Not for the first time, she was deeply grateful for making the decision to come back to Grand Oaks while Scott was deployed. Sure, she had Navy friends, but she and Scott had barely been in Newport News a few weeks before his ship departed. She'd made some casual acquaintances and knew two other wives from their time together in San Diego, but she wouldn't have had nearly the support system she had in her hometown.

The hardest thing for Paula to grasp, though, was how Ashleigh had stepped up as soon as she heard Paula was on bed rest. And then seeing Ashleigh here at the hospital last night had been a complete shock. To know she'd left her comfort zone to be on this floor when it held no good memories for her was inconceivable to Paula. Even more so now that Paula had begun to understand the devastation Ashleigh had endured.

Then there was the vibe she was sure she picked up on between Ashleigh and Kyle. As if something was going on with the two of them—and not their usual animosity.

How wonderful would it be if they got back together? Or at least if they could get along? Family gatherings could be happy occasions again.

Every once in a while Paula could actually see glimpses of the Ashleigh of old.

Oh, how Paula missed her sister. Would Ashleigh ever fully turn back into the sister Paula remembered?

ASHLEIGH ROLLED ONTO her back. She was alone.

She sat up abruptly and the sheet fell from her naked body. She looked around, squinting from the sunshine streaming through the window where the moon had shone earlier.

Definitely alone. Her lungs emptied with a whoosh. Kyle had somehow escaped the bedroom without waking her.

She listened carefully to see if she could hear him anywhere in the house. Nothing but the hum of the heat pump fan and the occasional car driving down the street.

No footsteps, no water running, not even his incessant whistling. Nothing.

She fell back onto the pillow. What a relief! Ashleigh wasn't sure she could have faced him if he'd been right there when she awoke.

She took a moment to consider her actions last night. As the aggressor, she took full responsibility for the outcome. Yes, Kyle had come to the door, but he would have left immediately if she hadn't pulled him into her lair.

There was nothing to stress about. After all, she was a big girl. Not a girl who had indiscriminate sex, but she and Kyle used to be married, for goodness' sake. Lots of divorced couples slipped back into old sexual habits at least once, didn't they?

She swung her legs off the bed and stood. The clock said almost nine. She never slept in that late.

Intent on gathering her strewn clothes, she realized they were neatly folded on the desk chair.

She slipped on her lightweight bathrobe. To be sure she was alone she snuck a peek out the front window. Kyle's truck was gone. She breathed normally again. Then she retrieved clean clothes and just for good measure, she called downstairs. "Kyle? Are you here?"

No answer.

The pounding in her chest slowed and she padded into the bathroom. In an effort to wash away every last memory of last night, she turned the water on extra hot.

Not that she regretted last night, but she had no intention of repeating that mistake.

Mistake? Yes, she decided, sleeping with Kyle had been a mistake and she didn't want to give him the wrong idea or any kind of hope for them as a couple. Was that the hint of regret she'd assumed was absent?

Damn.

She turned off the shower and froze in place as the water dripped down her body and into the drain. *She despised regret.* Not until goose bumps formed did she pull out of her stupor to towel off.

Once she'd moisturized, brushed her teeth and combed out her wet hair, she dressed in jeans and a lightweight, long-sleeved, sapphire-blue top.

Normally, she would have gone into the office for drop-in patients on a Sunday morning. Lucky for her, she'd been able to contact Cammie on the way to the hospital last night to ask if she'd put a note on the office door asking patients to call her answering service with any emergencies.

Ashleigh opened the bathroom door and was surprised to hear voices downstairs. Mark and Ryan. They were talking to Kyle.

He must have brought them home. To use them as a shield?

She was also surprised by the hint of color in her

cheeks that wasn't only from the overly hot shower. She quickly blew her hair dry, leaving it down rather than gathered up in her usual knot.

Before going downstairs, she checked the bedroom once more for signs of her and Kyle's activities. She made the bed and put everything else in its place—even the lamp they'd knocked over in their haste to be together.

She shoved away the memory. No use thinking about how deliciously sensual Kyle's mouth could be or how experienced he was at bringing her to climax in many and varied ways. There would be no repeat performance. It had been a one-night reprise of their former life.

She breathed in deeply, hoping to calm her racing heart.

She stood at the top of the staircase. No time like the present. *What a stupid saying.* If she were smart, she'd pack up and go back to Richmond right now. Paula could manage without her, and so could Kyle and the boys.

If not for being the lone pediatrician in the area, she'd have her suitcase in hand. She didn't care if a quick exit would have been the coward's way out.

Kyle probably thought he was quite the stud after she'd slept with him so willingly. Then again, she'd never been one to play hard to get where he was concerned.

Even the first time he asked her out, she'd barely

let him get the words out before practically yelling, "Yes, I'll go to the homecoming dance with you!"

That hadn't technically been their first date, because they had gone for ice cream two weeks before the dance.

Regardless, his ego was probably quite inflated after last night.

Instead of skulking out, she straightened her shoulders and went down the steps. Then she walked with confidence into the kitchen to face Kyle as if nothing had happened between them.

"Hi, Aunt Ashleigh!" Ryan greeted her. "Uncle Kyle is making pancakes!"

"I see." She couldn't stop the beginning of a smile at how enthusiastically the boys were eating. "You guys are chowing down like you're starving. I know I fed you dinner last night."

Both boys laughed and continued to bolt down their food. Ashleigh helped herself to a cup of coffee, ignoring Kyle at the stove flipping another batch of pancakes. He must have gone home before retrieving the boys because his jeans and Grand Oaks hospital 5K T-shirt weren't the clothes he'd stripped off last night.

Her face flushed at the memory of his solid chest and broad shoulders. She blew out a breath in an effort to cool herself.

"Good morning." Kyle's voice was deep and sexy. Damn him.

"Good morning." She tried for curt, but wasn't sure if it worked.

Kyle sidled up to her and whispered, "I didn't want to wake you."

"Mmm-hmm." She kept her eyes on the boys rather than on Kyle. His fresh-shower smell was difficult to ignore. "You didn't."

He ran his fingers through her hair and she stifled a moan. She was glad now that she'd left her hair loose.

"You're beautiful when you're sleeping." His arm came around her back and he pulled her closer to whisper in her ear, "You're even beautiful when you snore."

Her mouth formed an O and she jerked away from him and his teasing laughter.

"What's so funny?" Mark asked.

Ashleigh was startled by the question. She'd forgotten they weren't alone. "Your uncle thinks he's funny, but he's not."

"He tells funny jokes," Ryan told her.

"Yeah," Mark agreed.

Ashleigh opened her mouth to speak, but Kyle said, "Aunt Ashleigh's sense of humor isn't working this morning."

The boys shrugged as if this made sense and they went back to finishing off their pancakes.

"The neighbor keeping the boys called my cell early this morning, a little after seven-thirty," Kyle explained. "The boys were concerned about their mom, so I went and got them." He popped a piece of pancake into his mouth and kept his voice low. "I went to my place to shower and change first." He continued in a moderate volume. "I told the boys we'd visit their mom after breakfast." He offered her the plate of fresh pancakes.

"No, thanks."

He put the plate on the table in front of the boys. "Your car needed a new battery." Kyle's abrupt change of subject caught Ashleigh by surprise. "The auto club said they could do it, so I said okay."

Ashleigh stared at him. He'd taken care of her dead battery? "Thank you." She cleared her throat. "You've been busy this morning. Picking up the boys, calling the auto club..."

He walked over to her where she leaned her lower back against the counter. He glanced over his shoulder at the boys, who weren't paying them any attention. Then he kissed her quickly but deliberately on the mouth before whispering in her ear, "There was just one thing I didn't get to do this morning."

He pulled back, a mile-wide grin on his face and a sexy twinkle in his eye.

Damn if that indomitable heat of arousal didn't travel willy-nilly to every cell of her body. "Oh, yeah?" Her voice came out raspy. She fought for control of the situation...as well as her emotions.

He winked, acutely aware he'd gotten to her. "Yeah. Want details?"

She coughed, embarrassed to be so turned-on by

the man she'd been ready to completely ignore a few minutes ago.

"Hey, Dad, look at this." Ryan pointed to the pancake on his plate, getting both Kyle and Ashleigh's attention. "I mean Uncle Kyle."

Taking Ryan's slip in stride, Kyle replied with a chuckle, "Is that a monkey pancake?"

Unlike Kyle, she couldn't get past Ryan's slipup. Who would Kyle find to give him children to call him "Dad"?

The rest of their exchange didn't register. Ashleigh had become light-headed.

Her hand grabbed the counter so forcefully that she might have left indentations.

Who was she kidding? She had no business getting involved with Kyle again. They had no chance for a future.

She could never make Kyle a father.

CHAPTER TEN

ASHLEIGH HAD GONE PALE. "Are you okay?" Kyle placed his hand at her waist, afraid she might keel over. "What's wrong?"

He took her hand that gripped the counter into both of his and brought it to his lips. Her unfocused gaze centered on his collarbone.

To get her out of earshot of the boys, he guided her into the living room.

"Hey." He lifted her chin until she had no choice but to look him in the eye. "Talk to me," he whispered. "If you're having second thoughts about last night—"

His words must have reached her, because suddenly she glared at him. "Are you kidding?" If her eyes had been lasers, he'd be dead. "You think I'm upset about last night?" She jerked away from him and hissed, "I can't believe you don't understand what happened in there just now."

He crossed his arms over his chest, waiting for her to explain. Anything he said right now would be wrong.

Ashleigh cleared her throat and in a slightly calmer

but shaky voice she said, "Didn't you hear Ryan call you 'Dad'?"

"Kids make mistakes like that all the time." Kyle didn't see what all the fuss was about. "When Scott and I were kids, people were always confusing us. I bet I remind the boys of him."

Ashleigh's color heightened as if she were about to burst an artery.

"It's all right, Ash." Kyle spoke soothingly. "Ryan knows Scott is his dad and not me."

She swung her arms out, palms up, punctuating each word. "Don't you think I know that?" she practically shouted. Then she lowered her voice as if remembering the boys were in the other room and added through clenched teeth, "If you weren't being so dense, you'd realize I'm upset because I'll never be able to give you a child to call you 'Dad.'"

He froze, stunned by her admission. She flew past him, jerking away when he put a hand out to stop her. She ran up the stairs and slammed the door.

He was torn between going after her and giving her some space. He took a few steps toward the stairs and stopped himself. Better that they not kid themselves by getting close. Last night had been a mistake that would be best not repeated, no matter how perfect their time together had been.

He couldn't assume she'd stick around because of one night together.

A long time ago, he'd accepted they'd never have a child together. She obviously hadn't.

TOM HAD SPENT the past hour in his hospital office laboring over a contract the hospital administrator insisted had to be vetted by Monday morning.

Would have been nice if he had received the contract before the end of the day on Friday, but that tended to be business as usual around here.

Tom added a few more handwritten notes to the cover page he'd started and put it and the contract back into the manila envelope it had come in. After straightening his desk, he headed to the administrator's office to drop off the contract. He tossed it into the administrative assistant's in-box, glad to have that off his plate.

Next he would go see Stan—a visit was overdue. Tom pushed the elevator button to take him to the cardiac intensive care unit and quickly made a mental list of subjects to talk about since he didn't know the man that well. Ashleigh filling in for Stan, Washington Nationals opening day of baseball, the tornado that barreled through North Carolina yesterday.

He got off the elevator and waved to the female ward clerk at the ICU desk. "Stan Mitchell?"

"Hi, Tom," she said pleasantly. "Last cubicle on the right."

Tom entered the large room, waved to the two nurses near the bank of monitors in the center and continued straight to the glassed-in area considered Stan's room. "Hey, Stan!" he said from the entryway.

Stan's complexion was pale and his light gray hair matted. His bed was raised to a partial sitting position and he had tubes and wires coming from several areas on his body. "Tom! Nice of you to stop by." He waved him in.

"Looks like they're taking good care of you." Tom gestured to the blinking and beeping machine where electronic numbers kept changing, as well as the IV pole and various paraphernalia next to Stan's bed.

"Nothing like having a doctor as a patient." Stan smirked. "They want me healed and out of here as soon as possible because I'll know if they make a mistake. The only thing keeping me from complaining are the painkillers."

Tom chuckled. "I'm sure you're anxious to go home. How are you feeling?" He couldn't imagine what Stan had been through and decided right then and there that he'd have the fruit plate for lunch instead of the Reuben he'd been planning to order. The hospital exercise room also sounded like a good plan. Or maybe he should get his bike out since it was finally spring. He'd been only halfheartedly exercising these days.

Now that he thought about it, regular exercise hadn't been part of his routine since Theresa called off their engagement several months ago.

"You know, almost dying makes you take a long, hard look at your life," Stan said. "You realize what's important and what's not." His sudden drug-induced philosophizing made Tom a tad uncomfortable.

"I haven't been a very good husband," Stan went on. "In fact, I almost singlehandedly destroyed my marriage."

"Maybe I should let you get some rest." He didn't want Stan to confide more than he would when not medicated.

"No, no, I'm fine," Stan insisted. "My wife, Linda— have you two ever met? She and my daughters are around here somewhere."

"Yes, we have. At a hospital fund-raiser, I believe."

"Anyway, Linda's the best wife I could ever ask for and I've treated her like dirt." He lowered his voice. "Even worse than dirt, but she doesn't like me to use bad language." He smiled as if revealing a secret. "You know, just in case I slip in front of one of my patients. Parents don't like their children exposed to bad language, especially from their pediatrician. Can you imagine?" He let out a loud guffaw.

Tom couldn't help but smile. "That makes sense." He didn't know where Stan's rambling was headed. "Maybe I should leave so you can rest," he suggested for a second time.

Stan ignored him. "Back to my wife. You know, that's why we moved here. She said I worked too much out there in California and never had time for her. She was actually going to leave me if I didn't change. Said I took her for granted."

"You grew up here, didn't you?" Maybe that would turn the conversation in a different direction.

"She said I knew I could count on her to have dinner waiting for me whenever I got home. Sometimes I didn't even call if I wasn't going to make it home to eat it." Again Stan ignored Tom's question, choosing to continue focusing on Linda instead. "She always attended social functions with me, even if that meant changing her own plans. The woman's a saint."

Tom considered Stan's words, reminiscent of what Theresa had said to him when she called off their engagement.

"Did you know she saved my life?" Stan became animated and Tom worried he'd unhook a wire or something. "Without her giving me CPR, I wouldn't have made it to the hospital." He swiped at a tear and his mouth turned down as his emotions overwhelmed him. "All I've put her through and she has stayed right by my side through all of it."

Finally, the arrival of a nurse to check on Stan gave Tom an excuse to leave.

"Thanks for stopping by." Stan gave him a cheerful wave, apparently recovered from his melancholy—and oblivious to Tom's rushed departure. Stan's words were like a slap upside the head. A wake-up call.

Tom was exiting the elevator on the first floor when he ran into Kyle and Ashleigh and their nephews. "Hey, what brings you all here?" Tom forced himself to act naturally. He peered at the boys and gestured to Ryan's cast. "One of you hurt again?"

"We came to see our mom," Mark told him, his usual smile missing.

"Is she in the hospital?" Tom looked to Kyle and Ashleigh for an answer.

"Early labor," Kyle told him. "They stopped it but decided to keep her here." Kyle shifted the overflowing reusable shopping bag he carried from one hand to the other.

"You should stop by and say hi," Ashleigh said. "I'm sure Paula would appreciate visitors."

"I'll do that," Tom promised. "I'll be up after I grab some lunch."

They went their separate ways and after lunch, true to his word, Tom headed directly to Paula's room.

Laughter spilled into the hallway as he neared her door and he couldn't help but smile.

The expression froze on his face when he suddenly came face-to-face with his ex-fiancée. Theresa was just leaving Paula's room.

"Hi" was all he could think to say as he stepped back so she could exit completely and shut the door behind her.

Before the lunch with Ashleigh, he hadn't seen Theresa in a month or even longer. And then, only in passing. Now she seemed to be everywhere.

"Hi, Tom." Again he noticed her new haircut. She looked different, and possibly even more beautiful.

Her eyes sparkled with laughter, even when her joy turned to surprise at seeing him.

"I can come back later." He didn't want his presence to make her uncomfortable.

"No, no, that's not necessary," she said. "I'm leaving." She gestured to Paula's room. "Ashleigh, Kyle and the kids are in there now."

"How have you been?" He wanted to prolong their conversation.

"Good. How about you?"

"Busy with work, as usual." He swallowed. "I like your new haircut."

Her eyebrows rose and she touched a hand to her hair. "Thank you."

Pretty sad exchange. He didn't know how to broach the rumor about her and Kyle.

"Tom?" Her tone said she was waiting for his response. Her mouth mesmerized him—the pale pink color of her lipstick against her bright white teeth, the way her tongue flicked out to wet her lips.

He blinked to clear his mind. "What?"

"I asked if you were seeing anyone."

"Who, me? Um, no, not right now."

She nodded. "Oh, well, it was good seeing you."

"Yeah, you, too." This was the lamest conversation they'd ever had.

She gave him a little wave and sauntered down the hall toward the elevator.

He had this overwhelming urge to go after her. Though he still loved her, she obviously didn't feel the same. Otherwise, wouldn't she have stuck around to chat longer? Wouldn't she have shown a little more interest in him?

He'd been devastated when she broke off their engagement. Unable to function for quite a while.

She'd said he took her for granted. He didn't appreciate her.

How could she have thought that? They'd been together for three years. He'd planned to spend the rest of his life with her.

Would he always be unable to breathe around her?

ASHLEIGH DISTANCED HERSELF from the group in Paula's hospital room, standing in the far corner, only speaking to Kyle when necessary. He'd never understand how deeply saddened she was over not having a child who would call him "Dad"—or her, "Mom."

Paula had both her sons on the bed with her, one on each side with her arms around them to keep them from falling off. Kyle was on the other side of the bed and Tom stood awkwardly against the wall at the end of the bed. He hadn't said much since he'd arrived a few minutes ago.

The boys giggled, their laughter contagious. Paula was so good with her sons, teasing and joking around with them. And not once did they disrespect their mother.

Her sister kissed the tops of her boys' heads and Ashleigh automatically reached out to carefully straighten the kink in the IV line attached to Paula's arm.

Ashleigh's attention was drawn to the modern piece of artwork on the far wall. Her world spun. She'd been in this very room when her first miscarriage had been confirmed. She clutched at the unoccupied chair near her and lowered into it before her wobbly legs gave out.

Kyle gave her a concerned look from across the room, but she ignored him.

"Boys, why don't you hand me my purse," Paula suggested when they began to get riled up. "There's a snack machine down the hall." She rummaged in her wallet for change. "Pick something that's not all sugar. I'm sure your aunt and uncle would appreciate that."

Tom lifted his arm to check the time on his watch. "I'll go with them. Great seeing you, Paula. Take care of yourself." He waved and followed the boys into the hall.

As soon as the door shut behind them, Paula said to Kyle, "Did you see Theresa and Tom run into each other when she was leaving? I wonder if he's heard about the two of you." Paula immediately slapped a hand over her mouth, her eyes wide as she looked at Ashleigh. "I'm sorry, I didn't mean to blurt that out. It's not what you think."

Ashleigh spoke for the first time since entering the room. "That's okay," she said softly. "I know it's a rumor that Theresa perpetuated to make Tom jealous."

"How did you find out?" Paula asked. "You've hardly been in town more than a few days."

"Kyle sort of told me and then Theresa confirmed it." Ashleigh said to Kyle, "That's where I was when you couldn't reach me last night. We met at that piano bar right off the highway."

He took a step as if he were coming around the bed to her, but stopped when she drew back. She would crumble if he touched her. There were way too many emotions coursing through her right now.... How she longed for the solitude of her life in Richmond.

"Did you let Scott know what's going on with your pregnancy yet?" Ashleigh was anxious to change the subject.

Paula shook her head.

Ashleigh was surprised at Paula's answer. "Wouldn't he want to know?" She wasn't at home on bed rest anymore. She was in the hospital after going into labor. Scott had a right to know.

"I don't want to worry him," Paula said. "There's nothing he can do and he can't make it home any earlier than scheduled anyway."

Ashleigh and Kyle exchanged glances.

"And don't either of you tell him," Paula commanded sternly. "Promise?"

"Okay." They spoke in unison, but Ashleigh didn't agree with Paula's decision and Kyle probably didn't, either.

"What about Mom? Have you talked to her?" Ashleigh asked. "You know she wants to be kept up with what's going on while she's in Maryland with Grandma. Especially since she'll be staying at least another week now that Grandma's medications need to be adjusted."

"Good point," Kyle said.

Paula shrugged. "I guess I could call her and let her know. I figured her hands were full."

"When was the last time you talked to her?" Kyle asked. "Does she even know about your raised blood pressure?"

"Not unless Aunt Vivian told her."

"Speaking of Aunt Vivian," Ashleigh said. "She invited us all to dinner today. She may be going through physical therapy, but she says she's still able to cook one of her legendary Sunday meals." Ashleigh looked pointedly at Kyle. "She included you in that invitation, but don't feel obligated." Hopefully he'd take the hint.

"I'd love to come," he said, "but I'm working to-night. What time did she say?"

Ashleigh hoped her relief didn't show. "She didn't, not yet. I said I'd call her to let her know if we could all make it. I didn't know what Paula's situation would be." Ashleigh pulled her cell from her purse. "I'll do that as soon as we get outside."

The boys came back into the room. Any further discussion Paula wanted to have about Ashleigh and Kyle's status was now impossible.

"We should let your mom get some rest," Kyle suggested to the boys a few minutes later.

"Aww!" the boys complained as they munched on their snacks.

"Listen to Uncle Kyle," Paula warned. "He and Aunt Ashleigh are in charge."

They playfully frowned and Ashleigh couldn't keep from smiling because they reminded her of Kyle and Scott.

She sobered and swallowed the lump in her throat. That's probably what her children with Kyle would have looked like.

Children. Babies. Pregnancy. She sucked in a breath and her hand flew up to cover her mouth. All eyes were suddenly on her, but she didn't care. Her main concern at the moment was her stomach, which was about to rebel.

"Excuse me," she muttered, and hurriedly left Paula's room, hoping to make it to the more private bathroom down the hall before she lost the contents of her stomach.

Alone in the restroom, she splashed cold water on her face, grateful her stomach had settled without incident. She blotted her face with a paper towel and placed a hand on her abdomen, terrified beyond belief.

What a stupid, *stupid* idiot she was. How could she have acted so irresponsibly? Why hadn't Kyle thought of it, either?

They hadn't used birth control last night.

She could be pregnant.

She could lose another baby.

The possibilities made her stomach churn again.

CHAPTER ELEVEN

"WHAT A GORGEOUS DAY," Kyle commented to the boys when they reached the hospital parking lot. He looked at Ashleigh, who'd just ended her call to Aunt Vivian. "Everything okay?" When she'd finally returned to Paula's room after her sudden departure, her face had been flushed, but she'd offered no explanation.

She avoided his question. "Aunt Viv said to come around five. I told her you had to work."

The boys ended any further discussion when they began to pick at each other after they were all in Kyle's truck. He suspected that was their way of dealing with not having their mother at home.

"Hey, guys, how about we go to the park?" He looked at Ashleigh to see if she was interested, but she had her face turned away and was staring out the side window.

The boys' loud chorus of "yay!" made Kyle's ears ring. "You in?" he asked Ashleigh.

She didn't answer at first, and as he opened his mouth to repeat his question, she said quietly, "Okay."

Good. He hated seeing her upset. If she'd let him in, he was sure he could help her. They needed more time together, even if it meant exposing feelings. "Let's stop by my place and get a basketball. The boys' soccer equipment is still in my trunk."

"Do you and the boys go to the park often?" She surprised him with her interest.

"When the weather's nice," he said. "Their soccer practices started two weeks ago and I've been helping coach their teams."

The remainder of the short ride passed in silence. Even Mark and Ryan finally gave it a rest.

Kyle left Ashleigh and the boys in the idling truck while he dashed into his second-floor apartment. He quickly filled some water bottles for them all and jogged back down the stairs to get the basketball from the shed out back near the alley.

Alone with his troubled thoughts after last night he didn't want to consider that Ashleigh would leave again, but the outcome was inevitable. He needed to remember that. She would be in town for a few weeks, and after that it was a crapshoot. Better to distance himself from her sooner rather than later.

He told himself they were spending the afternoon together strictly because of the boys, but he couldn't help feeling good about their extra time together.

Could his thoughts be any more conflicted?

Kyle returned to the truck and much to his surprise, Aunt Ashleigh was laughing at the boys' antics as they did a spot-on imitation of two of their favorite cartoon characters. Kyle put the truck into Drive and prayed Ashleigh's uplifted mood would last.

For the next hour they alternated between soccer and basketball, though playing basketball one-handed turned out to be frustrating for Ryan. Before the boy lost it completely, Kyle suggested they get some ice cream from the small snack stand near the playground equipment.

"That was fun," Ryan said as they walked along the dirt path. "Aunt Ashleigh, you're pretty good at soccer! You even scored a goal."

She smiled. "You act like you're surprised."

"Well, you are just a—"

With her hands on her hips, she looked Ryan squarely in the eye. "If you're going to call me a girl, young man, then you better realize I used to be head cheerleader in high school and I threw girls bigger than you into the air." She tossed her hair over her shoulder. "Sometimes I caught them—" she paused "—and sometimes I didn't."

The boys' eyes were as round as softballs when they cried out, "Whoa!"

Kyle couldn't help but laugh. Chalk one up for Aunt Ashleigh.

In an obvious effort to change the subject, Mark asked, "Did you see how much better I can dribble now, Uncle Kyle?"

Kyle laughed. "Yeah, where was that skill during basketball season?"

Ashleigh looked at Kyle. "Did you coach basketball, too?"

"Assisted." He tried to make light of it after how

upset she was when Ryan had called him "Dad." He wished she didn't feel guilty about her infertility, but he wasn't sure how to help her. "With my hours at the hospital, I can't make it to every game and practice. So I never take on anything more than assistant coach."

Ashleigh said nothing and he didn't have to imagine how left out she felt—even if it had been her decision to distance herself from all of them.

"Hey." He grabbed her hand and entwined their fingers without thinking it through. "They're our nephews. I'm just doing my duty by being their favorite uncle." He hoped to cheer her up with his teasing, but he wasn't sure it was working.

After everyone got their ice cream, they chose a nearby picnic table under a shade tree. Ashleigh faced Kyle, and the boys sat next to each other on Kyle's side.

"Shut up," Mark suddenly hissed at Ryan. He gave his younger brother a shove. "You don't know what you're talking about."

"That's enough, boys," Kyle said sternly. "What's going on?"

Ryan said in a singsongy tone, "Mark's girlfriend is over there." He pointed to a group of girls over by the carousel on the far side of the ice-cream stand.

"She's not my girlfriend," Mark insisted, but his face reddened and he kept glancing over at the girls.

"Then why do you have a picture of her in your room?" Ryan behaved in true sibling fashion.

"Stop going through my stuff!" Mark's embarrassment was turning to anger at his nosy younger brother.

Kyle coughed to cover up the laugh he couldn't keep from escaping. He remembered what it was like to have younger siblings and so he mercifully took the heat off Mark. "Hey, guys, did I ever tell you about the first time I saw Aunt Ashleigh?"

"Summer before freshman year," Ashleigh stated confidently. "You were running football drills in the gym on a rainy day. I was practicing with the cheerleaders on the other side of the divider. Somehow a football was thrown through the door of the divider and when I went to give it back, I almost ran into you coming from the other direction."

"Nope," Kyle said, noting the boys were paying close attention to the story while licking their cones.

Ashleigh's head tilted and her eyes narrowed. "No?"

"That was the first time I ever *spoke* to you," he stated. The first time he'd had the nerve. "The first time I ever *saw* you was near the beginning of eighth grade."

Ashleigh's eyes widened. "Is that true?"

He grinned. "Uh-huh." He looked pointedly at Mark and confided, "I was scared to death to talk to her."

"Tell us more." Ashleigh's lips twitched and Mark was noticeably interested, too. "Eighth grade?"

He winked at her. "Oh, yeah." He swallowed and

continued his story, that day so clear in his mind. "I was in the school cafeteria, sitting with a couple of my buddies, when one of them said, 'Hey, look over there.' He was talking about some kid who was throwing up in the trash can in the corner." Mark and Ryan giggled. "But all I could see was you."

"Bobby something, wasn't it?" Ashleigh asked. "It's not every day a kid throws up in the middle-school cafeteria."

"Yeah, that was him. Bobby Jordan, I think." Kyle scratched his head and continued. "Anyway, all I could see was this cute little blonde with blue-and-white flowered pants and little white sneakers—"

Ashleigh's lips twitched at the nineties reference.

"—and a blue off-the-shoulder top I later discovered was a perfect match for her eyes."

The boys groaned.

"Keep quiet and listen," Kyle teased.

"My white Keds." Ashleigh laughed. "That was back in my *Saved by the Bell* days. I was sure I was the blonde Kelly Kapowski." She gestured with her hands. "My hair was huge, out to here back then."

"Kelly who?" Mark asked.

"TV show before your time," Ashleigh explained.

She and Kyle shared a smile before he continued. "Anyway, that was the day I first noticed Aunt Ashleigh, boys." He waggled his eyebrows at her. It was also the first of many nights he'd dreamed about her.

"And here I always thought it was the next summer

in the gym," Ashleigh said. "I figured you were too cool to notice me. Why did it take you so long to talk to me?"

"Sheer nerves." He chuckled, tapping Mark on top of his head. "If Tom hadn't thrown the ball into your side of the gym so I'd have to get it, it would have taken me even longer."

"Tom knew?" she asked.

"That I had a major crush on you?" He winked. "Heck, yeah. The entire freshman football team knew. And most of the other cheerleaders, too."

She chuckled. "I can't believe I never heard this before. Was I so out of touch I didn't notice your interest in me?"

"Hey, you were busy, what with all the clubs and activities you were involved in. Drama, debate, orchestra." He couldn't remember the rest.

"Debate wasn't until high school, but you're right." She sighed. "I had piano lessons and gymnastics lessons, and of course, cheerleading began in middle school."

"You had no time for me," he joked, "even if I'd been able to form a sentence in your presence."

"Well, if you'd had the nerve to talk to me I would have made time for you," she insisted.

"Can we go play on the swings?" Ryan asked suddenly. "I'm bored."

Kyle chuckled. "Sure," he said, and the boys took off. "Don't go any farther than the playground equipment," he yelled to their retreating backs.

Ashleigh's quick intake of breath caught Kyle's attention. "What's wrong?"

The color drained from her face. "Nothing. I'm fine," she said, but her voice trembled.

Kyle turned to look at what had upset her. A couple pushing a stroller was headed for the ice-cream stand. The woman turned and he noticed that she was quite far along in her next pregnancy. Kyle looked again at Ashleigh. Her eyes were closed and she was breathing deeply in an obvious effort to calm herself.

Just like in eighth grade, Kyle was clueless as to what to say to her.

Tom slammed his damp towel into the container in the men's locker room next to the hospital's fitness area. His muscles burned from a workout he'd taken to the extreme after running into Theresa.

How could that woman still affect him so strongly?

He'd tried to get over her, but no one could come close to matching Theresa's love of life and generosity of spirit.

On the drive home, he halfheartedly paid attention and ended up in front of the home he and Theresa had almost bought. She had fallen in love with the house at first sight, but Tom hadn't thought they should rush into purchasing when property values were so volatile.

He edged the car to the curb, turned off the engine and got out. He stood on the sidewalk, taking in the surroundings. Someone else had bought the house.

There was a child's bike in the driveway of the two-bedroom yellow-and-white bungalow and a barking dog at the window.

"May I help you?" A young woman, maybe late twenties or early thirties, suddenly appeared on the sidewalk behind him.

"What? Oh, no, I'm fine," he said. "Do you live here?"

She smiled tentatively. "Yes, we moved in a few months ago."

"That's good. It looks like a nice neighborhood."

"We think so," she confirmed. "Are you planning to move here?"

"No, no, I—" He didn't know how to finish the sentence. Didn't know how to make it clear he wasn't a stalker or child predator or something. *I was a fool and now you're living in the house meant for me* would sound stupid. "I'm just looking around. You know, trying to find the right place in the right neighborhood." He gestured to the other houses nearby. "Houses come on the market all the time. I want to pick the area first. You know what they say. Location, location, location." He forced himself to stop babbling. "I better let you go."

"Well, good luck," the woman said with a little wave. "I highly recommend this neighborhood. We have a block party in two weeks and there are several other social functions during the year."

Tom had no doubt Theresa would have learned

about the neighborhood before she'd even looked at this house.

He took one last glance at the property before getting into his car. He shifted into Drive and slowly pulled away from the curb.

That could have been his and Theresa's dog, their child's bike, their happily ever after. What had he been thinking? Theresa had begged him to reconsider, but he hadn't listened.

According to her, he hadn't heard a lot of what she'd said. Treated her like a piece of furniture.

Is that what he'd done? He certainly hadn't meant to.

Stan said he'd taken his wife for granted. The same words Theresa had used when she broke off their engagement.

"You never consider my feelings," she'd said. "I'm not asking for romance every single day, but when was the last time we went out? Not for a business obligation or with family and friends. I'm talking about a date for dinner, a movie, a ball game, a walk in the park. Time for the two of us."

She'd caught him off guard. He'd come back with some defensive retort about how she simply needed to tell him when and where and he'd be there. She'd stormed out and wouldn't take his calls. The next time he saw her was when she hurled his engagement ring at him.

He drove the few blocks to his apartment on the third floor of an old Victorian house built in the twenties. He turned into the alley behind the house and parked in his assigned space.

He took the outside metal stairway to reach his apartment and unlocked the door.

Slamming his keys on the kitchen counter, the emptiness in his life stared him in the face.

He'd screwed up big-time.

ASHLEIGH HAD STRUGGLED all afternoon to keep her fear of a possible pregnancy to herself. Listening to how involved Kyle was in his nephews' lives had been painful. An in-her-face reminder that she couldn't give Kyle what he wanted most—children to coach, to play with, to love. Even if she were pregnant, there was only a minute possibility of a full-term pregnancy.

How would she survive another heartbreaking miscarriage?

There was so much Kyle didn't understand about her. She couldn't bear to have him minimize her fear of yet another pregnancy. She had to admit she was surprised when he hadn't even been a little bit curious about whether or not she was on birth control.

A few months ago, Ashleigh had gone off birth control pills because she couldn't tolerate some of the side effects. She hadn't been involved with anyone and had made the conscious decision not to get serious. From the time she and Kyle were married, they'd been so intent on starting a family that they hadn't used birth control.

Last night had been reminiscent of those days, so she'd never given protection a thought.

When he finally dropped her and the boys off at Paula's house before heading to work, she was relieved to be free of his constant scrutiny.

"Come on, boys," she called upstairs. They were supposed to be showering in preparation for dinner. "We need to get going. Aunt Vivian is expecting us by five."

She went into the kitchen, poured a glass of water and studied the various pictures of her nephews Paula had displayed on the refrigerator. Some were together, some alone and some with family members or friends. All had one thing in common. They were happy. Paula was such a great mother. Her boys were well behaved and polite, but at the same time they knew how to have a good time.

Especially with their uncle Kyle. She wished she could stop picturing what it would have been like if the boys Kyle coached had been theirs. She blinked to clear her eyes.

"You guys look great," she told Mark and Ryan a few minutes later as they walked out the front door. "Do you go to Aunt Vivian's often?"

"Sometimes," Mark answered. He opened the sliding door of Paula's van and hopped in.

"Yeah, we like to see her animals," Ryan added as he got in the other side of the van.

"You know, your mom and I used to go to her house every Sunday when we were growing up."

Ashleigh waited for the boys to buckle their seat belts then backed into the street.

"Really?" Ryan's interest was piqued, so Ashleigh continued.

"Really," Ashleigh repeated. "We'd spend the afternoon playing with our cousins while my grandmother—your great-grandma—would cook a huge meal and we'd gather around the long table in the dining room."

"Why did Great-Grandma cook at Aunt Vivian's house?" Mark asked.

"Good question." Ashleigh chuckled. She went on to explain how the house had belonged to their great-grandparents. "When Great-Grandpa died almost ten years ago, Aunt Vivian moved into Great-Grandma's house to help her out."

Aunt Viv, never married and childless, was the oldest of the three sisters, and Ashleigh's mother, Melanie, was the youngest. Aunt Lynne was the middle sister. Her three boys were a little older than Ashleigh and Paula, so the boys had been great at teaching the girls how to hit and throw a ball and how to ride the horses their grandparents used to keep on the property. Paula's boys would have loved learning to ride, but caring for the horses became too much for Aunt Viv when her knee problems began.

Ashleigh turned onto the two-lane road that would take them to Aunt Viv's.

"Why doesn't Great-Grandma live there now?" Ryan asked.

How to explain Alzheimer's to a child when it was a difficult concept for adults to grasp? "She needs some special help, so my mother, your Grandma Melanie, is moving Great-Grandma into a special hospital in Maryland."

The drive to Aunt Viv's took about fifteen minutes, as the ten-acre property sat on the outskirts of Grand Oaks, surrounded by farms and thickly wooded areas. As a child, Ashleigh had imagined fire-breathing dragons and handsome princes in those woods.

As an adult, she knew that even the most handsome and courageous of princes couldn't rescue her from everything.

Aunt Viv's chocolate labs, Harry and Isabel, came galloping toward the van to greet them when they pulled into the winding stone driveway. She pulled over to the side to park and the boys were unfastening their seat belts before the engine stopped.

Aunt Viv wasn't far behind the dogs and she hugged each of the boys before getting to Ashleigh. Aunt Viv whisked Ashleigh away toward the house. "Now you boys know where I keep everything." Her aunt spoke over her shoulder while directing Ashleigh to the front door of the sprawling ranch home. "There's a surprise back near the barn," she told them, then turned back to Ashleigh. "They've been here enough that I trust them to stay out of trouble."

Aunt Viv continued marching Ashleigh across the

entryway and dining room and through the swinging door that separated the dining room from the kitchen. The house looked exactly as Ashleigh remembered it.

"I adopted a rabbit from one of the neighbors who couldn't keep it anymore," Aunt Viv confided to Ashleigh. "The boys will love it."

Her aunt was barely five feet tall, but she'd always possessed the spunk and vivacious personality of someone much taller and younger. Her salt-and-pepper hair was elfin short and she wore her trademark red penny loafers and white socks with navy cotton pants and a powder blue, short-sleeved top on her petite frame. If Ashleigh hadn't known about her aunt's recent knee replacement, her slight limp would have gone unnoticed.

"Tell me everything." Aunt Vivian handed Ashleigh a potato peeler and a five-pound bag of potatoes before propping herself on a counter stool to get started on the fresh green beans.

"Well, I wasn't there when Paula's labor began—"

"Oh, my dear, I don't want to hear about Paula," Aunt Viv exclaimed. "I've already talked to her myself."

"Then what?" Ashleigh was afraid to hear what was coming.

Aunt Viv lowered her voice to a whisper, even though no one else was in the house. "Tell me what's going on with you and Kyle."

She couldn't possibly know about last night, could she?

Ashleigh decided that was only likely if Kyle had mentioned it, and she couldn't imagine him doing so.

"There's *nothing* going on with Kyle and me." She emphasized "nothing" for the sake of both her aunt and herself. Last night had been a fluke, a moment of weakness. Even if she were pregnant, she'd deal with it alone. Maybe it wouldn't hurt so much if he didn't know.

She'd survived this far, she could do it again.

She scraped at the potato's skin as if she wanted to hurt it. Waterworks threatened and she blinked to clear her vision, but not before Aunt Vivian noticed and misunderstood the reason.

Her aunt hopped down from her perch to put an arm around Ashleigh's waist and squeezed. "Oh, sweetie, I didn't mean to upset you."

"I'm fine," Ashleigh told her, pausing midway through the potato she was peeling to look at Aunt Viv. "I'm just not feeling like myself. It has nothing to do with Kyle. We're divorced and that's that."

Aunt Viv raised an eyebrow in obvious disbelief. She put a hand on Ashleigh's shoulder. "Are you sure you're not upset about something with Kyle?" Then she quickly added, "I'm not trying to pry. It's just that when I talked to Paula, she thought things had gotten better between you and Kyle. A truce, maybe?"

"We're doing all right," Ashleigh said. "For a divorced couple." She attacked the next potato.

After a few minutes of uncomfortable silence, Aunt Viv said, "Did I ever tell you about Clint?"

"Clint?"

Aunt Viv walked to the oven to check on the chicken roasting there. "He was the love of my life." Her words were quiet and simple, but the anguish in Aunt Viv's voice was evident.

Ashleigh was afraid to ask, but she did anyway. "What happened to him?"

"He died a few years ago." Aunt Viv's back was to Ashleigh as she wiped up a spill on the countertop. "A blood clot travelled to his heart."

"I'm so sorry." Ashleigh didn't know what else to say. She waited for Aunt Viv to continue.

"We grew up together. His parents owned a farm down the road. You know the one, with the fruit stand in the summer and Christmas trees in the winter."

Ashleigh stopped peeling. "I remember. Walker Produce. Didn't they go out of business several years ago?"

Aunt Viv nodded. "When Clint's parents got too old, there was no one else to manage the farm anymore because Clint had moved away and he had no intention of moving back. So they sold the land to developers." Aunt Viv removed a large salad from the refrigerator and set it on the counter.

"Clint didn't want the farm?" Ashleigh asked.

"He couldn't take care of it." Aunt Viv's tone became somber. "He was paralyzed from the waist down in a car accident shortly before we were supposed to get married."

Ashleigh's sudden intake of breath was audible. Her hand flew to cover her mouth. "That's terrible." She choked out, "I'm so sorry."

She waited for Aunt Viv to continue, not wanting to push for details in case her aunt wasn't comfortable supplying them. Ashleigh had never heard this story, couldn't imagine why no one in her family had ever talked about Clint.

Aunt Vivian continued to tell her story while she cut up tomatoes for the salad. "We delayed our wedding while Clint recuperated." She spoke softly and Ashleigh strained to hear. "I wanted to get married right there in the hospital, but Clint wouldn't hear of it. I suggested it again when he was moved to a rehab facility and again he said no. He said he wanted me to have the wedding of my dreams, but he couldn't understand that none of that mattered to me anymore."

"You never married?" At this point, Ashleigh wasn't sure. She'd never heard even a whisper about this part of her aunt's life.

Aunt Viv's head shook slowly. "No, we never married." Her voice was wistful. "It would have been thirty-nine years next month if we had." She paused so long, Ashleigh didn't know if her aunt planned to continue or not. Finally she spoke in a strained voice. "By the time Clint was discharged from rehab, he'd decided he didn't want to be a burden to me."

Ashleigh's eyes welled up and no words would come.

Aunt Viv continued. "No matter what I said, he

wouldn't change his mind. He refused to give in, refused to recognize that I loved him enough to change the image I had of our future together. He decided to move to Kentucky to continue his therapy and he never once contacted me after that." She dumped the tomatoes into the salad bowl. "If I hadn't kept in contact with his sister, I never would have known what happened to him."

Ashleigh finally voiced the question that nagged her. "Why hasn't anyone mentioned this until now? Surely the entire family knew."

"I swore them all to secrecy," Aunt Viv said. "I never wanted to be reminded of that part of my life again."

Then Aunt Vivian walked over to Ashleigh and straightened to her full height. She grabbed Ashleigh's upper arms and gave her a slight shake. "You need to understand how much Clint hurt me by leaving. I was crushed beyond belief. Don't you see? He did to me what you did to Kyle."

CHAPTER TWELVE

HOW COULD AUNT VIVIAN be so cruel as to compare what Clint had done to her with Ashleigh and Kyle's situation? Ashleigh's intentions had been to look out for Kyle's best interests. Clint had only thought of himself.

Ashleigh looked Aunt Viv in the eye. "How can you say that? I did Kyle a huge favor. Once I was out of the picture, he was free to find someone else to fall in love with and start a family. Just because he hasn't found someone yet doesn't mean he won't someday find that happiness."

If she hadn't left, then Kyle would have been miserable because they couldn't have children. That would have made Ashleigh miserable, too. So she chose the shortest path to the end of their marriage.

"Did you ever look into adoption?" Aunt Viv's tone softened. "I'm sure Kyle would have been open to that."

Ashleigh had heard this suggestion multiple times, mainly from Kyle. She was sick of it. It might be the perfect solution for so many people, but she refused to consider it.

She steeled herself and took control of her emotions before speaking. "As a pediatrician, I've seen several adoptions. Many have been successful, but some have gone horribly wrong. One family in my practice tried private adoption three times before it finally worked out."

Ashleigh took a breath, recalling the woman's emotional distress as if it had happened yesterday. They'd originally met when she came in for an interview appointment to decide if Ashleigh was the right pediatrician for her new baby. "Two different birth mothers changed their minds a few weeks before their babies were born." She took a breath before continuing. "There was another family who brought their newborn home. Right before the child turned six months, the birth father returned and the birth mother wanted the baby back."

Aunt Viv opened her mouth to speak, but Ashleigh put a hand up to stop her. "I've also seen unsuccessful foreign adoptions break families in two."

She'd witnessed firsthand the utter destruction of a childless couple when their foreign adoption of an older child fell through. This particular husband and wife had spent three years diligently doing everything right, only to lose the child when she died in an earthquake that demolished the orphanage. They were told they'd need to start the process all over again, but the stress had been so great that the couple divorced.

"That doesn't necessarily mean *you* would have a bad experience, too," her aunt scolded, her head shaking.

At that moment the boys came crashing through the front door, ending any more discussion of the matter.

Ashleigh had sustained too much pain and heartbreak with her failed pregnancies to suffer through the possibility of more with adoption. Simply talking about it made her sad.

No one had ever understood that, not even Kyle.

Especially Kyle.

ASHLEIGH AWOKE THE next morning to the alarm clock on her cell phone. She groaned, grabbed the phone from the nightstand and touched snooze. Morning came way too soon after a restless night of troubled thoughts and vivid memories.

When she'd first climbed into bed last night, she'd been surrounded by reminders of her previous night with Kyle. The way they'd lain together, spooning their naked bodies, where a single caress had been all it had taken to ignite a fire within them.

Ashleigh had spent the night turning this way and that, kicking off the covers and trying to find a position that didn't make her feel bereft and alone. Every movement brought forth more erotic memories as she inhaled Kyle's scent on the sheets.

And those memories led her back to reality. They hadn't used protection and there was a definite chance that she was pregnant. She'd done the math in her head several times and it always came out the same—this was her fertile time of the month. She may have been unable to carry a baby to term, but they'd never had trouble conceiving.

Shoving the possibility of pregnancy aside, her thoughts had turned to the story Aunt Viv told of losing her long-ago love. After the boys had interrupted them to tell Ashleigh about the rabbit, she hadn't been able to figure out if Aunt Viv understood her stand on adoption or not.

She turned off her alarm before the snooze sounded and dragged her body out of bed. Monday mornings never bothered her, but this wasn't her usual work morning where she stayed in her pajamas, drank coffee and answered emails until midmorning.

Today she needed to get the boys off to school before heading to the office to see patients. Although the arrangement was temporary, this version of playing house was fulfilling in a way she never thought she'd experience.

She slipped her silky robe on over her pajamas and was tying the belt as she went across the hall to wake the boys. "Hey, guys, time to get up." They tossed, turned and moaned. She understood where they were coming from. They should have left Aunt Viv's earlier last night, enabling the boys to wind down sooner before finally getting to bed. "What do you want for breakfast?"

They mumbled two kinds of cereal into their pillows, so she headed downstairs to make coffee and get breakfast. Pressing a hand to her abdomen, she made decaf even though she could use the caffeine.

With a cup of coffee in her hand a short while later, she went back upstairs for a quick shower and to check on the boys' progress.

Amazingly, they all got to where they needed to be on time.

Later, over her lunch break—shortened because she'd run behind while seeing patients—she updated charts, returned phone calls and signed prescriptions. All while she nibbled at the grilled chicken wrap Cammie had ordered for her.

The afternoon went by quickly. With no time to spare, Ashleigh went to the front desk to speak to Cammie. "Would you mind calling my sister's house to find out if my nephews made it home from school?" She gave Cammie the phone number. "Emma should be there with them."

A few minutes later, there was a knock on the door of exam room two.

"One second." Ashleigh looked up from examining her young patient. She held up a finger to her young patient's mother. "Excuse me."

Ashleigh opened the door and slipped out to see Cammie.

"Emma said the boys are fine. They're finishing their homework before Dr. Kyle picks them up for soccer practice. She gave them a snack to hold them until dinner."

Ashleigh said, "Thanks," and returned to the exam room.

Close to six o'clock, Ashleigh finally finished with her patients. She still needed to run by the hospital to consult on a young patient admitted last night, but she'd do that after dinner when she brought the boys to see their mother.

Her cell phone rang. Caller ID showed it was Kyle calling. "Hello?" she answered.

"Hey, Ash," Kyle said cheerfully. The boys were chattering in the background. "Soccer practice just ended and I'm taking the boys to their house. We wondered if you were going to make it home for dinner." His question sounded domestic enough to make her grimace. She ached at the normalcy of their situation, similar to a real family.

"I have a few things to finish up here at the office. Then I'll be on my way." She hadn't expected their paths to cross again so quickly. She took a calming breath as the possibility of pregnancy jumped to the forefront of her mind. Still not a subject she wanted to discuss with Kyle until she was sure.

"Good," he said. "I'll throw one of these casseroles in the oven and it should be ready by the time you get home."

"Sounds great." That was the truth. She hadn't had dinner waiting for her when she arrived home since she and Kyle had been married. "Do you need me to pick up anything?"

"No, we're good. See you soon." Kyle disconnected before Ashleigh could say she'd planned to take the boys by the hospital.

Dinner went smoothly, with the boys taking up much of their attention. Ashleigh was again able to keep her troublesome thoughts at bay.

"Homework all done?" she asked the boys when they were cleaning up after dinner.

Both Mark and Ryan answered in the affirmative.

"Good, then get your backpacks and clothes ready for tomorrow and let's go see your mom!"

The boys cheered and Kyle put his hands up for high fives from them as they passed his chair.

"Oh, I forgot," Mark said. "I have a note from my teacher."

Ashleigh's head pounded. A note from a teacher could mean anything. It could be disciplinary or complimentary or even refer to a forgotten homework assignment.

"Let's see what it says." Kyle rose, ever the calm one. That's why he made such a great E.R. doctor.

Mark dug through his backpack and came up with a wrinkled piece of paper with a note attached.

"Uh-oh," Kyle said after reading it.

"What?" Ashleigh tried to read over his shoulder, but she was too short.

"It's a permission slip for a class trip tomorrow."

Kyle passed it to her. "Says he was supposed to have it signed last week, but he never returned it."

Ashleigh read the note from the teacher attached to the permission form. "It also says he needs to bring in his diorama tomorrow or he can't go on the field trip." She looked pointedly at Mark. "Diorama? Did you do a diorama?" Her stomach churned as if it were her own project to turn in.

Mark scrunched up his face. "Not exactly."

"Exactly how far did you get with it?" Kyle's patience seemed endless.

"I have a shoe box," Mark said with enthusiasm.

Kyle looked to Ashleigh and they rolled their eyes.

"I guess we need to get to work," Kyle said.

Ashleigh's cell phone rang. She checked caller ID. "It's the hospital." She touched Answer on the screen. "Dr. Wilson."

"This is Julianne Harper at Grand Oaks hospital. I'm sorry to disturb you, Dr. Wilson."

"That's okay," Ashleigh assured her, trying to recall if she knew the woman. "What can I do for you?"

"We had a single-car accident. The patient is approximately thirty-six weeks pregnant and has gone into labor. Dr. Bausch requested you come in because the baby looks to be about five pounds on the sonogram and might need to be admitted to the NICU."

Ashleigh asked a few more questions and checked the time. "I should be there within thirty minutes."

"Good," she said. "The patient's labor is progressing quickly."

Ashleigh ended the call and turned to Kyle.

"I've got this covered," he said before she could open her mouth. "I'll take the kids over to see Paula after we get Mark's diorama done."

Ashleigh didn't respond.

"Problem?" He'd apparently overheard her side of the conversation and filled in the blanks.

The honest answer was "yes," but it had nothing to do with going to the hospital to care for a newborn. She answered more sharply than she'd hoped. "Everything's fine." She softened her tone. "Thanks for taking homework duty," she said, and meant it.

How did people juggle careers and kids? Was this how it would have been for them if they'd had children? One of them constantly being called to duty, leaving the other with the kids?

No. Because she would have gladly put her career on hold to raise their children. If only that had been meant to be. She would have happily done whatever necessary to have this kind of life.

AFTER CARING FOR her NICU patient and doing the consult on the teenager, it was a little after ten-thirty and Ashleigh was ready to go home. Then she remembered she'd never checked in on Paula.

"Hey." Ashleigh spoke quietly from Paula's doorway when she saw the TV on. "Am I disturbing you?"

"No, no." Paula waved her in and muted the TV. "Please, come in. I'm so bored, but I can't sleep because I'm not doing anything to make me tired." She heaved a sigh. "Staying in this bed is torture."

"I wish I could do something to help." Ashleigh wasn't lying. No matter their differences of opinion, she hated seeing her sister confined to a hospital bed.

Particularly now, when her boys needed her at home.

"Did Kyle bring the boys in tonight?" Ashleigh asked.

Paula's features softened. "Yes. They even brought in the diorama to show me and I signed the permission form. I'm so sorry, I completely forgot about both of those things."

"You obviously have other things on your mind." Ashleigh chuckled, relieved now that the pressure was off. At least as far as the boys were concerned. "You must go through this all the time."

"More times than I'd like. It's not easy keeping on top of things," Paula said. "Kyle told me about the emergency you had to take care of. Everything go okay?"

"As well as can be expected," Ashleigh said. "The baby appears healthy, but I admitted him to the NICU as a precaution. Unfortunately, his mother has multiple injuries and will need help caring for him for a while."

"What a terrifying experience," Paula said. "It's one thing to fear for your own life, but when you're carrying a life inside you—"

Ashleigh didn't hear the rest of Paula's sentence over the persistent ringing in her ears.

Was it possible she had a life inside her? Was she once again responsible for another life besides her own? If that were the case, then she'd need to take care of that precious life, even though her chances of miscarrying were high.

While it was a few days too early to even get an accurate blood test for pregnancy, first thing tomorrow she needed to make an appointment with her ob/gyn to get her professional opinion.

Rosy Bausch, both friend and doctor, was the one person she could confide in right now.

PAULA'S HOUSE WAS DARK except for the outside light and a dim lamp in the living room. Ashleigh entered quietly and placed her medical bag and purse right inside the front door.

Kyle was asleep on the living room couch. Lying on his back, his breathing was heavy but he wasn't quite snoring. His legs were crossed at the ankles and elevated on the opposite arm because he was too long for the sofa. The floor lamp in the corner was turned on to its lowest setting, bathing the room in shadows.

Ashleigh slipped off her shoes to walk barefoot across the room. She sat on the coffee table in front of Kyle, watching him sleep for the first time in years. His facial muscles were relaxed, his lips slightly curved as if he were having pleasant dreams.

Ashleigh's chest tightened. Had Aunt Vivian been

right? Had Ashleigh hurt him by leaving? She still didn't believe she had. He would be better off with a woman who could give him the family he deserved.

Not a physically defective woman like herself.

No matter how much he said he loved her whether she could bear children or not, she knew that wasn't true. She'd seen him interact with Mark and Ryan, as well as other children. Ashleigh knew he'd never be happy without children of his own to love.

She wiped a tear from her cheek before reaching out to touch Kyle gently. His eyes opened suddenly, startling her.

"Hey." His smile was sleepy, his voice deliciously deep and sexy. "I didn't mean to fall asleep." He slowly sat up and lowered his feet to the floor. They faced each other for a few long moments, knees touching.

The heat built in Ashleigh from that single connection. She couldn't fall under his spell again. No matter how easy it would be to succumb.

"I opened a bottle of wine." He gestured to the bottle and now empty glass at the other end of the coffee table. "It's your favorite merlot. Want me to pour you a glass?"

"No, thanks." She panicked momentarily, thinking he'd want an explanation. Like with caffeine, she needed to pay attention to what she put in her body—just in case. But she didn't want to stumble over her words and make him suspicious. "I'm pretty tired." No need to worry Kyle unnecessarily or cause him to feel obligated to her when they both knew a successful pregnancy would be improbable.

Kyle covered his mouth when he yawned. "I only wanted to close my eyes for a minute. What time is it?"

"About eleven-fifteen." Ashleigh hadn't stayed long in Paula's room once she'd made the conscious decision to care for the life she might be carrying. She worried she might give away her possible condition if she stuck around. Paula would definitely have an opinion about what Ashleigh should do and she didn't need outside interference right now. Not when, as always, her opinion would be biased toward Kyle's best interests.

"How's your patient?" he asked.

"NICU" was the simple answer. Then she added, "He's got strong vitals. His original Apgar score was six, followed by a ten at five minutes. NICU was a precaution after surviving what I heard was a pretty bad car accident."

"There were pictures on the local evening news," he said. "I can't believe there were no fatalities."

"I know," she agreed, and changed the subject. "I stopped to see Paula on my way out. She said you came by and everything is set for tomorrow with the boys."

"Turns out the diorama needed to be a scene from colonial history," he said, "so Ben Franklin and his potbellied stove are made from Legos. I'm sure his teacher will give him a break once we tell her his mom is in the hospital."

Ashleigh smiled. "Good call. I'll write her a note to send along with Mark. Does he have everything for his field trip?" His class was going to a working dairy farm in the morning.

"I think so." Kyle yawned again. "We dug through his closet and found his raincoat since there's a chance of drizzling rain tomorrow."

"Nothing like tromping around in mud," Ashleigh quipped.

"Hopefully it's mud, since there are dairy cows on the farm." They shared a smile and Kyle rose from the couch. "I better get going. I'm on at six tomorrow morning."

After a momentary sense of physical loss, Ashleigh also rose and walked with him to the front door. "Yeah, morning came way too soon today. I'm not used to being up and out so early anymore, not to mention the rush involved in getting the boys on their way."

Kyle turned to her when he reached the door. "I'll touch base tomorrow sometime. I've got a meeting with Tom about the lawsuit after work. You okay by yourself with the boys?"

"Of course," she said. "I'll let Emma know if office hours run late. She's been a lifesaver."

He turned to the door and back to Ashleigh again. "I promised myself I wouldn't do this." He placed his large hands at her waist and pulled her close, covering her mouth with his before she could think, much less protest.

Instead of objecting, she enjoyed the kiss and her arms circled his neck without conscious thought. This might well be the last time she would experience his mouth, his strength, his sheer masculinity. She wanted to savor every second.

He deepened the kiss and she became lost in the heat fueled by their passion.

Without thinking, she moved her hips ever so slightly against his erection. He groaned and removed his mouth from hers. He leaned his forehead against hers and whispered, "I should go." He gave her one last chaste kiss before he disappeared out the front door.

Ashleigh braced her back against the wall when she became light-headed, overcome by mixed emotions about his sudden departure.

THE NEXT MORNING, as soon as she got to work, Ashleigh called her OB and was put right through after giving her name. "I need to see you, Rosy."

"Let me check the appointment schedule," she said.

"I don't want anyone to know," Ashleigh said quickly.

"Oh." Rosy paused for a second. "Is everything okay?"

"That's difficult to answer."

"Do you need an exam or advice?" Rosy asked.

"Can you break away for lunch?" Ashleigh mentally calculated what time she might be free.

"I've got our monthly staff meeting over lunch," Rosy said. "What about dinner?"

Ashleigh considered it. The boys would need her home because Kyle already said he would be working and then meeting with Tom about his lawsuit afterward. She needed to remember to see what she could do about getting Kyle funding for the charity, since she felt responsible for him losing it in the first place.

"I can't do dinner tonight," Ashleigh said. "I have to watch the boys."

"What if I come over to your office as soon as I'm done seeing patients?" Rosy suggested. "I'll give you a call when I'm on my way."

"Are you sure? Office hours have been running until almost six."

"That's perfect," Rosy said. "I'll bring something to keep me occupied if you run late."

They ended the call and for the first time, Ashleigh was confident that she was headed down the right path as far as her possible pregnancy was concerned.

The day dragged on, though. Not until a little boy of four came in for his yearly physical with a picture for her wall did she rediscover some of the joy she used to experience as a pediatrician. She'd barely gotten out a thank-you over the lump in her throat.

In the past, those times had been the most difficult. Stark reminders that she would never have a little boy or girl of her own to draw her pictures.

Even a pregnancy right now would only be the precursor to disappointment and overwhelming heartache. Not the answer to her prayers.

"Hey." Rosy popped her head into Ashleigh's office a little after six. "Cammie told me to come on back."

Ashleigh stood and waved her in. "Have a seat. Thanks for being so flexible."

They chatted a few minutes, hitting the highlights of their lives since Ashleigh had moved out of town. Rosy had been a close colleague when Ashleigh had been in Grand Oaks since they were often involved with the same patients.

Rosy and her husband had occasionally doubled with Kyle and Ashleigh, going out to dinner or to the movies. But as Ashleigh's pregnancy difficulties became more debilitating, she cut herself off from the outside world.

"So tell me what's going on with you," Rosy finally said. "Why am I here?"

Ashleigh swallowed, trying to still her racing heart. "There's a possibility that I might be pregnant."

Rosy's eyes widened enough that Ashleigh recognized her surprise. "You don't know for sure?" Rosy asked.

"It's too early to even do a blood test." Ashleigh recited dates.

Rosy agreed. "Seven days at the earliest. Ten would be better."

"This is stupid." Ashleigh rose from her desk chair and gripped the back of it for support. "I can't believe I let myself get into this position."

"Sit down and relax," Rosy suggested. "Getting upset won't fix anything."

Ashleigh sat, inhaling deeply. "I need your honest opinion, Rosy. Is there any chance I can carry this baby to term? That is, *if* I'm pregnant."

Rosy didn't say anything right away. She pursed her lips and didn't meet Ashleigh's gaze. Not a good sign.

"The honest answer is I don't know. Kyle did all the research," Rosy said. "You should be asking him."

"I can't," Ashleigh said quickly.

"You haven't told him?" Rosy narrowed her gaze at Ashleigh.

"Why would I tell Kyle?" Ashleigh became defensive and straightened her shoulders. "You're assuming the baby is his." She didn't know why she was denying that Kyle would be the father. Unless she was trying to protect him from one more heartbreak.

"Is it Kyle's?" Rosy raised an eyebrow. Before Ashleigh could answer, Rosy waved a hand. "No, sorry, that's none of my business."

Ashleigh expelled a breath. "Yes. If I'm pregnant, then it's Kyle's. I didn't plan it, it just happened." Her pulse sped up at the memory. "I went off the pill a few months ago because I didn't like how it made me feel. And why use birth control if you're not having sex, right?"

"You probably never even thought about it when you were with Kyle," Rosy guessed. "Because it was Kyle."

Ashleigh dipped her head, more than slightly embarrassed. At least being honest with Rosy eased the weight on her shoulders.

"Why don't you talk to him?" Rosy suggested. "Ask him if he's heard of anything new."

"I can't. I'm not ready to go through that again, Rosy. At least not until I know if I'm pregnant." A crushing weight on her chest made it difficult to breathe. The surgeries, the tests, medications. She couldn't do it again, knowing it would all be for nothing.

"I understand," Rosy said. "You already know that having both the incompetent cervix along with endometriosis makes it difficult to fix two things at once. The amazing thing has been that you've been able to get pregnant so easily. Statistics say forty percent of women with endometriosis can't even conceive."

"And what's the statistic for those who do conceive to actually carry to term?" Ashleigh asked.

"No one's sure because many women miscarry before they realize they're pregnant. They assume their periods are late." The odds had been against Ashleigh from the beginning. Rosy added, "And you've also been through an unsuccessful cervical stitch because your cervix is extremely thin."

That had been during her last failed pregnancy. The one she'd hoped to carry to term.

Ashleigh cleared her throat. "So the straight answer to my question would be that there's no better chance of me carrying this pregnancy to term than there was before."

"Unfortunately, I think that's correct." Rosy spoke softly, her eyes glassy with emotion. "I'm sorry I don't have better news."

Ashleigh raised her gaze to stare at a point on the wall above Rosy's head.

"What are you going to do?" Rosy asked.

Ashleigh narrowed her eyes. "What do you mean? Are you asking if I want to end the pregnancy because there's a huge chance I'll miscarry anyway?"

"I wasn't asking that," Rosy said calmly. "If you are pregnant, will you stay here? Or do you want me to find a specialist for you somewhere else?"

"Oh, sorry." Ashleigh blew out a breath. "I guess I jumped to the wrong conclusion." She swallowed her embarrassment. That had been the actual advice from a former friend after hearing about her miscarriages.

"No need to apologize, Ashleigh," Rosy told her. "Being told you'll never carry a baby to term must scare the hell out of you now that you might be pregnant."

"Thanks for understanding, Rosy. But back to your question, I think I'll go back to Richmond after Paula delivers and once my pediatric replacement arrives."

"Well, a new environment might be less stressful."

This was why she was such a fan of Dr. Rosy Bausch. She got where Ashleigh was coming from.

They talked a few more minutes until Rosy said, "I should get home to my kids."

"Let me lock up and I'll walk you out." The single thing Ashleigh had accomplished by talking to Rosy was having someone to share her secret with. Her burden lightened ever so slightly.

They were coming out the front door when Kyle suddenly appeared. Ashleigh froze. Her heart started pounding so loudly that she was sure Kyle and Rosy must hear it, too.

"I wanted to stop by before my meeting with Tom," he told Ashleigh. "Hey, Rosy, what brings you here?"

"Just visiting with an old friend," Rosy said smoothly.

"We were, um, catching up." Ashleigh hoped she didn't sound as loud and fake as she thought. She breathed deeply, trying to slow her racing pulse.

Kyle's brow furrowed. "Okay. Well, I wanted to make sure you'd make it home to have dinner with the boys. I'll postpone my meeting with Tom if you need me to."

"No, no." Ashleigh's words spilled out louder than she anticipated. She hastily moderated her tone. "I'm on my way there now." She turned to Rosy. "Thanks for stopping by." She looked at Kyle but avoided his eyes. "Thanks for checking in."

He grinned and gave her a wink.

Her breath caught when she glimpsed the ever cheerful man she'd fallen in love with years ago. She hated to admit it, but she'd missed his positive attitude and sense of humor.

"Is everything okay, Ash?" Kyle asked.

She swallowed. "Yes, why wouldn't it be?"

Kyle appeared unconvinced, but he said, "Okay, see you later then."

Ashleigh watched Rosy and Kyle walk to their respective cars before turning to lock the front door. Her rubbery legs barely carried her to her own car.

Keeping the truth from Kyle—if she was pregnant—would be more difficult than she'd imagined. She'd never carried so much guilt in her life, while at the same time she was even more determined not to upset the thriving life he'd forged for himself.

CHAPTER THIRTEEN

KYLE STARTED THE ENGINE of his truck and hesitated before putting it into Drive. Had he imagined Ashleigh's anxiety? He didn't think so. Something was definitely off about her. More than usual.

But what?

He shifted into Drive and pulled into light traffic on Market Street, which was considered the main drag in Grand Oaks from before the town was founded in 1720. Historians claimed everything imaginable had been bought and sold on this stretch of road, from food to animals to humans.

Kyle's tenth-grade history teacher spent a lot of time on Grand Oaks's history. He wanted his students to be clear about where they lived and how things had changed in this part of southern Virginia.

Kyle hadn't understood at the time, but he came to learn that it's important to understand why things evolve the way they do. Mostly, it's vital to not repeat mistakes.

That was why he'd left Ashleigh so abruptly last night. He didn't want to repeat their mistakes of the past. If she was going to take off at the first opportunity—and he was sure that she would—then he needed to guard himself. He couldn't allow her to crush him like she had two years ago, even if it would require forgoing a physical relationship with her.

Was that why she'd been uncomfortable when he showed up unexpectedly at her office? He hadn't meant to make things awkward between them. Maybe he should have explained why he left last night.

Then again, how did you phrase something like that? *I need to keep my distance from you so you don't crush me like a bug again* probably wouldn't go over well.

As these thoughts went through his head, Kyle continued on his way to meet with Tom, who had recently opened a private law office located two blocks off Market Street. Kyle found a parking spot nearby. He jogged up the half dozen steps to the door of the town house and went right in. The former three-story row home had been converted into offices, with Tom's located on the second floor. Through the open doorway, Tom was visible behind his desk. His gaze traveled from what he was reading to Kyle, a welcoming smile lighting up the man's face.

"Hey, Kyle, come on in." Tom rose, waved him in and pointed to a burgundy leather chair in front of his mahogany desk. Kyle shut the office door and they shook hands before taking seats across from each other.

Tom pulled out a folder from his file cabinet and opened it. "The reason I wanted to meet again so soon was that I've talked to the plaintiff's lawyer and they'd like to settle."

Kyle raised his eyebrows. He hadn't done anything wrong. Why settle? "Talk to me." He tried to keep an open mind.

"We've discussed the two-million-dollar limit the state of Virginia puts on medical malpractice compensation. Even though they were asking for five mil, they were expecting to get two if they won. And that would include any punitive damages." Tom took a sip from the soda can next to him. "Want one?" He gestured to his drink.

"I'm good," Kyle said. "Give me the bottom line."

"They're willing to settle for a million."

Kyle must have heard wrong. "Are you freaking kidding me?" He shot out of his chair and paced back and forth in Tom's small office. He stopped and pounded a fist on a filing cabinet, making the planter teeter. "I didn't do anything wrong, Tom. In fact, I saved the guy's life. I'm sorry he started abusing prescription drugs again, but that's not my fault."

"I know, I know," Tom said. "Sit down and relax. All you need to do is say you don't want to settle and we continue on to court."

"But what if the judge doesn't rule in my favor?" Kyle asked. "He could award this jerk the two million dollars and my insurance company would likely drop me."

"Take it easy, Kyle," Tom said. "If I thought that was going to happen, then I'd advise you to settle.

But I'm confident we can find someone to say this guy made it a habit to take off his medical-alert bracelet when he didn't want people to know he was a former addict."

"Really?" Kyle tried not to be too hopeful.

"Yes," Tom said. "I have a P.I. I've worked with before and she's hunting down people who know him. She even talked to the guy's sister, who didn't sound convincing when she said she was positive he never took the bracelet off." He leaned forward. "She's had some addiction problems, too."

Kyle still had his doubts about the outcome of his case, but he trusted Tom completely.

Kyle returned to his seat and they went over a few other details.

"Thanks, Tom," Kyle said. "I'm actually feeling a little better than when I walked in here."

Tom shifted nervously in his seat. "Now that we've settled on where to proceed, would you mind if I asked you about Theresa?"

Kyle had warned Theresa he wouldn't lie to his best friend when she came up with this crazy plan. She could have chosen any number of other guys to play the part of her boyfriend to make Tom jealous.

"Sure, what's up?" Kyle asked.

"I've been hearing things about you and her," Tom said.

"Don't believe everything you hear."

"I've heard the two of you are dating—"

"I wouldn't call it dating," Kyle corrected.

"No?" Tom said. "Then what is it?" His voice got louder. "Are you sleeping with her?"

"No, no!" Kyle could barely keep a laugh from bursting forth. "Jeez, Tom. I'm not involved with Theresa. She's been working on the nonprofit with me and someone started the rumor that we were seeing each other. She only asked me to go along with it so you'd be jealous."

Tom's eyes nearly popped out of his head. "She did?" The muscles in his face relaxed and he grinned. "She's trying to make me jealous?"

Kyle laughed. "Yeah, so what are you going to do about it?"

Tom sat back down and opened his laptop. He clicked a few keys and turned the screen in Kyle's direction. "This is what I'm doing about it." He pointed to a real estate listing. "I'm going to contact the listing agent to see this house. It's in the same neighborhood as the house that Theresa wanted to buy last fall."

"I KNOW, MOM." Paula dialed back the whine in her voice while talking on the phone with her mother. "I really don't want to worry Scott."

"But, Paula, he's your husband. The baby's father." Her mother repeated what everyone else had already said. "He has a right to know what's going on."

"I'll tell you what." Paula's patience was dwindling. "I'll think about it."

That answer placated her mother, but then she hit

another sensitive subject. "How's it going with you and your sister?"

"Ashleigh and I are doing fine." Paula decided that wasn't even a lie. They tolerated each other and avoided any conflict so that they didn't get into a heated argument.

"Well, that's a relief," Mom said. "Now you can ask her to be your birth coach. I'm sure she'll agree."

"Mom!" Paula's head was about to explode. Birth coach? Where did that come from? "I can't ask Ashleigh. I thought you were going to do it." Her mother was an R.N., the logical choice to fill in for Scott if he couldn't make it in time.

"I can't leave your grandmother yet, dear," Mom said. "I need to see what the doctors decide to do about her leaking heart valve. If they do surgery, then I'll stay. I need to be sure she's going to be okay."

Paula's mother had done extensive research to discover Copper Ridge, an outstanding Alzheimer's care facility affiliated with John Hopkins in rural Maryland, only to find out Grandma had heart problems.

"I still have a few weeks until this baby is due," Paula reminded her mother. "You'll be back by then."

"But what if I'm not?" her mother asked. "You've already gone into labor once. Next time they might not be able to stop it and you'll be on your own."

"I've done this before," Paula said. "I know what I'm doing."

"But what if decisions need to be made? Like a

Cesarean?" her mother said. "You'll have no one to talk those things over with."

"I'm a big girl, Mom."

"And big girls know when to ask for help."

She hated when her mother was right. Even having someone available to get her ice chips or a wet washcloth would make labor much more tolerable.

"I'll figure out someone to be with me during labor, okay?" Hopefully that would pacify her mother. How could Paula ask Ashleigh to do it when this floor had so many awful memories for her sister?

"Ask Ashleigh," her mother repeated insistently. "It's about time the two of you made up and put this feud behind you."

THE NEXT DAY, after spending a busy morning in his hospital office, Tom hung up the phone. He leaned back in his desk chair and folded his hands behind his head. He'd spoken with a loan officer from his financial institution. Preapproved for a mortgage sounded like a step in the right direction.

Tom immediately dialed the listing Realtor for the house he'd seen online. "Two o'clock would be perfect," he told the woman when she suggested the time to see the house.

The day dragged until he was able leave for the appointment. He had work to complete, but his head wasn't into it. All he could think about was whether the house would look as good as on the Realtor's website.

And whether Theresa would love it as much as the one she'd wanted last fall.

When he could stand it no longer he left the hospital, well aware he would be early for the appointment.

He got to the neighborhood and passed the house Theresa had loved, two blocks from the one he was seeing today. He drove around the area, viewing it from a different perspective than he'd ever looked at other properties.

The elementary school was within walking distance. There was also a fairly new tot lot and some tennis courts in the vicinity. There were two nearby swimming pools and the new branch of the library was less than a mile away. Several grocery stores and pharmacies were in either direction.

Tom headed to the house he was about to tour, located at the end of a cul-de-sac. He parked on the street rather than the cement parking area on the right front side of the house.

From his rearview mirror, he saw the Realtor pull up behind him.

"Great house, isn't it?" The real estate agent reached out a hand to shake his. "I'm Shirley Johnson." She was probably mid-forties with coal-black hair pinned up in a sloppy knot. Her hairdo contradicted her stylish black skirt and matching fitted jacket worn over a tailored red blouse. Shiny black patent leather heels brought her nearly eye to eye with him.

"Tom Patterson," he said. "How long has the property been on the market?" He knew the answer from the website, but wondered if it had been on the market previously and taken off to lower the price.

"This house was actually sold six months ago in a short sale and the new owners gutted the inside to flip it."

Tom hoped the workmanship was good. Several lawsuits were pending where flipped houses hadn't been done to code. Insurance companies were going after the flippers to pay for water and electrical damages.

"Shall we go inside?" Shirley held the key to the lockbox in her hand. "Are you searching for a home for yourself, Tom, or do you have a family?"

"A fiancée." His shocking reply was automatic.

"Wonderful!" she gushed. "When are you getting married?"

"We haven't picked a date yet." That was definitely true.

Tom followed her to the front door. The home was a white Cape Cod with a dark green door and matching shutters. There were flowers, pansies maybe, in the window boxes on the first level. The brass doorknob and house numbers were shiny and inviting.

They stepped inside the front door onto a slate area that transitioned into gleaming wood floors. The smell of fresh paint lingered in the air. The living room was spacious, set up with what was probably rented furniture staged to make the house easier to imagine as your own.

Not that he owned much furniture. He had a one-bedroom apartment and his major purchases had been a bed, a leather recliner and a flat-screen TV.

"This is a wonderful space," the real estate agent said. "Do you think your fiancée will like it?"

"I hope so." He eyed the room. "I'm wondering if she'll let me keep my furniture or if she'll want to start fresh."

The Realtor smiled. "Ah, a typical disagreement among newly married couples."

He was jumping too far into the future but couldn't help himself.

"As you can see," the Realtor said, "the kitchen has been completely redone with black lacquer cabinets, stainless steel appliances and beautiful granite countertops."

Tom could appreciate the kitchen, even though his small galley kitchen had mostly empty cabinets.

"Does your fiancée like to cook?" the Realtor asked.

"She loves to try new recipes she finds on the internet," Tom answered.

"There's even room for a small table and chairs in front of the window," Shirley said. "Let's look at the backyard while we're here." She opened the door from the kitchen and they stepped outside onto a patio made of cement pavers. The yard was well maintained and fenced in, with room for a swing set or a soccer goal. Actually, it was much better than the tiny, unfenced backyard at the house Theresa had wanted him to buy. It would especially be good for the dog that she desperately wanted.

"There's a powder room over here next to the coat closet." Shirley pointed it out when they went inside and down the hall toward the master bedroom. "And there's a full bath off the master."

They stepped into the master bedroom, which was quite spacious for the size of the house. Like most of the first floor, the walls were painted a neutral khaki color and the hardwood floors were all refinished.

"Can you see yourself and your fiancée here?" she asked.

"Actually, I can," he said.

The Realtor smiled and said with enthusiasm, "Then let's go check out the other bedrooms."

Tom was equally impressed with the two bedrooms upstairs with window seats in the dormers and the shared bathroom between them that the Realtor referred to as a "Jack and Jill" bathroom.

"What do you think?" she asked when they came up from inspecting the partially finished basement. "That would make a perfect playroom for your future kids."

"I like it a lot," he admitted, "but I have a few other properties to look at." A lie, but it made good business sense not to appear too eager.

"There are a few other parties interested," she said in likewise business fashion, "so I'd suggest you make an offer quickly. Why don't you bring your fiancée to look at it?"

"I'll definitely do that." He also needed to call a real estate lawyer or at least another Realtor to look out for his interests.

"The owners will be back in town this weekend," Shirley said. "I'll be bringing all offers to them at that time. They're anxious to move forward with a sale."

Tom was sure that was true. The people who'd flipped it wouldn't want to make any more mortgage payments than necessary.

He shook Shirley's hand before they went their separate ways.

Tom squashed his urge to call Theresa to tell her about the house. He wanted it to be a done deal first so she would know he was serious about treating her better and putting her needs first.

FOR THE PAST twenty-four hours, Ashleigh had been able to avoid Kyle. At least in person. They spoke on the phone a few times, mostly to coordinate schedules but also to share updates about their nephews.

Ashleigh began to look forward to those phone calls. The normalcy of them, the implied intimacy. That close connection with another human being had been absent from her life in Richmond. She hadn't missed it until now.

Talking on the phone was perfect. Kyle couldn't see her to judge whether she was hiding anything. Which, of course, she was.

She'd finished her last appointment and was seated

at her desk in her office when her cell phone rang. Expecting Kyle, she was surprised when it was Paula.

"Hi, Paula," Ashleigh greeted her. "Is everything okay?" Paula tended to go through Kyle when she had something to convey to Ashleigh.

"Everything's fine," Paula grumbled, "if sitting in this damn hospital bed is your definition of fine."

"O…kay." Ashleigh was unsure what to say next.

Luckily, Paula spoke up again before Ashleigh could say anything else. "Sorry," she said. "Anyway, are you planning to come to the hospital either tonight or tomorrow?"

Ashleigh mentally reviewed her schedule. "I need to stop by tonight to see my patient in the NICU. I'm also off tomorrow afternoon." They'd never scheduled appointments on Thursday afternoons from the time her father owned the practice so he could play golf. She'd kept the tradition since she often worked weekends and evenings. "What did you need?"

Paula didn't speak right away. Then, as Ashleigh was about to ask if she was okay, her sister said, "I need to talk to you about something."

Ashleigh was curious now. "I'll stop by later this evening. Kyle will have the boys for dinner and I'm sure he won't mind staying until I get there. I'll let him know I'll be a little longer than expected."

"Thanks, Ash, I really appreciate it."

"Is there anything I can bring you?" Ashleigh scoured her brain for ideas to cheer up her sister. "Orange Creamsicle milk shake?" That had always been Paula's favorite flavor at The Dairy Barn on Market Street.

"No, thanks." Paula's voice held a touch of melancholy. "I'm fine."

Ashleigh was pretty sure that wasn't the whole truth, but she didn't want to push her when their relationship was so strained.

They ended their call and Ashleigh straightened her desk before heading out.

She went directly to the NICU when she arrived at the hospital. Reviewing the newborn's chart, she was pleased with his progress.

"He's had a good day," the young R.N. assigned to him told Ashleigh.

"If I don't find anything during examination, I'll transfer him," Ashleigh told the nurse. She collected herself and called on her internal strength to get her through the tiny baby's exam.

"His mother came to see him this afternoon." The nurse adjusted her dark-framed glasses. "She was brought over in a wheelchair and I could see she was itching to hold him."

"That's wonderful." Ashleigh was relieved the woman had made enough progress to be able to come see her son. Last night when Ashleigh stopped by, the mother was in a great deal of pain and barely able to process what Ashleigh told her. "She'll be glad when I move him to the regular nursery then." She would stop by to give the mother the good news before going to see Paula.

The nurse nodded. "I was happily surprised when she was able to come up here with the injuries she'd sustained. I guess motherhood provides women the strength to overcome a tremendous amount of adversity when their child is involved."

"Very true." Ashleigh always thought if she'd done *more,* then maybe she would have carried to term. Discovering what "more" encompassed was what she'd never been able to ascertain.

She examined the infant, wrote the order for transfer to the regular nursery and went to see the baby's mother.

She knocked quietly on the woman's open door. "Mrs. Small?" She and the man sitting next to her turned in Ashleigh's direction. "I don't know if you remember me from yesterday," Ashleigh began.

"You're the pediatrician," the woman said groggily. The left side of her face was dark with bruises and her left arm was in a cast from her hand to above her elbow. "This is my husband, John."

Ashleigh entered and reached out to shake the man's hand. "I'm Dr. Wilson." She stood at the end of the bed. "I wanted to update you on your son's condition."

"His name is Matthew," Mrs. Small told her with a hint of a smile. "It means 'gift of God.'"

Ashleigh smiled in return, while her heart was breaking. She would never receive that kind of gift from God. "That name suits him," she said. "He came through with flying colors. In fact, I'm hoping to transfer him out of the NICU after his next exam since he's doing so well." She looked at the husband. "Because his bilirubin is slightly elevated, I'd like him to spend at least another twenty-four hours in the hospital before I discharge him."

"No hurry," Mr. Small joked. "He's our first child and I'm not sure I can handle him without my wife."

"You'll be fine," Ashleigh assured him. They discussed how much longer Mrs. Small might be in the hospital according to what they'd been told by her doctor earlier that day. Ashleigh assured them that if Mrs. Small was physically up to it, she could still breast-feed. They discussed options and Ashleigh answered their questions.

"Thank you so much, Dr. Wilson." Mr. Small rose to shake her hand before she left. "We appreciate all you've done."

Ashleigh left the new parents and as she walked down the hospital corridor, she experienced an enormous rush for the first time in several years. She'd forgotten how great she could feel when giving parents good news about their child.

Her mood was still buoyant when she reached Paula's room.

"Come in," Paula said as soon as Ashleigh arrived. "I just got off the phone with Mom. Since I told her about being in the hospital, she's been calling or texting me every few hours to see if my labor started again."

Paula rolled her eyes. "At this rate, she's going to be the one responsible for starting my labor."

"How's she doing?" Ashleigh hadn't spoken to her mother since before she moved Grandma to the Maryland facility.

"She's anxious to come home," Paula answered. "But now that Grandma has been diagnosed with that heart valve thing, she wants to stay to speak with the doctors in person."

"Are they talking surgery?" Ashleigh asked. Even though her mother was a retired R.N., you'd think she'd at least call her doctor daughter for advice.

"Mom thinks that's going to be what the doctors recommend," Paula said. "I'm surprised she hasn't talked to you about it."

"Mom and Dad were never big on consulting with me," Ashleigh told her, inwardly grimacing at their slight. "I guess it's the age thing. They figured I still had a lot to learn."

"Funny," Paula said. "Whenever I was with them, they couldn't speak highly enough about you. I never thought I had a chance at competing with you."

Ashleigh's eyes widened at Paula's admission. "You're kidding!"

"Oh, no, according to them, you were the greatest thing since heart transplants."

"That's crazy," Ashleigh said. "Because I always heard about *you* when I was with them."

Paula's eyes opened wide. "Really?"

"I remember this one pediatric conference that Dad and I attended together," Ashleigh said. "He pulled out pictures of Mark and Ryan every chance he got."

"He was always partial to his grandsons." Paula smiled pensively.

"But then while people were ogling your kids," Ashleigh continued, "he would go on and on about what a good mother and wife you were. He raved about how you so willingly embraced the role of an officer's wife to support base families while spouses were at sea."

Paula stared at her sister.

"It's true," Ashleigh said enthusiastically. "I guess our parents didn't want us to get big heads, so they only complimented us when we weren't around."

"I guess so." Paula still appeared bewildered.

They were interrupted by a nurse's aide who came to record Paula's vitals.

After she left, they enjoyed a few more minutes of pleasant conversation until Ashleigh finally said, "You mentioned on the phone that you wanted to talk to me about something." If it happened to be a contentious subject, Ashleigh wanted to deal with it sooner than later.

Paula hesitated a moment. Then she inhaled and began speaking. "Well, since Scott isn't here, Mom agreed to be my labor coach."

Ashleigh didn't need to be clairvoyant to know

where this was going. Did her sister have a clue how painful it would be to witness the birth of her niece or nephew? She allowed Paula to continue in case she was wrong.

"But now that Mom might not be back before this baby decides to arrive, she suggested—"

Ashleigh raised her eyebrows as she waited for Paula to spit it out.

"I mean, I was wondering if maybe you'd consider being my labor coach."

"Are you sure you want me?" Ashleigh asked. "Isn't there someone else who has experience who can do it?" She'd delivered babies as an intern, but she'd never coached a mother through birth.

Paula's eyes were suddenly glassy from unshed tears. "That's fine." She spoke quickly, waving her hand and looking away. "I can find someone else. I shouldn't have asked you. Of course you wouldn't want to do it after—"

"No, no," Ashleigh said immediately. "You misunderstood." Not the first time for either of them. "I'm not sure I'm the right choice. I've never coached before or even attended Lamaze classes." She'd never gotten far enough along in her own pregnancies to sign up for classes.

"But you're a doctor," Paula said. "You've delivered babies before, right?"

"Yes, but that's different." Ashleigh paused a moment. "Can I think about it?"

Paula stiffened.

Ashleigh had screwed up again.

"I understand." A tear rolled down Paula's cheek.

CHAPTER FOURTEEN

THURSDAY AFTERNOON, KYLE bought a new pair of soccer shorts for Mark. Now he was on his way to Paula's house to drop them off, fully aware that Ashleigh didn't have afternoon office hours and he might run into her.

He pulled into the driveway, unsure if he was relieved or not to find Ashleigh's car missing. He'd gone out of his way to not see her the past few days and now here he was actively going against that plan. There'd always been the possibility that she'd gone to the hospital to visit patients or was still at the office. Maybe he wouldn't see her at all.

He hesitated. He could come back later with the shorts as an excuse but then decided against it. This wasn't high school. He didn't need an excuse to see Ashleigh.

More importantly, he needed to protect himself from getting too close to her. Which translated into avoiding her.

He grabbed the shorts from the passenger seat, as well as Paula's house key from the truck's center console, and left the vehicle.

Ashleigh pulled up next to the curb.

He waved as she got out of her car. She wore a prim navy suit that hugged her body, but the wisps of hair that escaped from the clip on the back of her head softened her look. His hands itched to release her hair and run his fingers through it. He mentally shook the images from his mind.

When she came near enough that he didn't have to yell, he said, "Mark tore his soccer shorts the other day at practice. Crazy kid climbed a fence to get the ball and caught the edge. So I picked up another pair for him." He held out the plastic bag and she took it.

They stood in awkward silence until she finally spoke. "Want to come in?" Her invitation forced him to make a crucial decision.

He could leave, say he had things to do before work tonight. Why torture himself with what he couldn't—or shouldn't—have?

"Sure," he said instead, following her to the front door. "I already have my key out." He leaned around her to unlock the door, automatically putting a hand on the gentle curve of her waist. Her nearness and the light floral scent of her body lotion made his body come to life automatically. "I didn't think you'd be home."

She turned her head in his direction and her warm breath tickled his cheek. "Oh," she said.

Was that disappointment in her voice? Or was his physical reaction to her influencing his thoughts?

They entered Paula's house and he closed the front door.

"I thought I could get some fund-raising work done this afternoon at the office." She sounded a little breathless and averted her eyes. "But I left my files upstairs in my briefcase. Otherwise, I would have stayed."

"You're going back to the office?" he asked. Good. They could both turn around and just leave.

Except there was something on her mind. She had the same demeanor as right before they'd split up. As if she would crumple if he said the wrong thing.

"No, I'll work here since the boys won't be home for a few hours." She checked her watch. "I also have a conference call at two-thirty."

"Ashleigh, is there a problem?" he asked.

Her head jerked in his direction. "A problem?"

She was definitely behaving exactly the same as she had two years ago. He hadn't forced a conversation back then and wasn't about to now.

"Never mind. But I could use some of your iced tea." That would give him time to give her a gentle nudge. "Do you have any in the fridge?"

The widening of her eyes suggested her surprise that he wasn't taking her hint about him leaving so she could work. There was definitely something bothering her. "Sure. I made some yesterday."

He followed her to the kitchen, tugging at the neck of his T-shirt when the enticing view of her from behind raised his body temp.

He removed two glasses from the cupboard while she opened the fridge and took out the pitcher. She set it on the counter and closed the refrigerator. Like individual robots doing their tasks.

Kyle filled the glasses with ice, brushing her arm when he set them back on the counter. Why couldn't he simply step away from her and avoid the temptation to take her into his arms?

Dropping off Mark's soccer shorts had definitely not been one of his best ideas.

After Ashleigh poured tea into both glasses, he picked them up and placed them on opposite sides of the kitchen table while Ashleigh put away the pitcher. He took a seat and Ashleigh did the same, crossing her legs. At least she was far enough away that he couldn't reach out and touch her.

He was fascinated by her hands holding her glass of tea. She set it down and ran her finger up and down the outside of the dewy glass.

"So what's up?" he asked.

Her head jerked up. "What do you mean?"

"You're acting like there's something on your mind."

She didn't say anything for a long moment. Finally she spoke. "Paula asked me to come to the hospital last night."

Kyle narrowed his eyes, waiting for her to continue.

"She wanted to ask me something." Ashleigh took a long drink of her iced tea and finally set it down again. "She wants me to be her birth coach."

"Wasn't your mom going to do it?" He doubted

Paula had thought this idea through. Didn't she realize how hard that would be on Ashleigh, watching her sister do what she could never do herself?

Ashleigh filled him in on her grandmother's condition. "Paula is worried Mom won't be back in time. Actually, my mom may have made the suggestion."

"What did you tell her?" he asked.

"I said I'd have to think about it. She wasn't real happy with my response."

Kyle wasn't surprised, and Paula shouldn't have been, either. "Isn't there someone else who could do it?" No one came to mind, though.

Her eyes narrowed and her tone sharpened. "You sound like you think it's a bad idea."

"I'm worried," he explained. She'd somehow gone from thinking about it to arguing that it was the right thing for her to do. "Labor and delivery holds a lot of bad memories for both of us. I'm not even sure I'd be comfortable doing it."

"So you think I'll fall apart in the middle of her labor?" she snapped.

This wasn't going well at all. He spoke slowly and deliberately. "No, that's not what I think."

"Then tell me why you're so against it," she challenged, rising from her chair.

"I'm worried about you." His response was louder than he wanted. He rose, also, regulating his volume. "Watching your sister give birth won't be easy. This isn't just any baby. This will be your sister's baby. Our niece or nephew."

"You don't understand," she spit, turning her back to him and crossing her arms.

He came around the table and put his hands on her shoulders. "Try me."

"I'm working at it, Kyle, really I am." She turned to face him. "I want us all to get along. I don't want to dread the labor and delivery floor anymore." She put a hand flat on his chest. "I feel like I need to coach Paula or she'll hate me forever."

"It takes time for things to heal, Ashleigh," Kyle said softly.

She met his eyes. "I don't have that kind of time. I won't be in town for much longer and I need to fix things before then."

He dropped his hands and walked back to his iced tea. His throat had closed up and he could barely swallow the cold liquid.

There it was. She'd said it out loud. She would be leaving. He always knew that would be the outcome, but her words still came as a crushing blow.

Why had he thought she finally realized how much she had missed by moving away?

"Why don't you drop in on a Lamaze class at the hospital," he suggested once he could speak calmly.

"I was going to do some reading about it," she told him, "but observing a class would be better. That's a good idea. Thanks."

Before he could question the wisdom of his idea, he said, "Would you like me to go with you to a class?" He'd keep his distance, thinking of it more as a clinical workshop with a lab partner.

Her eyes widened. "You'd do that?"

He deliberately acted nonchalant. "Maybe you'd feel more comfortable with a partner." He hoped he sounded casual. He and Ashleigh had never gotten far enough along in their pregnancies to even discuss Lamaze classes.

"I'd like that." She stepped toward him and put her arms around his torso. Before he could address his lack of judgment, he hugged her back.

When she lifted her head and met his gaze, he knew he never had a chance of getting out before tasting those inviting lips of hers.

He lowered his head and did just that. Her body melted into his as she kissed him in return. He took a step back to brace himself against the kitchen counter, pulling her along with him.

She felt so right in his arms. The taste of her was so familiar, the touch of her skin a sensuous memory as she caressed the back of his neck.

"Is this what you want?" His words came out as a breathless whisper and he wasn't sure what he wanted her to say. His head said to leave, protect his heart. But his body screamed to take her upstairs. Take her now.

She whispered back, "Surprisingly, yes."

He began to move them out of the kitchen when she stopped him. "What is it, Ash?" He wasn't sure he could bear it if she'd changed her mind.

She paused. "Do you have protection?"

"Protection?" He had assumed she was using something. She'd always used birth control pills when they weren't trying to get pregnant. "But we didn't use anything—"

The intensity of her gaze laid the truth out in front of him.

He choked on his words. "The other night?"

She shook her head.

He dreaded the next question, terrified to hear the answer. He spoke over the blood pounding in his ears. "Could you be—"

The frightened look on her face was the answer to his unfinished question.

ASHLEIGH'S HEART RACED WILDLY. She hadn't planned to tell Kyle about a possible pregnancy, but he'd already put the puzzle pieces together.

He had a firm grip on her upper arms. "When did you figure this out?" His tone was sharp, suddenly accusatory.

Her throat tightened. "The morning after."

He practically shouted. "The next morning?" His face flushed a bright red. He removed his hands from her arms. "When were you going to tell me?" He glared at her. "Or were you *ever* going to tell me?"

"Why would I tell you before I knew for sure? It's just a small possibility at this point."

"Even so, don't you think I'd want to know, especially with our history?" he asked.

"Please understand." She hated that he'd put her on the defensive. "I was trying to keep you from worrying until there was actually something to worry about."

"And when is that?" he snapped.

"A few more days."

He stalked out of the kitchen.

"Let me explain." She followed close behind.

He turned when he reached the front door. "Go ahead, explain."

"Maybe I should have told you as soon as I realized it," she began, "but I still think I was right to wait until I knew for sure." She told him about how she'd gone off the pill and reminded him how they hadn't needed birth control in years. "I never thought about using protection the other night." Her concentration had been on how perfectly and naturally they'd come together, but she kept that to herself.

His eyebrows furrowed. "Are you in the habit of having unprotected sex?"

The question stung, but she deserved it. "No, you don't have to worry. I have never had unprotected sex."

"It's just with me that you forgot?"

She bristled at his implication. "This was a two-player game, Kyle. I didn't see you asking if I was on anything."

He had the grace to appear sheepish. "You're right." He rubbed the back of his neck and tugged at his collar. "I'm as much to blame as you are. I'm sorry I took the news poorly," he said. "I guess I'm in shock."

"Join the club," she said glumly. "Can we sit down and discuss this rationally?"

He put a hand out for her to lead the way into the living room.

"How are you feeling?" he inquired when they were settled. He was on the sofa and she sat on the upholstered chair at a ninety-degree angle from him. She removed her wedge heels and tucked her legs under her.

"Nervous," she answered honestly. "I'd like to know one way or the other."

"Other than that?" He cocked his head and his features tensed. "Hey, wait, was that why Rosy was at your office last night?"

"I wanted to talk it over with her," Ashleigh explained. "See what she thought my chances were of carrying a baby to term."

"You talked to her before me?" He shot up from his seat.

"Please calm down." What an exhausting discussion.

He paced the small living room like a caged animal and finally returned to his seat. "What did she say?" His tone projected controlled fury.

"Ironically, she suggested I talk to you," Ashleigh said, "because you've done all the research."

"I haven't kept up with it," he admitted. "Not since we divorced."

"I figured you hadn't," she said. "Why don't we take this a step at a time and deal with it when and if I'm pregnant."

"I never thought I'd hear those words from you ever again." He ran his hands through his hair. "At least the part about you maybe being pregnant."

"Me, either," she said. "But it's good that you know now."

She wanted to reach out to him, but he was still hurt and angry. Sharing a burden was supposed to make it easier to bear, but she wasn't sure it was true in this case.

AFTER HE'D CALMED DOWN and they discussed their situation in Paula's living room, Kyle gained a different perspective on his relationship with Ashleigh. They might be having a baby. In a million, trillion years, he never thought that was even a possibility.

Their chances of actually having a child were slight. Plus, they didn't even know for sure if she was pregnant.

But if she was?

Kyle was determined to find out if any headway had been made in the past two years in the research area having to do with Ashleigh's combined difficulties.

"What other advice did Rosy give you?" Kyle asked.

"Nothing, really," Ashleigh said. "First we need to find out if there's an actual pregnancy."

"Okay."

"She also offered to find me a specialist in Richmond." Ashleigh's words were so casual that Kyle questioned his interpretation of them.

"Richmond?" The thought was ridiculous. "Why would you go to Richmond? If you're pregnant, then you're staying right here." As soon as the words left his mouth, he realized how overbearing he sounded.

Ashleigh leaned forward and glared at him. "You can't dictate where I should live."

Kyle held up a hand. "You're right, I'm sorry. Please don't get upset." He softened his tone. "I didn't mean it the way it sounded."

"Go on."

"I want to be there for you, Ash," he said. "And I can't do that if you're in Richmond."

Ashleigh was quiet for a long moment. "I know, but I can't promise I'll stay here, Kyle. I've got a job and a life in Richmond."

"But you've got family and a support system right here in Grand Oaks," he countered.

He knew he'd found a possible chink in her armor with that statement when she concentrated on her cuticle instead of smacking him with a comeback.

"I'm not sure I can handle being here for another pregnancy," she finally said in a choked voice. "I know there's not much chance I'll carry to term, but I would be reliving the nightmares of the past by staying here."

He took her hand, rubbed the top of it with his

thumb. "Don't think of it that way. Consider it a second chance. Maybe something has come to light since the last miscarriage."

She pulled her hand from his. "No!" She looked pointedly at him. "No more experimental treatments. I can't go through that again."

"But what if—"

"No!" She rose from her chair and turned to him with her hands on her hips. "Absolutely not."

Before he could respond, her cell phone rang.

"It's my conference call," she told him. "I need to take this."

"We'll finish this later." He saw himself out the front door and headed home to see what he could find on the internet in the way of new treatments. Then he'd also consult with a friend, who was an expert in infertility at Women and Infants Hospital in Providence, Rhode Island.

Tom hung up the phone in his private office, leaned back in his chair and folded his hands behind his head. He was ready to proceed with the purchase of the house he'd toured. He smiled broadly.

An old law school friend recommended the real estate lawyer he'd spoken to. The guy had a good head on his shoulders and turned out to be the author of the current Virginia real estate contract, acutely aware of every nuance in the document.

The notes Tom wrote down during his phone conversation were definitely thorough. Offer full price or more if he thought other offers would be high and the local market could handle it. Include contingencies for a house inspection by a professional of Tom's choice, as well as an independent appraisal of the property's value.

He had some work to do since he wasn't using a real estate agent, but his lawyer promised to be present at closing to review all documents for accuracy.

He pulled out the business card the listing agent had given him and dialed her office number since it was almost a quarter of five in the afternoon.

A few minutes later, after a quick conversation with the agent, he hung up the phone. She would draw up the contract to his specifications and he would stop by her office by six o'clock to review and sign it.

Now to make the call he'd both looked forward to and dreaded. He dialed Theresa's cell phone from memory, his stomach acid churning while he waited for her to pick up.

"Hello," she said after the third ring.

Tom cleared his throat. "Hi, Theresa, it's Tom. How are you?"

"Um, fine," she said.

"Good," he replied, wondering why he hadn't thought this through better. "I hope I'm not interrupting anything. I figured your students would be gone by now."

"Yes, I'm at home." Her tone carried a touch of puzzlement. "Did you want something in particular?"

Exactly like the Theresa he knew. Get to the point. "Actually, yes." Could she detect his nervousness? "I wondered if you would meet me for a drink."

There was silence on the other end.

"Theresa?" Had the call been dropped?

"I'm here," she said quietly.

"We could meet at that restaurant you always liked. The bar is usually pretty quiet. The Grey Goose?"

"Why?" she said.

He swallowed with difficulty. "I don't know. I want to see how you're doing. You know, catch up."

Again, silence.

"You know I'm seeing someone." A statement, not a question.

"Yes." Tom was glad she couldn't see his grin through the phone. "This is just a drink, Theresa. Please?"

No answer.

"I don't think so," she finally said. "I have a lot of schoolwork to do for the end of the year. I don't have time."

Tom didn't know what to say next. He had not anticipated that she would turn down his invitation. Kyle said she was using him to make Tom jealous. Didn't that mean she wanted to get back together? "Can't you spare even a half hour? I have some news I'd like to share with you."

"Well, okay," she said. "Half an hour."

Tom shot up from his desk and silently danced

around his office, waving his arms. "That's great." He kept his voice steady. "What time works for you?"

They settled on seven o'clock, which worked out perfectly since he was meeting the real estate agent at six.

ASHLEIGH WAS REVIEWING her notes after her conference call when it sounded like a herd of elephants was entering the house.

"Hi, Aunt Ashleigh," the boys greeted her, offloading their backpacks right inside the front door.

"Hey, Mark, hey, Ryan," she said. "Why don't you take your things to your room? Emma will be here soon and she'll fix you a snack and take you to soccer practice." Then she remembered why Kyle had stopped by. "Oh, and Uncle Kyle bought you new soccer shorts, Mark," she called upstairs.

He came running back down the steps and she tossed the bag to him. "Thanks," and he was off to change.

The house was quiet again after they departed with Emma so Ashleigh went back to her notes. A few minutes later her cell phone rang. Theresa. "Hello."

"Hi, Ashleigh, do you have a minute?" Theresa's excitement came through loud and clear.

"Sure." Ashleigh put her notes aside.

"You're never going to believe this. Tom called and he wants to see me."

"That's great," Ashleigh said, "isn't it?"

"It's wonderful!" Theresa let out a giddy laugh.

"And I played it cool, too. At first I told him no and really made him work for it."

Ashleigh smiled. "Good for you."

"We're meeting for a drink at The Grey Goose tonight. He said he has news to share." Theresa's words came quickly. "I even reminded him that I was seeing someone—not that I am—and he still wanted to get together."

"He must really miss you." What would Ashleigh have said to Kyle if he had called her some time in the past two years and wanted to see her?

She wasn't sure.

Theresa made a promise to call Ashleigh later to let her know how it went and they disconnected. She couldn't help wishing her life was as on track as Theresa's was right now.

Ashleigh was about to get back to work on her hospital fund-raising duties but decided to take advantage of the quiet house and see if she could drum up some interest in contributing to Kyle's children's charity.

She found several people interested, but not ready to write a check without more information. She offered to provide it very shortly—just as soon as she could pull it together. Perhaps a leaflet would be useful. She added a note to the file she'd already begun for the charity.

Kyle would be furious if he discovered she'd gone against his request for her to stay out of it. But she felt it was something she had to do—plus, the charity was important to her, too.

Her cell phone rang—it was Jack, her boss in Richmond. She couldn't avoid the inevitable so she answered.

"Ashleigh Wilson."

"Ashleigh! I've been trying to get you for days," Jack said. "You haven't returned my calls."

"Sorry, Jack, I've had family business to take care of." In an attempt to gain some sympathy, she added, "My sister was admitted to the hospital."

"So sorry to hear that," he said.

Ashleigh went right into a rundown of what she'd been doing for her clients and, thankfully, Jack sounded pleased with her progress.

"When are you coming back to Richmond?" he asked. "We need you here as soon as possible."

"I'm not sure." She was taken off guard to discover she wasn't as anxious to leave Grand Oaks as she'd once been. She placated Jack by promising to be better at keeping in touch and they disconnected.

She had no sooner set her phone down than it rang again. This time Kyle's name appeared on the caller ID. "Hello?" Hopefully he didn't want to continue discussing the possible pregnancy.

"It's Kyle," he said unnecessarily. "We're finished with soccer practice." Was it that late already? Ashleigh checked her watch. 6:15 p.m. "I was going to take the boys to my house for a quick dinner if you want to join us."

"Thank you, but I'll pass," she said. "I'm trying to catch up on work."

"I know you don't want to hear this, but I hope you're not skipping meals."

Ashleigh didn't know how she felt about his warning. She said simply, "No, I'm not."

Kyle was silent for a split second before saying, "I'm working tonight and the boys want to see Paula. Can you meet us at the hospital to bring them home?"

"Sure, no problem."

"Great." He named a time.

They disconnected. Unlike when Tom wouldn't let Theresa say no to a drink, Kyle had taken her "no" to dinner much too easily.

She shook her head. She didn't play games. There truly was a lot of work for her to catch up on. Kyle had simply been his polite self, offering to include her in their dinner plans. She had done the same the other night.

Ashleigh cleared her head and focused on her clients. She still had a few phone calls to make, but most people had gone home for the day and she'd take care of them tomorrow.

Knowing Kyle's shift began at eight that evening, Ashleigh made it to the hospital ahead of time. She was standing at the bank of elevators when a familiar voice greeted her. "Hello, Dr. Wilson."

Ashleigh spun around. "Hello, Mrs. Thornton," she said. "How are you?"

"I'm visiting a dear friend," the older woman explained. "You reach my age and your friends start spending more time in the hospital than at home."

"That must be difficult for you." This was the perfect opportunity to broach the subject of the funding for Kyle's charity, but how could Ashleigh do it casually without being too pushy? Kyle might think she "played" people to get what she wanted, but it wasn't a skill she consciously used.

"I hate to say it." Mrs. Thornton lowered her voice as they both entered the empty elevator. "But it doesn't upset me nearly as much as it used to. Better them than me." She maneuvered her walker to face the doors.

Ashleigh drew herself up and gathered her courage. "Mrs. Thornton, do you have a minute for us to speak about something?"

Mrs. Thornton puckered her lips and narrowed her eyes. "If this is about the funding for Dr. Kyle's charity, then we'd both be wasting our time."

"But Mrs. Thornton." Ashleigh spoke quickly when the elevator doors began to open on Mrs. Thornton's floor. "You don't know the whole story."

"Dr. Kyle is being sued for malpractice and I can't put my support—financial or otherwise—toward someone who may not be able to follow through on his obligations."

"Wait," Ashleigh begged as Mrs. Thornton was about to step onto her floor. "Have you read the allegations? It's an unwarranted lawsuit and he and his lawyer are sure the suit will be thrown out." Ashleigh pressed the door-open button so hard her finger began to hurt.

Mrs. Thornton turned away from Ashleigh.

"At least let me send you some information so you have a better idea of the case." Ashleigh sucked in a nervous breath, prepared to chase her down the hall if necessary. "There are lots of needy children counting on you, Mrs. Thornton."

The older woman's head spun in Ashleigh's direction. "All right, Dr. Wilson, send me everything you have." Her voice was stoic. "But I'm not promising anything."

"Thank you, Mrs. Thornton, thank you!" Ashleigh called out as the woman was already making her way slowly down the hallway to see her friend.

A few minutes later, Ashleigh arrived at Paula's room and stood at the open doorway. The curtain was drawn around Paula's bed. Ashleigh didn't hear the boys, but Paula was speaking to someone.

"I didn't want to worry you, Scott." Her sister spoke in a choked voice.

"I can handle it, P." Her husband's voice was as clear as if he were in the room instead of through the computer by video chat, which Ashleigh assumed was going on. "I want to be there for you. You don't have to handle everything by yourself."

"I know." Paula sniffed.

"You should have told me how bad things were,"

he said. "I had the feeling there was something you weren't telling me when Ashleigh showed up."

"I'm so sorry," she said. "I should have been honest."

"There's nothing we can't work through together," Scott told Paula, his voice thick with emotion. "I love you so much."

Ashleigh stepped backward into the hallway and leaned against the wall for support. Without turning her head in their direction, she knew Kyle and the boys were coming down the hall toward her.

Scott's words to Paula kept repeating in her head. *There's nothing we can't work through together.*

Would Ashleigh's life be different if Kyle had said that to her?

CHAPTER FIFTEEN

ASHLEIGH DIDN'T PAY ANY notice to her nephews because her attention was on Kyle in his green hospital garb. He strode confidently toward her down the hallway.

"Hey," Kyle greeted her. He had a nephew on either side of him and he rubbed their heads. "These guys wanted to come with me while I changed for work. Sorry we weren't here when you got here."

"That's okay." Her voice sounded funny to her ears. She cleared her throat and hoped her next words came out stronger. "Paula's talking to Scott." She gestured toward Paula's room with her head.

"Yeah, the boys have already talked to him. We got lucky that he was available to chat." Kyle lowered his voice, although the boys were preoccupied with small wooden mazes anyway. "Paula had no choice but to let Scott in on what's been going on."

She lowered her voice. "How did he take it?"

"We didn't stick around," he said. "They needed to discuss it privately, but Scott sounded more worried than angry that she didn't tell him earlier."

"That's good," Ashleigh said. "Paula doesn't need any more stress."

"True. I'm glad Scott knows now, though." Kyle gave Ashleigh a pointed look that she couldn't help translating as his disapproval.

He checked his watch. "I'm on duty soon." He looked at the boys and back at Ashleigh. "You good?"

"Yes."

"Thanks for meeting us here."

"You're welcome." Her tone was more formal than she intended.

Kyle gave a little wave and lightly tapped each of the boys on the head. "Behave for Aunt Ashleigh. See you tomorrow."

Kyle jogged down the hall in his typical effortless manner. His arms were bent at the elbows and pumped rhythmically at his sides, his back straight. His well-muscled legs, hidden by scrubs, made him appear to smoothly glide away from Ashleigh.

She wanted to speak to Paula for a minute, having decided, with Kyle's backing, that she would coach her sister through childbirth. She stood at the doorway and didn't hear any voices. Turning to the boys, she said softly, "I'm going to talk to your mom a minute. Can you two stay out here quietly?"

Both boys nodded but didn't look up from where they were now sitting on the floor, backs against the wall, and concentrating on their mazes.

Ashleigh's lips curved into a smile as she enjoyed her nephews' quiet time before knocking lightly on Paula's doorframe.

"Come in," Paula called out in a scratchy voice from behind her curtain as if she'd been crying.

"Hey." Ashleigh tried for a cheerful tone as she pulled the curtain back. "How are you?"

Paula shrugged. "They say my blood pressure is a little higher than they'd like, but the baby looks good on the last ultrasound they did."

"That's good," Ashleigh said. Paula clearly didn't want to talk about her conversation with Scott. "Did they say how big the baby is?" She mentally prepared herself to care for her new niece or nephew in the NICU.

"They're estimating five and a half pounds," Paula said. "If I start productive labor again they'll let me deliver."

"That's good," Ashleigh said. "Are you having any contractions at all?"

"Just some annoying Braxton Hicks." Paula referred to the "practice" contractions most women experienced for up to several weeks before actual labor began. She suddenly changed the subject. "I talked to Scott and he knows everything."

Ashleigh was unwilling to raise Paula's blood pressure even more by saying *it's about time*. Instead she asked, "How did it go?"

"Better than I expected." Paula's mouth turned down and she sniffed. "I'm afraid he'll worry too much. He has enough to be concerned about as the ship's XO."

Ashleigh came closer and clasped a hand on her sister's shoulder. "He's a big boy. He can handle it."

Paula brushed at the tears on her cheeks. "Are the boys still with Kyle?"

"No, they're right outside, playing with mazes. I told them I wanted to speak to you a minute."

Paula smiled slightly, her eyes red rimmed. "Mom got those for the boys and I put them away and forgot about them. A few days ago I told Kyle where they were and he must have been saving them for when he needed to keep them occupied."

"They're working like a charm." Ashleigh was anxious to get to the point of why she'd come in to talk to Paula. She drew in a fortifying breath, suddenly parched. "I wanted to talk to you about being your labor coach," she began.

Paula waved her away. "Don't worry about it," she said.

"But—"

"My friend Stephanie is going to do it." Paula reached for the water pitcher on the portable bedside table.

"Oh." Ashleigh's response was barely a mumble through the crushing ache in her chest. She'd agonized over Paula's request. She'd set aside her own painful memories and mixed feelings to support her sister. All for nothing.

"Stephanie's a nurse and has had two kids." Paula poured water into her cup, oblivious to Ashleigh's discomfort. "You were hesitant to do it and I don't blame you. I know how hard it would have been for you. I'm sorry I wasn't more considerate of your feelings."

Ashleigh swallowed the lump in her throat and drew in a shaky breath. "It's…okay. I…I wanted to tell you that…that if you didn't have someone else—"

"I know, you could find someone for me." Paula sipped her water through a straw. "Don't worry. I have plenty of other friends who can fill in. Thanks for the offer though."

"Sure." Ashleigh clamped her mouth shut, ignoring the urge to lash out at her sister. Anything she said right now would upset Paula. Her health, as well as her unborn baby's health, was more important than letting her sister know how much she'd crushed her. "I better get the boys home. I'll send them in to say good-night." She cleared her dry throat and tamped down her feelings. "While they're in here, I have to check on something, but I'll be back to pick them up in a few minutes."

She rushed out the door. "Go say good-night to your mom," she told the boys as calmly as possible.

Then she hurried down the hall in the same direction Kyle had taken. Her brain said stop, but her legs wouldn't listen.

KYLE WAS ABOUT TO enter curtain three to examine a patient complaining of a low-grade fever with no other symptoms. From the corner of his eye, he saw Ashleigh at the end of the hallway that intersected with the main corridor. Her head turned frantically in all directions as if searching for someone or something.

They made eye contact as he walked toward her and she practically threw herself against him. In order to avoid making a public spectacle in front of the few people in the waiting room, he guided Ashleigh into the small office used for dictating patient's charts and updating their computer check-ins.

He pulled the single desk chair out and directed her into it. She covered her face with her hands.

He squatted in front of her, placing a hand on her knee. "What's wrong? What happened?" A sudden thought dawned. "Did you take a pregnancy test?"

She shook her head vigorously. "No," she said in a choked whisper. "I…I should have listened to you." She sobbed openly. "I don't know what made me think I would be the right person to coach Paula through labor."

He waited for Ashleigh to continue because he wasn't sure what he should say.

"I went in to tell Paula I'd do it—" She hiccuped. "But before I could say anything she said her friend was going to fill in."

She doubled over and her head ended up on Kyle's shoulder. He brought his arms around her, wanting to comfort her but he didn't know how.

When she finally sat up again, he retrieved a box of tissues from the desk drawer and offered it to her.

She removed one and gently blotted her cheeks and under her eyes.

"Don't get mad at me for saying this, Ash," he began.

Her eyes narrowed, but she didn't say anything.

"Maybe it's better for someone else to coach her—" He held up a hand to silence her when her mouth opened as if to speak. "Let me finish." Her lips locked shut and he continued. "This way you can still be there for her when she's in labor, but if it gets to be too much, you're not obligated to stick around."

Ashleigh stared at him. "Well, it doesn't matter now anyway. I have no choice. She found someone else."

"True." He waited a few seconds. "Can you accept that?"

Her mouth softened and she nodded. "I guess so."

He rose, his stiffening joints rebelling, and he pulled her up into his arms. She came willingly and wrapped her arms around his waist.

Her heart thudded against his chest and his beat as if in reply.

There was a quick rap on the door and they drew apart, but Kyle kept a hand on Ashleigh's lower back. The E.R. ward clerk popped her head in. "Sorry to disturb you, Dr. Jennings, but we have a febrile two-year-old. She's lethargic and nonresponsive." The clerk then said to Ashleigh, "The patient is Kayla Pratt. Her mother said you prescribed amoxicillin for a possible strep throat yesterday, but she's gotten worse. Your service referred her here."

"Thanks, Betty." He turned to Ashleigh. Their eyes locked in silent communication. Kyle again turned to Betty. "Would you mind calling Maternity and ask them to let Paula Jennings know that Dr. Wilson has been delayed with a patient?"

"Yes, Doctor," Betty said. "The patient is in curtain one."

"Thanks," he said.

He turned back to Ashleigh when they were alone and squeezed her hand.

She blinked a few times and he wiped a smear of mascara from under her eye with the pad of his thumb.

"The child's quick test was negative," she told him, "but I put her on antibiotics because I was pretty sure the overnight test would be positive. She probably needs a stronger antibiotic like Ceclor." Ashleigh wiped at her cheeks with her hands. "Give me a few seconds to freshen up and I'll be right in."

She turned her back to him. Her words were professional. Not as one lover to another.

As if the comfort he'd provided and their ability to communicate nonverbally had all been in his imagination.

TOM LEFT THE listing real estate agent's office with a spring in his step and a lightness of spirit. Signing a contract to buy a house was a huge step in anyone's life, but he had no doubts. He'd offered full price and with his large down payment and loan preapproval, he was confident about his chances for getting the home.

He drove the few miles to The Grey Goose, the quaint restaurant where he was meeting Theresa. The parking lot was half-full and there was no sign of her car.

The dashboard clock said he was nearly twenty minutes early. Oh, well. There were no messages on his cell phone so he pocketed it. Several cars pulled into the parking lot, none of which were Theresa's, but he decided he should go in to get them a table before the establishment became too crowded.

He stepped through the large, wooden double doors to enter the colonial-inspired restaurant with its dark wood tables and turned spindle chairs. The furnishings were enhanced by the backdrop of pale green walls and a white chair rail, crown and picture-frame moldings, as well as the abundance of fox hunting–theme prints.

"Hi, how are you? I'm meeting someone," he told the hostess who greeted him with a warm smile. "I'll wait for her in the bar."

The hostess directed him with a wave of her hand to the right side of the room. "Through that doorway. You can take an empty table if there's one available."

"Thank you." He went into the bar, pleased to discover there were only a few other patrons in the quiet space. He chose a small table next to a window where he could watch for Theresa's arrival. He drummed his fingers on the table, his pulse rate elevated, as he waited. He requested a soda when the server came to his table, deciding to avoid alcohol at least until Theresa arrived. In his mind, he pictured them toasting to their new home.

About two minutes before their appointed time, Theresa's car pulled into the parking lot. She strolled confidently across the asphalt wearing a flowing abstract top under a deep blue shrug. Skinny jeans and tan wedge sandals completed her outfit. She smoothed back a lock of hair that blew into her face.

He'd desperately missed her, he realized.

And he'd do anything to get her back.

He got out of his chair to go and meet her at the entrance. "Hi." He smiled as Theresa entered the restaurant, tamping down the urge to hug her—he didn't want to scare her off.

"Hi." A tentative smile formed on her lips.

He put a hand lightly at her lower back and guided her to the table in the bar. "Is this okay?"

"It's fine." Theresa took the seat across from him. "What did you want to talk to me about, Tom?" She got right to the point as she hung her purse on the back of her chair and folded her hands on the table in front of her.

"We'll get to that later," he answered, his eyes drawn to the hint of cleavage at the edge of her neckline. "First, tell me how you've been."

Their server interrupted before Theresa could answer. He ordered a Scotch and soda, while she ordered a margarita. "Are you hungry?" At her nod, they decided to order the artichoke appetizer to share.

"I've been really good. I'm actually going on a cruise in the Caribbean," she said when the server left. "We depart the Friday after school is out."

"How exciting." He tried to act as if it was exciting, but all the while he wondered who she was traveling with now that he knew it wasn't Kyle.

"A few of the teachers at school organized the trip and invited me to join them," she said in answer to his unasked question.

"That's great." His entire body relaxed. She was probably using the money she'd saved to put toward their wedding to pay for the trip.

"We're getting a group discount, so I decided to go for it," she said.

Should he mention that he knew she wasn't seeing Kyle? "How's your job going?" he asked instead. "Happy the school year is almost over?" The last two months before summer break had always been the most stressful for her.

She groaned. "I can't remember a year like this one. I'll be extremely happy to promote the entire class and let some other unsuspecting teacher deal with them next year."

Tom laughed. "That bad?" Their drinks and appetizer arrived and he enjoyed her company as she told him tales of her third-graders.

"It's funny now." She told him about one incident where several of her students decided to fake being sick to avoid giving oral reports. They all headed to the nurse's office right after lunch. "But when their parents had to leave work to pick them up and discovered they weren't actually suffering from upset stomachs from the cafeteria food, they got in more trouble than they'd bargained for." Theresa put her hands over her mouth when she couldn't stop laughing. Her eyes widened to saucers when she admitted, "They were the first ones I called on to give their reports the next day."

Tom and Theresa continued to catch up on each other's lives as if they'd never been apart. He couldn't believe how smoothly they slid into the easiness of their former relationship. At least the way it had been before Theresa had become so unhappy.

She checked the time on her watch and Tom's chest constricted. He wasn't ready to let her go yet.

"Do you have to be somewhere?" he asked.

Startled, she looked at him almost guiltily. "No, I didn't realize we'd been talking for so long."

Both of their glasses were empty and they'd devoured the artichoke dip. "I'm having a good time and would love to continue talking," Tom ventured. "Would you like to order dinner?"

Theresa hesitated a few seconds longer than Tom's heart could bear. "Sure," she finally said.

"Do you want to stay here or get a table in the dining room?" he asked.

Theresa looked around the bar, still pretty quiet. "Let's stay here."

Tom agreed and got the attention of their server. "Can we get some menus, please?" He looked at Theresa. "Another margarita?"

"Actually, I could use a glass of water," she said, and he ordered a soda for himself.

After they placed their food orders, Theresa said, "You still haven't told me what you wanted to tell me."

Now was as good a time as ever. Their time together had been going much better than he'd expected.

"Well." He inhaled deeply. "I put in an offer on a house."

"You did?" Her demeanor changed slightly as she shifted in her seat.

He plowed on, hoping to get her as excited about the house as he was. "Yes. It's about two blocks from the one you looked at last fall."

"The one you wouldn't buy six months ago because you didn't think we were ready to take on that kind of debt?" Her tone was sharp, but he began telling her about the house anyway.

Before he could finish, she held up a hand and said between gritted teeth, "Stop! I can't sit here and listen anymore."

"What's wrong?" Why wasn't she happy he was seeing it her way?

"What's wrong?" She glared at him. "Are you crazy? Did you think I'd be happy for you simply because you're doing what I wanted you to do last fall?"

He was confused. "Yes, I guess that's exactly what I thought."

She blew out an exasperated breath and lowered her voice to where he had to strain to hear her. "I loved that house, Tom. I wanted to share it with you, but like always, you couldn't see it any way but your own."

"But you don't understand," Tom said quickly. "That's why I want to buy this house."

Her brows furrowed. "Go on."

"I'm trying to make things up to you." Flop sweat formed at his temples.

"Prove it."

"I understand now why you called off our wedding." Stan's advice came back to him. "I'm trying to put you first."

Their food arrived. She waited until the server left before speaking. "Why now? Because I'm seeing Kyle?"

Should he admit he knew their relationship was fake? "I know you aren't seeing Kyle."

Her eyes widened, but she didn't say a word.

"I'm so sorry that you had to drag Kyle into this. I know I hurt you and I want to make it up to you. I want you back, Theresa. I'll do anything to prove it to you."

"I don't believe you," she shot back. "Every time you've said that in the past you've reverted to your old ways. I don't need to come first all the time, Tom. Once in a while is enough for me. But you never consider my feelings and that's unacceptable."

"I'm trying to put you first now, Theresa. I'm buying the house for you." He reached out to take her hand which was cold and stiff in his. "I want to make you happy."

"I can't believe you thought buying a house without me even seeing it would make me happy." Tears gathered in her eyes and she pulled her hand away. "I'm sorry. I want to believe you but I can't."

Before he could stop her, she dug through her purse and withdrew a few bills that she anchored with her drink glass. She rose quickly and her chair nearly fell backward. She left her untouched food on the table and departed the restaurant without so much as a goodbye.

AFTER ASHLEIGH WAS ASSURED that her young patient was settled into a room in Peds, which included a cot set up for the child's mother to spend the night, she rounded up her nephews and headed for her car in the parking lot. Pulling out her cell phone for the first time in hours, she saw she had three missed calls from Theresa but no voice mail messages.

Somehow it seemed Ashleigh had become the woman's closest confidante. Without turning on the car, Ashleigh sent Theresa a text message to say she'd call as soon as she got the boys into bed.

"Hi, Ashleigh," Theresa said in a subdued tone a short time later.

"Hey, Theresa, is everything okay?"

"Not really." There was a hitch in Theresa's voice.

Ashleigh settled on the couch in Paula's living room while she waited for Theresa to continue. She wasn't sure why Theresa was being so friendly when the majority of the town had given Ashleigh such a cool reception. She didn't even know Theresa that well. Maybe she recognized a kindred spirit.

"I'm sorry. I shouldn't be burdening you with my problems," Theresa said.

"I don't mind." Ashleigh meant it. "I'm happy to listen, even if I don't have any good advice to impart. You've met me, right? I'm the pariah of Grand Oaks." She tried to lighten Theresa's mood.

Theresa chuckled softly. "It's not that bad, is it?"

"Eh," Ashleigh grunted.

"Well, I personally would love it if you moved back to Grand Oaks for good." Theresa sounded adamant. "I was just getting to know and like you when you moved away. It's hard moving to a new town and meeting people, but you were always nice to me."

Ashleigh was taken aback. Theresa was probably the only female in her life who wasn't a colleague or a relative. Even in Richmond, she had acquaintances but not any close friends.

"I doubt very much that I'll be staying in town." She had no reason to stay once her pediatric replacement arrived and Paula had her baby. "But we should

stay in touch. Maybe you can visit me in Richmond."
Ashleigh paused and decided it was time to change
the subject—she doubted Theresa had called three
times just to discuss Ashleigh staying in town. "So
what happened tonight with Tom?"

"Oh, Ashleigh, it was terrible," Theresa began.
"Not at first," she added quickly, relaying how well
their time together at the restaurant had gone—how
easy the conversation had been. "But then he told
me that he's buying a house."

"That's wonderful," Ashleigh said, "isn't it?"

"No, it's awful," Theresa said. "Last fall I found
the perfect house for us, but he said we weren't ready
to buy one. Now he's put an offer on a house two
blocks away from the one *I* wanted to buy."

"Are you upset because it's in the same neighborhood or because he's buying a house after saying no
to the one you wanted?"

Theresa sniffled. "I don't know. Both, I guess."
She paused. "He told me he wants me back."

"That's great news, Theresa. It's what you wanted."
Ashleigh was truly happy for her. "Isn't that why you
schemed with Kyle?"

"Yes, but I can't get over the fact that Tom put a
contract on a house that he wants me to live in, yet
it didn't even cross his mind that I'd want to have a
look at it first."

"Good point," Ashleigh agreed. "I'd be upset, too."
Not that Kyle would ever do such a thing.... He had
no reason to want her to stay in town. He no longer

had feelings for her. He only wanted her for the possible child she was carrying.

"Now I don't know what to do," Theresa said. "I want to be with him, but I can't get over the house thing."

Ashleigh made a suggestion. "Maybe you should come at it differently."

"What do you mean?"

"Why don't you look at the house. Maybe you'll love it."

"Maybe." Theresa didn't sound convinced.

"You know you love the neighborhood. You might just be happy with the house, too. You can always make changes to the house or find another one to buy."

"True." Again Theresa sounded skeptical.

"Look, Theresa, most women would be thrilled that a man loved them so much that he'd go against his own wants in order to make her happy." That's what Ashleigh and Kyle had—a long time ago. Before things had spun out of control. "You know that's all he was trying to do. He loves you. And you love him. Don't let a stupid house stand in the way of your happiness."

Theresa was silent as if considering Ashleigh's advice. "Okay," she finally said. "I guess I can at least look at the house and see if it has potential. The one I wanted was a fixer-upper and I was looking forward to spending the time with Tom working on it. You know, making it our own."

"Well then, give it and Tom a chance," Ashleigh advised. "If you don't, you'll never know if things would have turned out differently for the two of you."

They agreed to talk soon and then ended the call. As Ashleigh went upstairs to get ready for bed, she couldn't help thinking about all that she would miss *if* she left Grand Oaks. Up until now, she hadn't considered staying.

She also hadn't considered that her feelings for Kyle had been rekindled. Her heart constricted at the thought of not seeing or talking to him daily.

Was she falling back into love with him?

CHAPTER SIXTEEN

AFTER ASHLEIGH LEFT the E.R. to admit her young patient, Kyle experienced an unusually quiet night. He got home a little after nine the next morning and went straight to bed. He'd taken a few catnaps during the night, but nothing long enough to keep him going the rest of the day.

He woke to the ding of a text message on his phone, which was recharging on the nightstand. The time on his alarm clock read a few minutes past noon and he checked the message on his phone.

Maddie. His older sister. They hadn't spoken in a few weeks. She probably wanted to know the scoop on Paula. Her message read, Give me a call when you have a few minutes.

He figured he'd slept just long enough to get by, so he took a quick shower before calling his sister.

"Hey," he said when she answered. "What's up?"

"I wanted to check in and see how Paula's doing."

"Thanks for being so concerned about your brother," he teased.

She giggled and, as always, it made him smile.

"Sorry." Her tone became serious. "How are you, *brother?*"

He wasn't sure how to answer. How was he? Confused. Anxious. Excited. Worried. He could go on and on, but he wasn't sure he wanted to get into it with his sister. At least not right now.

"I'm hanging in there," he answered instead. "How are you? Anything new in the way of treatment for Jeremy?" Maddie's six-year-old son had been diagnosed right before his second birthday with Angelman Syndrome, a genetic disorder that caused developmental disabilities and neurological problems. Jeremy's delayed motor skills and lack of balance had been enough to make his pediatrician begin tests at an early age.

"He was recently chosen for a research trial of topoisomerase inhibitors." Maddie stumbled over the medical term in her excitement. "We're all very encouraged."

"That's great! Are his seizures under control?" Jeremy began having seizures about two years ago, another common symptom of the disorder.

Maddie and Kyle spoke for the next few minutes about the research trial and the tests Jeremy endured to better evaluate his seizures.

The conversation got Kyle thinking about his charity and the fact that he needed to spend time finding alternate funding now that Mrs. Thornton had backed out. There were other kids in need of medical care who didn't have Jeremy's family's health insurance and financial resources.

"Okay," Maddie said. "Your turn. First tell me about Paula."

He gave her the abbreviated version of Paula's status.

"I wish I'd been able to come help her out," Maddie said, "but with Jeremy—"

"Everyone understands, Maddie," Kyle said quickly. "No one expected you to drop everything. You have your hands full as it is."

"You're right. But I'm glad she's doing okay. So, how's your lawsuit going?" she asked.

Again, he gave her the short answer and included the search for proof that the guy made a habit of not always wearing his medical alert bracelet.

"That's encouraging," Maddie said. "Sounds like Tom has everything under control."

"I hope so." Kyle wished the whole thing would go away and he would have one less thing to worry about.

"How's it going with Ashleigh?" Maddie finally got to the question he knew was coming but had hoped to avoid.

"Complicated," he said, which was the simple answer. "It's been tough on her since she's been back. Seeing her sister pregnant, treating patients again…"

The possibility of another pregnancy.

Maybe he should confide in Maddie about it. He desperately wanted to talk it over with someone and Maddie had always been good at keeping his confidences.

"She might be pregnant," Kyle blurted out.

There was a long silence before Maddie finally said, "Might be?"

"It's too early to know," he explained.

"Oh." Another long pause. "Is it yours?"

"Of course it's mine." He practically yelled into the phone.

"Sorry!" she said quickly. "You *have* been divorced for two years. How am I supposed to know if she's been seeing anyone?"

Kyle calmed himself. "I know. But if there's a pregnancy, then it's mine."

"Well, it's good to know the two of you are getting along again."

"I wouldn't go that far," he told her.

"Obviously you went far enough...."

There was a teasing tone in her voice and his mouth softened into a smile. "You need to promise you won't say anything to anyone. We don't even know for sure yet."

"What if she is pregnant?" Maddie was serious again. "Is there any chance she'll be able to carry it to term?"

"The short answer is that I don't know." He ran a hand over the back of his neck. "During my free time at work last night I did an internet search for anything new in the field over the past two years."

"Did you find anything worthwhile?"

"There was a woman in England with a weak cervix, identical to one of Ashleigh's problems, who from five months on spent most of her pregnancy in a hospital bed with the foot of the bed elevated so her legs were higher than her head. She delivered a healthy baby six weeks early by Cesarean section."

"Wow," Maddie said. "That takes determination. Would it work for Ashleigh?"

"The problem is that Ashleigh has never gotten that far along in a pregnancy," Kyle said. "The longest she's ever carried was fourteen weeks."

"What about her endometriosis?" Maddie asked. "I know she had surgery a few months before that last pregnancy, but has she had any problems since?"

"I don't know," Kyle said honestly. He and Ashleigh hadn't talked about it. "Endometriosis often recurs and sometimes requires further surgery for a successful pregnancy."

"Does this mean you and Ashleigh are back together?"

"No," he said quickly. "I mean, nothing's changed."

"But what if she's pregnant?" Maddie asked. "Won't you be there for her?"

If she'll allow it. But Kyle kept the thought to himself. Ashleigh had already told him she wouldn't be sticking around.

"We have differing opinions on that," he said.

TOM ARRIVED AT Theresa's apartment shortly after noon. He sat in his car, parked in the lot in front of her building and looked up at the third floor. He hadn't called before coming over, taking a chance that she would be there. Giving her a warning probably wasn't a good plan after she ran out of the restaurant last night.

He reached for the bouquet of fresh flowers on the passenger seat of his car. Black-eyed Susans—the state flower of Maryland, where Theresa grew up. They were also her favorite.

Walking across the parking lot, doubt kept nipping at his heels. What if she wouldn't speak to him? What if she didn't want to hear what he needed to say? What if she's not even home? Or not alone?

His heart thudded in his chest, so loud he was sure the man who jogged past him heard it. Tom took the two flights of stairs at a rapid but steady pace, not wanting to break a sweat or be winded by the time he reached Theresa's apartment.

He shifted his weight from one foot to the other in front of her door—3B. How many times had he stood in this very spot over the years? They'd enjoyed such good times together.

He straightened his shoulders and raised a fist to knock on the door. He refused to give up without a solid effort.

The door opened before he could knock.

"Oh!" Theresa held a laundry basket overflowing with clothes in her arms. "I didn't hear you knock."

"I was about to," he said.

"Oh," she repeated.

They stared awkwardly at each other and Tom finally stuck out his hand with the flowers. "For you."

Like a five-year-old who'd collected wildflowers to present to his first girlfriend.

Theresa stared at them. Her hands were full and, after an awkward moment, Tom said, "Here, let me take that." He set the laundry basket in the hallway and handed her the bouquet.

"Thank you." She ran a hand through her hair. "I wasn't expecting you."

"I didn't want to give you the chance to tell me not to come over," he explained. "I want to work things out with you, Theresa."

"Oh." She swallowed and said thickly, "How do we do that?"

"First, I'd like you to look at the house I put an offer on. If you truly don't like it, then I'll withdraw my offer."

"You'd do that for me?"

"Of course I would." He wanted to reach out and touch her but was afraid of pushing too fast.

"When?"

"When what?"

"When do you want me to see the house?"

He was surprised at her urgency. "I can call the Realtor right now, if you want." Theresa nodded her head and he pulled his cell from his pocket. The Realtor picked up on the first ring.

"We'll see you in an hour," he said when the real estate agent told him that was the only time she had free. "Thanks," he said, and disconnected.

Theresa let out a gasp and covered her mouth with her free hand.

"What's wrong?" What had he done this time to upset her?

"I need to shower and change," she said. "I can't go like this."

He hadn't noticed anything beyond her gorgeous blue eyes and dazzling smile. Now he took in her ratty T-shirt and gray sweatpants. "Isn't that my T-shirt?" The corner of his mouth turned up.

Her bare face reddened and she put her free hand on her hip. "What if it is? It doesn't fit you anymore anyway."

He lowered his voice. "I always loved seeing you wear it."

Her gaze moved to his lips and he found himself leaning in to her.

"Well good afternoon, you two." The elderly, hard-of-hearing woman across the hall spoke loudly as she exited her apartment and locked the door. "It's nice to see you both again."

"You, too," they said in unison.

After she disappeared into the stairwell, Tom and Theresa looked wide-eyed at each other and laughed.

"Why don't you grab a shower and I'll put these in water." He reached for the flowers and their hands touched.

"I'll be quick." She took off before he could put into motion any other ideas he might be entertaining about spending the afternoon in her bed.

Hours later they found themselves at a coffee shop not far from the house. They'd spent a lot of time looking at every inch of it, but Tom had no clue whether Theresa liked it or not.

"It has a nice backyard," Tom said tentatively when they settled at a table with their coffees. "Good for a dog."

Her eyebrows rose. "A dog?"

He grinned. "Sure."

She narrowed her eyes at him. "A dog that needs to be walked and fed and cleaned up after?"

"Of course."

"Since when?" she asked.

He wasn't sure what to say, so he was honest. "Since I realized I can't live without you." He sucked in a breath. "And if it takes a dog or a house or anything else to make you happy, then I'm prepared to do that."

She stared at him.

"What do you think of the house?" he asked. "I know it's not anything like the one you found, but we can change whatever you don't like about it."

He waited anxiously for her to say something. Anything. All he wanted was some sign that she was willing to start over with him. Her silence caused him to fill the void. "Or we can keep searching until we find one you like." He started to reach out to take her hand, but instead he spoke from his heart. "I'm so sorry, Theresa. I know I've hurt you. I know I never listen, but I promise I'm trying. I can't guarantee I won't ever be a jerk and disregard your feelings, but I'm working on it. Tell me what I can do to make up for my mistakes."

Finally, her mouth slowly widened into a grin. "I love it!"

He stumbled over his words. "You do?"

Her head bobbed vigorously, her eyes wide with excitement. "I do!"

He couldn't believe it.

"I love the backyard, the updated kitchen, the finished basement for when we have kids—" She stopped suddenly and put a hand to her mouth. "I'm sorry, I didn't mean to jump—"

He reached out for her hand. "If you're jumping, then you've finally reached the point where I've been waiting for you for quite a while now." He smiled at her. "I love you and I want us to spend our lives together."

Her shoulders relaxed and she put her other hand over the one covering hers. "I love you, too."

KYLE THOUGHT LONG AND HARD after speaking with his sister until he came to a decision. He and Ashleigh needed to be proactive. They needed to discuss the possibility of a pregnancy and what they'd do if she was actually pregnant. No holds barred.

There were too many unknowns floating through his head. How had her health been over the past two years? Had her endometriosis returned? How far would she be willing to go to protect this pregnancy? What kind of role did she see him playing?

Was there some way to convince her to stay in Grand Oaks if she turned out to be pregnant?

The idea of her going back to Richmond hit him squarely in the gut. He'd gotten used to speaking with her at least a few times a day and seeing her in person often. How would he deal without her in his life in some capacity? How would he deal with losing her again?

He needed her in his life.

It was a shocking revelation. He was falling back in love with his ex-wife, no matter how much he'd tried to avoid that exact thing.

How had it happened? And what was he going to do now?

Too many questions and not enough answers. He picked up his cell phone and sent a text to Ashleigh. Call when you have a minute.

Not two minutes later, his phone rang.

"Hey," he said. "That was quick."

She chuckled, a sound that lightened his heart. "You caught me at the right time. I just finished with my last patient of the morning. One to two is supposed to be lunch, but I have a few calls to return before I begin afternoon appointments."

"Don't forget to eat." He snapped his mouth shut as soon as the words came out. She was sure to be angry if he kept nagging her about eating, but he couldn't help it. Skipping meals had been her standard operating procedure during her internship.

"Don't worry. Cammie already ordered lunch for me." Luckily she wasn't offended by his concern and once again she let his worry pass without a bad reaction. There was shuffling on her end of the line. "Hold on a minute."

After muffled conversation, Ashleigh came back on the line. "I've got to take another call. Can I call you back?"

"Sure. I actually wanted to get together and wondered if you were free for an early dinner tonight."

"I can't tonight, how about tomorrow night?" she suggested.

"Sure. Saturday's better anyway because I'm off all weekend." Then he added, "I'll talk to Emma about watching the boys."

"That's great," she said. "Gotta go."

They disconnected and he was satisfied with the outcome. He called Emma right away to make sure she was free to babysit, but she wasn't.

Instead of scrapping the plan altogether, he took a chance and called Ashleigh's Aunt Vivian.

"I'd love to watch the boys!" Her excitement was obvious when she said loudly, "All right!"

Kyle chuckled. "What time would you like them?"

They spent a few minutes discussing the arrangements before disconnecting.

Next, he considered what he would cook for them. Ashleigh tended to eat light, avoiding red meat except on rare occasions. So he settled on an Asian chicken salad with peanut sauce that she loved.

He dug through a drawer in his kitchen for the recipe he'd saved but hadn't made since before their separation. He jotted down a grocery list. He could stop at the store on his way home from work in the morning.

With a free afternoon before he had to go to work, he cleaned his apartment and went for a long run. By the time he showered it was time to head to the hospital.

As long as he kept busy, he didn't have time to stop and overthink any life-changing events that might or might not happen.

ALL DAY SATURDAY, Ashleigh had been both nervous and excited about spending time alone with Kyle. Their relationship had gone in all different directions since she'd come back to town. They'd fought, they'd made love, they'd possibly made a baby.

She sucked in a breath.

Kyle would want some kind of agreement about their future. She was pretty sure that's what he had in mind to discuss over dinner. He wouldn't want to be left out of any decisions that affected him, but she didn't want to face it.

What did she want? She didn't have a clue, except to avoid the heartbreak of another miscarriage.

By late afternoon, Ashleigh was on her way to drop off the boys. Aunt Viv had asked to have them spend the night, maybe hoping to give Ashleigh and Kyle more time alone.

Mark and Ryan had stuffed their backpacks with pajamas, clean clothes and all the necessities, as well as a few toys they couldn't live without.

Ashleigh laughed at their excitement. They couldn't wait to go see Aunt Viv's animals, chattering about them the entire trip.

After a brief visit with Aunt Viv, Ashleigh left for Kyle's, but first she had a quick stop to make. If Kyle was going to press her for decisions, then she needed to get answers. Specifically, was she even pregnant? That was the operative question.

She pulled Paula's minivan into the hospital staff parking lot, hoping she wouldn't get towed since there wasn't a sticker on it. Her errand shouldn't take more than a few minutes as she hurried to the basement level where the lab was located.

"I need to have some blood drawn," Ashleigh said to the young woman who greeted her. She handed the technician the request that had been signed by Rosy earlier in the week, with the provision Ashleigh wait at least seven days to have the pregnancy test done.

Today marked a week since she and Kyle had made love. A week of agonizing and wondering and waiting.

"How long before I can get the results?" Ashleigh preferred to not use her temporary position at the hospital to get special treatment. The fewer people who knew about her possible pregnancy the better. Hospital gossip traveled faster than the speed of light.

"We're pretty backed up right now," the tech said. "You might hear from your doctor later today or tomorrow but most likely Monday."

Not fast enough for her stomach to stop doing flips.

ASHLEIGH ARRIVED AT Kyle's apartment complex and found a visitor spot for the van. She'd never been in his apartment—hadn't made it farther than this parking lot the other day.

Why were her nerves jangling? This wasn't a date or anything. They were simply meeting over dinner, two friends who used to be married and who now might be having a baby together.

How strangely civilized was that?

She made her way to his door and raised a hand to knock. She drew in a deep, calming breath. No need for him to know how anxious she was about being here.

Would he see through her facade and discover her feelings for him were deeper than either of them expected?

She knocked briskly on the door and he opened it within a few seconds. His warm smile greeted her and her heart melted even as it pumped her blood faster.

Nothing like a combination of love and lust in one smooth blast.

"Hi," she said as he moved aside for her to enter his apartment.

"Hi." His dulcet tone washed over her. "Can I get you something to drink?"

"Water would be great." Her mouth was suddenly parched from nerves, making speech difficult.

"Please, sit down and relax." He pointed to the living area and stepped away into what she guessed was the kitchen. The apartment was very masculine in its decor. There was nothing to soften the plain lines of his contemporary furniture. No pillows, no photographs, no touches of nature like flowers or sticks or even rocks. Nothing that said, *This is Kyle Jennings's apartment.*

She chose one end of the black leather sofa closest to the matching recliner. Kyle appeared with two large tumblers of ice water and he handed her one before choosing to sit in the recliner.

She took a long drink and looked around for coasters but didn't see any. When he set his drink directly on the glass coffee table, she did the same.

She needed to find a topic of conversation. They'd barely said more than a few words to each other since she'd arrived—not that it had been awkward. More like comfortable silence with someone you share a history with. "I like your apartment," she finally said.

"It serves its purpose." He gestured around. "I haven't spent much time decorating, as you can see."

She smiled, secretly glad he hadn't dated a woman who'd taken on the project.

"Would you like a tour?" he asked. "It would take all of a few minutes. Things aren't quite back in place after I painted last week, so excuse the mess."

"Sure." She rose from her seat. As they went from room to room, she didn't recognize any of his furniture. She'd left most of their furnishings for him, only taking a few items with personal meaning like the bedroom furniture passed down to her from her parents. When they got to the second bedroom that he'd made into his office, she finally asked, "Where's all the furniture? I mean, our furniture?"

"I put it in storage." His demeanor became guarded. "Too many memories."

"Oh." His answer caught her off guard and she didn't know what to say.

"We can eat anytime," he said. "I made that Asian chicken salad with peanut sauce you used to like."

"Sounds delicious," she said. "I could eat whenever you're hungry."

They were heading to the kitchen when someone knocked on the apartment door. "I'll be right back," he said. "Have a seat." He gestured to the round glass-and-iron table in his small kitchen, set for two.

He jogged off and mumbled words came from the entrance. He reappeared at the kitchen doorway. "My neighbor needs a hand moving a dresser from his truck. It should only take a few minutes."

"No hurry." She had nowhere else to be. Unless there was a major disaster, her answering service was referring people who couldn't wait until morning to the hospital emergency room.

She went into the living room and retrieved their glasses, refilled them with ice and water, and set them at their places on the table. She used the bathroom and when she came out she drifted into his office, remembering that she needed to call Mrs. Thornton to prod her into making a decision about funding Kyle's charity. She also needed to touch base with the others she'd approached about possible donations.

His battered wood desk was cluttered, not unusual for Kyle. She smiled. He'd always referred to it as "organized chaos" because somehow, at any given moment, he could put his finger on exactly what he needed.

A long metal table set up behind the desk was home to a printer and several framed items that were probably meant to be hung on the freshly painted walls eventually. There was a lone framed picture turned facedown on the other side of the printer.

Her eyes watered when she picked it up. Their wedding photo. Through her tears she saw the two of them, over-the-top blissful. Kyle in his sleek black tux and with a sexy smile. She looked carefree and serene in the antique cream satin gown she'd found accidentally at a consignment store downtown.

She focused on the photograph of the people they used to be. Neither of them had had a clue as to how their lives would change in such a few short years.

CHAPTER SEVENTEEN

"THANKS, MAN," HIS NEIGHBOR said as Kyle was leaving the young newlyweds' apartment after the two of them had manhandled a chest of drawers up two flights of stairs. "Gotta keep my wife away from flea markets."

"No problem." Kyle chuckled, waving back. "Glad I could help."

He smiled as he walked down the hall to his own apartment. Having Ashleigh waiting for him gave him the urge to skip like a schoolkid.

His smile froze when he opened his door and came face-to-face with Ashleigh's stormy expression and the pile of medical journals in her arms.

"What the hell do you think you're doing?" she shouted even before he was in the apartment and able to shut the door.

She flung the papers and journals on the floor in front of him. "I thought we agreed there would be no more experimental treatments, no more surgeries. Nothing." She stared him down, hands on her hips. "I don't need *you* going behind *my* back to find more ways to poke and prod me when the outcome never changes." She went from angry to emotional in one sentence as her eyes became glassy.

He clenched his jaw as he fought to control his own emotions. "This is my baby, too. You can't tell me to give up on my own child."

She stared at him with narrowed eyes, her lips puckered as if deciding how to respond. "So it's all right for you to talk me into doing some crazy new treatment you found? No matter what it might put me and my body through? I don't think so." Before he could stop her, she grabbed her purse and slammed the apartment door as she left.

ASHLEIGH MADE IT TO Paula's minivan before processing her anger. Kyle was doing what he always did. He was trying to fix things. Why should she be surprised?

He didn't understand. Unlike her car the other night with its dead battery, she wasn't fixable. She was broken beyond repair.

She leaned her head on the steering wheel and allowed the tears to flow. He just couldn't accept her, completely—failures and all.

The passenger-side door suddenly opened. Ashleigh straightened, her breath caught in her throat.

Kyle slid into the seat next to her and closed the door.

Neither said anything for a few minutes. Ashleigh swiped at the tears on her cheeks. Kyle turned his entire body in her direction.

"Go away." Her voice was hoarse and her words didn't come out as strong as she meant them.

"I'm not going anywhere. We have things to straighten out. And you're in no condition to drive."

"Stop trying to control me."

He ran his hands through his hair. "The last thing I want to do is control you." He paused. "I think deep down you know that."

She reached in the console to pull out a tissue to wipe her runny nose. "If you're not trying to control me, then what is it you're doing?" She knew what she wanted him to say, what she'd always wanted him to say. That he loved her despite her not being able to give him a baby.

"Let's go back upstairs and finish this."

KYLE OPENED HIS apartment door, standing back so she could enter first. He'd picked up the scattered journals before going after Ashleigh. He didn't want them to add fuel to her anger if he was able to talk her into coming back.

He motioned for Ashleigh to sit on the sofa while he sat at the opposite end. As much as he wanted to take her hand, he was safer sticking to his explanation and keeping his hands to himself.

"You know me," Kyle began. "I can't sit around and wait for something that may or may not happen. I had to see if there had been any new discoveries in the past two years."

Ashleigh smirked. "You couldn't even wait till we found out if I'm actually pregnant?"

"No." His single-word answer made her eyes widen. "Every second counts. We don't have time to wait and see."

Her medical training must have kicked in because she appeared to be considering his argument.

When she didn't disagree, he asked, "Would you like to know what I found out?"

She stared at him for a long moment before nodding. Her gaze moved to her hands, folded on her lap.

"Unfortunately, I didn't discover anything useful," he said.

Her eyes widened. "Nothing?" He had her attention now as she watched him carefully.

He went on to tell her about the woman who'd remained bedridden in the hospital with the end of the bed elevated for months before delivering a healthy but premature baby.

"That sounds appealing," Ashleigh muttered sarcastically.

"Pretty much what your sister's doing—minus the elevated foot of the bed—but for a much longer time."

Was she considering the idea? Her silence was difficult to read.

Kyle glanced at his watch. Almost seven o'clock and they were at an impasse. "Would you like to have dinner? Maybe we can table this discussion until afterward?"

She didn't say anything, but instead rose from the couch and walked toward the kitchen. He followed her and retrieved the salad and homemade peanut dressing from the fridge.

"Can I do anything to help?" she asked sullenly.

"I'm going to toss the salad." He pointed to a cupboard. "There's a loaf of bread on the counter and a cutting board in the cabinet down below if you want to slice it."

They went about their tasks, carefully avoiding any physical contact. When they finally sat at the table across from each other, the table was so small that their knees nearly touched. He'd only eaten there alone in the past.

His body was screaming at their nearness, craving the pleasure of touch. Skin-to-skin contact was preferable, but right now he didn't even care if it was through clothing.

The fact that she was still angry didn't matter to his overly sensitive body parts in the least.

"This is great," Ashleigh finally said, a few bites into the meal, forcing Kyle to focus on food rather than sex. "I haven't had this salad since—" She cut herself off, obviously realizing she'd have to refer to when they were still married. She pushed lettuce, shredded carrots, chicken and crunchy chow mein noodles around with her fork. "I haven't made it since

I moved to Richmond." She concentrated on the salad as she spoke.

"I haven't made it since you moved to Richmond, either."

She lifted her head and their gazes collided. "Oh."

He stared into her eyes and a realization became clear to him. He loved her. He *still* loved her. He had never *stopped* loving her, no matter how devastated he'd been when she left.

He swallowed, unable to speak. He went back to eating his dinner and she did the same.

Eventually they began talking about Mark and Ryan, trading funny stories about their nephews. The tension had eased slightly, but they still avoided any uncomfortable subjects.

And just like they did back when they were married and even before, they worked together to clean up the kitchen once they were finished eating.

He put the leftover salad in the fridge, turned quickly and collided with Ashleigh. He caught her upper arms to steady her and as soon as she gazed up at him, his urges acted before he could control them.

His mouth was on hers without considering the consequences.

Instead of pushing him away and rebuffing him, Ashleigh wound her arms around his neck and pressed her body to his. The heat they produced was nearly hot enough to cook by.

He cupped her face with his hands, controlling the angle and intensity of their contact. She moaned as he deepened the kiss, exploring her mouth as their tongues clashed. She tasted like peanut and... Ashleigh—warm, sweet, and flavorful and, most of all, sexy.

He spun them around a hundred and eighty degrees so her back was against the refrigerator and his entire body was flat against hers. His heavy erection pressed into her abdomen. He ran his hand from her face and down the side of her neck until he was cupping her firm breast. Even through her bra and cotton blouse, he felt her hardened nipple and teased it with the pad of his thumb.

She moaned again and he moved his mouth in the same direction his hand had traveled until he reached her nipple. He bit the nub playfully and caught her around the waist with one arm when her knees buckled.

She arched her head back against the fridge and he licked at the skin on her neck. His hands roamed over her upper body, finding their way under the back of her blouse.

He wanted her now more than he'd ever wanted her before, at least that's what his body was screaming at him.

"I want you." The words weren't his but instead came in a gasp from Ashleigh.

He wanted to ask if she was sure, but he couldn't get the question out. His mouth descended on hers. With two hands on her firm rear end, he hoisted her up and she wrapped her legs around his waist. His bedroom wasn't far. He carried her the few steps and they fell onto his bed with her beneath him.

He cupped her face again, stroking her cheeks with his thumbs. He was finally able to find his voice. "You're so beautiful." He was lost in her deep blue eyes. Her legs were still wrapped around him, his erection pressed tightly against her. The heat from her core scorched him even through their clothes. "Are you sure?"

She didn't speak, merely squeezed her legs tighter. He couldn't catch his breath.

"Before...we continue." He sucked in air. "I need to say something." His body was screaming at him to shut up and get on with it, but his brain wouldn't listen.

She froze, her eyes wide and unfocused less than half a foot from his. "What?" she said softly. "If you're wondering about using a condom—"

"That's not it. I've got that covered."

She giggled at his choice of words and gave him a puzzled look. "What is it then?"

He swallowed. "I love you."

There it was. Right out in the open. No taking it back, no filtering it with *I think I might have feelings for you*. Nope, he'd said it very clearly, so there was no room for misunderstanding.

Funny thing was, he was okay with it. Like a weight off his chest. A weight that had been vexing him for a long, long time.

Ashleigh stared at him wide-eyed. Her mouth

opened slightly, but before she could speak he put a finger to her lips.

"You don't need to say anything," he said. "I just needed you to know. I didn't want you to think I was saying it, you know, in the heat of passion." The words kept flowing. "I've never stopped loving you."

Ashleigh's mouth curled into a smile. He removed his finger and she said, "Kyle?"

"Hmm?" he said.

"I love you, too. I always have."

He wasn't sure he'd heard her correctly. "What did you say?"

Her smile widened. "I said I love you, too."

"You do?"

She grinned. "I do." Then she sobered when she added, "That doesn't change anything. Love wasn't enough before and nothing's changed."

He gave her a quick kiss. "At least it's a start."

She smiled in agreement. This time she cupped his face with her hands and squeezed him with her legs. "Now can we get back to what we were doing?"

They both laughed as he rolled onto his back and pulled her with him, his heart light and his body hot for her as he kissed her and ran his hands under the back of her blouse to touch the soft skin there. His hands moved lower, cupping her butt cheeks and squeezing gently.

She sat up, straddling him while nestling his rock-hard penis tightly against her. She crossed her arms, catching the hem of her blouse in her hands, slipping it over her head and tossing it onto the floor. He reached around her back to unfasten her bra, but she was too quick for him. She released it and slipped it down her arms, flinging it on the floor to join her blouse.

He cupped both breasts in his hands, tasting and teasing each breast in turn. "You're gorgeous." He spoke against her skin, a catch in his throat that was pure emotion.

Rolling her onto her back, he continued to lick and suckle her breasts before slowly moving down her body to trail kisses to her belly button. He opened the button on her jeans and took his time as he slid the zipper down. Before pulling her pants off, he used the pad of his thumb to rub between her legs, causing her to raise her hips off the bed and pant desperately in anticipation. He touched the right spot and she moved in tandem with his hand until her entire body tensed and she cried out softly.

While Ashleigh caught her breath, he drew his T-shirt over his head and stripped out of his constricting jeans and briefs before sliding her jeans down her legs. He caught her brief wisp of pink satin panties in his teeth before teasing her with his tongue. He tossed the bikinis, then spread her legs, which were bent at the knee, and used his mouth to propel her into a frenzied state. He licked and thrilled her over and over again, until she let out an unabashed shriek of ecstasy.

He made his way back up her body and she grasped

his erection in her hand. She slowly ran her fingertips over his shaft.

"Careful," he gasped into her neck, automatically grabbing her hand to stop her before this encounter ended abruptly.

She chuckled deep in her throat and replaced her hand with the heat between her legs when she spread them. He slipped on a condom then entered her swiftly and deeply. This time they both moaned. He needed a second to get back under control.

He kissed her, their tongues sparring, until she began moving her hips, anxious to continue.

He obliged her and moved slowly in and out at first, building to a crescendo using both acceleration and force, thrusting into her until they were both spent.

ASHLEIGH MUST HAVE drifted off to sleep, because Kyle's bedroom was dark when she regained consciousness. His arm rested across her stomach as she lay next to him on her back. His breathing was slow and steady—definitely asleep. Turning her head in the other direction, the bedside clock said 9:33 p.m.

She carefully moved Kyle's arm and slipped out of bed. She grabbed the first piece of clothing she came to. Kyle's T-shirt. She put it on, loving the feeling of being covered in something that smelled like him, as if his arms were still around her. She hugged herself and smiled, truly happy for the first time in quite a while.

She pulled the bedroom door closed behind her and used the bathroom. When she tiptoed into the living room to find her purse and check her cell phone, she had two missed calls and one voice mail.

Nothing about her pregnancy test. They were all from the same person. Mrs. Thornton.

Ashleigh stepped to the farthest point in the living room away from Kyle's bedroom. She didn't want to wake him when she played Mrs. Thornton's message.

Right after she'd run into Mrs. Thornton at the hospital and convinced her to reevaluate her decision to not fund Kyle's charity, Ashleigh had sent the woman everything available that referred to the accident and subsequent lawsuit. Hopefully Mrs. Thornton had learned that Kyle had been a hero and wasn't the bad guy in the situation.

Ashleigh's heart was in her throat. She'd put some feelers out about other sources of funding while still hoping Mrs. Thornton would come through.

Ashleigh had hit Play on her cell phone to listen to the voice message when the phone in Kyle's office began ringing. She hadn't even known he had a landline. Unable to hear the message clearly on her phone, she hurried toward the office to pick up the phone, but it stopped ringing before she got there.

Kyle's voice was clear through the bedroom door. He must have an extension in there, too. Heat suffused her. She hadn't spent much time looking at details of the room when they'd been locked in each other's arms.

From what Ashleigh could hear on the other side of the bedroom door, Kyle wasn't saying much, mostly listening to whoever was on the other end of the phone. Ashleigh tried again to listen to Mrs. Thornton's message.

"Hello, Dr. Wilson, this is Edna Thornton. As persuasive as you've been, I'm afraid I'm going to have to wait until Dr. Jennings' lawsuit is resolved before I can consider donating to his very worthwhile charity. I'm sorry to disappoint you, but I'm sure you understand. Please let me know the moment you have good news."

As the message ended, Kyle opened his bedroom door. Ashleigh jumped, a combination of surprise and guilty conscience.

He grinned at her. A sexy, sleepy grin. "Hey."

"Hey." She smiled, unable to take her eyes off his bare chest and strong shoulders. He'd slipped his jeans on, but they were undone at the waist, drawing her eyes to the arrow of hair at his lower abdomen that led to what lay beneath.

"That was the hospital," he told her, kissing her cheek.

"Do they need you to come in?" she asked over her shoulder as she went into the living room to put her phone back into her purse.

"That wasn't about work," he said. "Paula's water broke."

Ashleigh spun around and her eyes widened. "You're kidding!"

"Nope," he said. "A nurse from Labor and Delivery called from Paula's cell phone. Paula asked her to call me and let me know that they were taking her to do an ultrasound to be on the safe side. You were going to get a call next, but I told her I'd handle it." He winked at Ashleigh and damn if she didn't melt at his sexy grin.

"Has her labor started?" She returned to what was important right at that moment.

"Not yet."

Ashleigh did a mental calculation. "She's a little over thirty-four weeks, right?" Her adrenaline pumped as reality set in.

"Sounds right." He reached for her and nuzzled her neck. "The baby's developed enough. Everything should be fine."

She pulled back. "We need to get to the hospital."

"No hurry." He tried to guide her back to his bedroom. "Stephanie is on her way to the hospital," he said, referring to Paula's labor coach.

"How can you think about sex when my sister is about to have a baby?"

His sexy grin alone was about to be her undoing. She slapped playfully at him and laughed. "I mean it. We need to get going." She looked down at herself and when she glanced back up, he was staring at her hardened nipples through his T-shirt.

"Well, you can't wear that to the hospital," he told her. He waggled his eyebrows at her and grabbed her around the waist with one arm. "And the moment you take off my T-shirt, you know I'm going to be all over you like white on rice."

Before she could react, he cupped her breast and leaned down to take her nipple into his mouth through the shirt. Then he ran his hand up the back of her leg and squeezed her bare bottom. Electricity coursed through her from her breast to her lower abdomen and beyond. Her legs gave way, but Kyle had her braced tight enough that she didn't fall.

"Okay," she panted. "You win. We might as well do this instead of sitting in the waiting room for hours."

"Now you're talking." He chuckled, the sound coming from deep within his chest and vibrating throughout her body.

"But you have to be quick," she told him, which made him laugh even more. "We still need to get to the hospital sooner rather than later."

"Paula's going to give birth to our niece or nephew whether we're there or not." He put an arm under her knees and picked her up, heading into his bedroom. "And I can be as quick as you want me to be."

With that said, he dumped her on the bed, stripped off his jeans and showed her how speedy—as well as how thorough—he could be.

IF HIS INTERNSHIP with its all-night shifts had taught Kyle one thing, it had been how to manage to stay awake even when he desperately wanted to sleep.

Especially after the physically exhaustive evening he and Ashleigh had shared.

He squeezed Ashleigh's hand as they once again sat together in the waiting area shared by Labor and Delivery and the maternity ward. He really hoped her anxiety over being back here again didn't return. He hadn't kept her in his bed as long as possible for sex alone.

She glanced over at him. "How much longer do you think it'll be?"

"No idea." They'd spent a few minutes with Paula before her doctor came in to examine her. He and Ashleigh had been sitting in the waiting room for about fifteen minutes now, but he tried to keep his concern to himself. "Rosy already started Pitocin. Something should be happening soon since this is Paula's third pregnancy."

Finally, Rosy came out of Paula's labor room. She closed the door behind her and crossed the hall to stand in front of Ashleigh and Kyle.

"How's she doing?" Kyle asked.

"Not as well as we'd hoped." Concern was evident in Rosy's tone. "Her labor is strong but not productive. She's not even dilated three centimeters yet."

Ashleigh shot up from her chair. "But it hasn't been that long," she said. "You're not worried, are you?"

Kyle rose, put an arm around Ashleigh's shoulders and squeezed gently.

"We're doing everything we can for both Paula

and the baby," Rosy said cryptically. "You can go in to see her now."

Rosy had turned to leave when Ashleigh said, "Wait." She glanced nervously at Kyle before looking at Rosy to ask, "I know this isn't the best time, but did you happen to get my test results yet?"

Rosy's eyes flicked briefly to Kyle before saying to Ashleigh, "I'll check with the lab to see if they have them."

Ashleigh nodded and Rosy headed in the direction of the elevators.

"Test results?" Kyle asked when they were alone.

"I had a pregnancy test done." Her voice was so soft he could barely hear her.

He swallowed. "So we might know soon, one way or the other."

Tears flooded her eyes.

He guided her back down into her chair and he joined her, holding her hand on his thigh. He ran his thumb absently over the length of hers.

He brought her hand to his lips and kissed the back of it before saying, "You know I invited you over for dinner tonight because I thought we had things to work out." He squeezed her hand. "Making love to you was never in my plan."

She turned her head to peer at him through narrowed, glassy eyes. "Never?"

He smiled. "Well, maybe not never."

Her mouth turned up slightly.

"Anyway," he said. "I know you said you wouldn't stay in Grand Oaks if you were pregnant, but—"

"Do we have to talk about this now?" She blinked several times. "Can't we wait until we know one way or the other?"

"We need to get this settled." Before their emotions took over.

She waited for him to continue.

"I know you've made a life for yourself in Richmond," he began. "But if you're pregnant, then that changes everything."

"No, it doesn't," she insisted.

He raised a hand. "Hear me out. I'm not done," he said. "I love you, Ashleigh. I've always loved you. From the moment I saw you in the middle-school cafeteria. I couldn't bear to have you hours away if you're carrying my child."

"I love you, too," she said, "but it doesn't change anything. We loved each other before and it wasn't enough."

The same words she'd used earlier. He hung his head and remembered to breathe.

"We both know the chances of me carrying to term are slight." She sounded a little desperate. "I might not even be pregnant."

"Let me ask you this." He took another approach. "Do you want to be pregnant?"

Again, she narrowed her eyes at him. "What are you asking?" A tear spilled down her cheek and she angrily swiped at it. "It's not like I have control over it. I'm either pregnant or I'm not."

"The question isn't a difficult one, Ash." He spoke gently, smoothing her hair back from her face. "I want to know now, before we find out for sure, whether you want this to happen or not."

She covered her face with her hands. "I don't know, Kyle. I don't know. I'm not sure I can handle another miscarriage."

"I'll be there for you. Every step of the way."

She removed her hands and her lips quivered. "I'm scared."

"Me, too," he whispered. He drew her closer and held her, but he still hadn't received a definitive answer.

A few minutes went by before he spoke. "Ash?"

She raised her head from his shoulder to look at him. "Hmm?"

"If you're pregnant, will you promise to stay in Grand Oaks?"

Her mouth formed an O and she didn't answer right away. "You mean stay with you?" she asked.

He hadn't thought that far ahead, but that sounded right. "Yes, with me. Give us another chance."

Her brow furrowed. Was she considering it? "But my job is in Richmond."

"We can work out all the details." Desperation surfaced. "Just say you'll stay with me if you're pregnant."

"*If* I'm pregnant," she repeated. There was a long pause. "What about when I miscarry?"

"All the more reason you should stay here." Then he added, "Think positively."

"But the chances—"

"Screw the odds," he said firmly. "No negativity."

"I have to think about it."

Not the answer he wanted, but at least she was considering it. "Of course."

Just then, Rosy came down the hall. Her gait was brisk and businesslike.

She stopped in front of them. This was it. In a heartbeat he'd know whether he and Ashleigh had a chance of having a future together.

Because he knew if she wasn't pregnant, then she'd be gone and out of his life again.

CHAPTER EIGHTEEN

ASHLEIGH'S PULSE POUNDED in her temples as Rosy came down the hall toward them. This was it. Either pregnant or not. Then they could proceed from there. She ran her sweaty palms over her jean-covered thighs and sucked in oxygen.

Kyle wanted her to stay in town if she was pregnant. He hadn't said anything about wanting her to stay if she wasn't.

What had she expected? He'd always wanted children and she was the least likely candidate to give him any. Why would he want to tie himself down with her again? That would be repeating past mistakes. She'd done him a huge favor when she'd ended their marriage. He couldn't help but feel an obligation to be there for her if the test came back positive.

She wished, not for the first time, that he had put up at least a bit of a struggle when she'd asked him for a divorce.

"Ashleigh?" Kyle's voice close to her ear brought her out of her introspection.

Rosy was standing in front of them. She'd probably spoken, but Ashleigh had been so into her thoughts that she'd shut out the rest of the world.

"Sorry," Ashleigh said.

"I was saying that I went to the lab for your results," Rosy said.

Ashleigh's chest constricted and she couldn't breathe. The sympathy in Rosy's eyes was evident before she said another word. The stunning realization came in that moment.

Ashleigh had wanted to be pregnant. Desperately. Even if she miscarried, she'd at least have a reason to stay in town. She'd get some more time with Kyle. The two nights they'd spent together hadn't even been close to enough.

"I'm sorry," Rosy continued in a doctor-giving-bad-news tone. She hadn't used her sympathetic "friend voice," possibly to steel herself from her own feelings. "The test was negative."

Ashleigh refused to let the outcome break her. "I'm not surprised." She remained as cool as possible, while inside she was crumbling. "There was only a slight chance I could be pregnant and with my history of endometriosis, that lessened my chances considerably."

She couldn't turn her head to look at Kyle, couldn't bear to know whether it was relief or pain in his eyes.

"Dr. Bausch?" A nurse called from a patient's doorway down the hall and waved her over.

"Excuse me." Rosy looked pointedly at Ashleigh. "We'll talk more later," she said before hurrying down the hall to the patient's room.

No need for any more talking. Not pregnant was not pregnant. Period.

"Ash?" Kyle's voice sounded far away, but it came from the chair next to hers.

She couldn't make her mouth form words.

"Are you okay?" he asked.

She finally looked at him and wished she hadn't. His eyes were red rimmed. She turned away quickly and her hands flew to her mouth.

A choking sound escaped before she could hold it in. What had she been thinking? No way was she going to get upset about not being pregnant. This was a relief. She wouldn't have to go through another miscarriage. Wouldn't that have been so much worse than not being pregnant in the first place?

Now she'd be able to make sure everything was in place here in Grand Oaks before returning to her life in Richmond. That had been her plan from the beginning.

Kyle should be thrilled that he wouldn't have to go through the heartbreak of another miscarriage with her. And he'd be free to move on without her... again.

No matter how much they proclaimed to love each other, Kyle would be relieved when he was able to process it. She was certain.

"Ashleigh?" Kyle said again as if from far away.

"Hmm?" She didn't look at him.

"I asked if you were okay."

"Why wouldn't I be?" She wished her voice was stronger. She tried to clear her throat, but the lump persisted.

She couldn't do this now. Not if she had any hope of keeping herself together. She rose quickly. Apparently too quickly because she became light-headed. She grabbed for the arm of the chair and missed. Kyle caught her around the waist before she lost her balance.

"Sit back down." He helped her into her seat. "Are you feeling all right?"

"I got up too quickly." She tried to rise again, but he put a hand on her knee to stop her. "I'm overtired with everything that's been going on." Lightening the mood and changing the subject became her objectives. "You were always better than I was at going on little sleep." She nudged him with her elbow and said out of the side of her mouth, "Especially after the evening we had in your bed." Hysteria rose inside her and it took all her willpower to keep it from bubbling out.

"Ashleigh, stop it." Kyle's voice was stern.

She lowered her voice but couldn't stop herself. "What's the matter? Afraid someone will find out we've been having wild sex?" Hysteria was winning.

"I mean it." He rose from his chair to stand in front of her.

"Hey, you should be celebrating." She feigned cheerfulness. "I'm not pregnant. Now you don't have to worry about me sticking around. You're a free man."

"Let's go get some coffee and find somewhere private," he suggested. "The E.R. has a new single-cup coffeemaker and we can sit in the conference room."

He'd always been a champ when it came to steering the subject away from sensitive topics.

"Sure, we'll 'talk.'" She used air quotes to punctuate her sarcasm. "Like we 'talked' every time I miscarried."

"We did talk."

"Oh, right. We talked about how to fix me, how to have children some other way. If that's what you mean by talking, then fine, we talked." She sucked in a breath. "Although I guess we never needed to talk about anything else. You made it quite clear that I'd failed you. You kept trying to fix the situation and I wasn't cooperating. You could never accept me, faults and all."

"That's not true. Not once did I think you failed me." He kept his voice low and deliberate.

"Oh, sure. That's why you wouldn't give up, wouldn't stop sending me for tests and procedures. Anything so you could have what *you* wanted."

"I didn't mean—" He reached for her but she pushed him away. "I wanted to give you what you wanted most in life."

"What I wanted?" Anger crept into her tone.

"Don't you want a child?"

She let out a laugh that sounded as fake as it felt.

"You don't understand, Kyle. I *can't* have a child. I've spent the past two years learning to accept that. You still haven't. You won't let yourself admit that we'll never have the perfect life we planned."

"That's not true."

"Then why did I find the medical journals and new research on infertility in your apartment? You're still trying to fix me. Trying to make me your perfect wife and the perfect mother of your children."

"What am I supposed to do? Ignore the fact that you might be pregnant and that there may be something new that might help you carry to term?"

"Well, I'm not pregnant, so there's no need for more research." She stood up on shaky legs. "You go get coffee if you want it. I can't do this anymore. This is the end for us. I'm not pregnant, so you're no longer obligated. You're free. We have nothing else to discuss."

She kept her head high, barely making it down the hall and into the vacant restroom before she doubled over and wept uncontrollably.

KYLE WATCHED HELPLESSLY as Ashleigh hurried away. He didn't know what more to say to her. Didn't know what to do to make her accept the fact that whether they had a child or not didn't matter to him. He wanted to reach out and hold her until life became tolerable, but she wanted nothing to do with him.

He could barely handle the news that there was no pregnancy—*she* had to be crushed. No wonder she'd lashed out at him. She couldn't possibly believe he thought she'd failed him by not giving him children, could she? That was ridiculous.

But he realized that this had been their one chance at getting back together. Now that she wasn't pregnant, she had no reason to stick around. No reason to stay with him.

He hadn't been able to keep her from leaving two years ago and now they were repeating history. He couldn't see any way to avoid the same outcome—at least not when she was so upset. Maybe when she calmed down he might have a better shot at making her see reason. Maybe.

He walked to the bank of elevators and went down to the E.R. to make them coffee. When he stepped off the elevator on the first floor, he ran into Stan and his wife, Linda, walking down the hall.

"Hi, Linda. Hey, Stan," Kyle greeted them. He forced a smile, not in the mood to have a friendly conversation, but he asked Stan, "How are you?" Kyle hadn't been to see his friend and colleague in a few days and he could see he was still a patient by the dark brown bathrobe over his hospital gown and tan moccasins on his feet.

Stan grinned and put an arm around his wife's shoulders. "Thanks to my lovely wife, I'm doing much better." He hugged Linda close and kissed her temple.

"He gives me too much credit," she said pleasantly, then smiled indulgently at her husband.

"Not true," Stan insisted. "If you hadn't noticed my shortness of breath when we did our daily walks around the hospital, then no one would have picked up that I had a touch of pneumonia."

"I'm sure your doctor would have," she said.

"Good catch," Kyle said. "I wondered why you hadn't been discharged yet."

"Listen," Linda said to both men before pointing to a bank of chairs next to the wall. "Why don't you two sit over there and catch up while I get our ice cream from the cafeteria?"

"She worries I'm overdoing it," Stan said in a stage whisper.

"There's no *worrying* involved." Linda grinned. "You're definitely overdoing it. And as a doctor, you should know better." She patted her husband's arm then asked Kyle, "Can I get you anything?"

He shook his head. "No, thanks. I came down for coffee. Ashleigh's sister is in labor."

"Is that good news?" Linda's eyebrows rose. "I knew they were keeping her here so she wouldn't have the baby too early."

"She's far enough along now." Kyle wished he didn't have to pretend that he hadn't just been kicked in the gut.

"That's good," Linda said, then told Stan, "I'll be right back."

When his wife was gone, Stan said, "I'm a lucky man, Kyle. Truly a lucky man."

Kyle smiled, unwilling to acknowledge a twinge

of jealousy. "Yes, you are, Stan." The guy had suffered a heart attack, open-heart surgery and now pneumonia, but still Kyle was envious because Stan had a happy marriage.

"Want to know the secret?" Stan asked.

A magic pill or potion? "Sure." Kyle was anxious to get back to check on Ashleigh, but he had a few more minutes for Stan.

"Don't be a mind reader." Stan laughed. "Don't assume you know what she wants or when she wants it."

Kyle waited for him to go on.

"Ask her what she wants," Stan said. "Don't do what I did. I almost learned that lesson too late." He stopped to turn his head away and cough into the crook of his arm before he continued. "I thought I knew Linda, but when we finally sat down to talk, I was dead wrong. Turns out all she ever wanted was me." He laughed. "Not the house, the cars, the vacations. Just time with me."

Linda came around the corner then, holding two cardboard cups of soft ice cream with spoons sticking out. "Is he boring you with his insights into life?" She handed a cup of ice cream to Stan, along with a napkin she pulled from her pocket. "Ever since he had his heart attack he's been telling everyone who'll listen about how to improve their lives."

"Simply offering a little advice." Stan took a bite of ice cream.

Linda rolled her eyes. Kyle stood so she could sit down next to Stan.

"I better get back with that coffee I promised," Kyle said. "Thanks for the advice, Stan. Bye, Linda."

Linda waved and Stan said, "Anytime," as Kyle retreated in the direction of the E.R. break room.

As he waited for the coffee to finish brewing, he considered Stan's advice and shoved it to the back of his mind. This was not the time to ask Ashleigh anything, much less what she wanted from him. He could pretty much guarantee she didn't want a damn thing from him right now.

Maybe ever.

ASHLEIGH HELD COOL, wet paper towels to her eyes in hopes of easing the redness and swelling from her crying. According to the large mirror in the ladies' room, the towels weren't helping. Her nose was red, too. She searched in her purse to see what makeup she had with her to mask the damage.

From the early days of her internship, she'd kept herself well stocked with makeup, snacks, toothbrush, hair ties and clips. Anything she might need to make it through twenty-four-hour or longer shifts. Back then she'd had a locker at the hospital for everything, but she'd never been able to break the habit of carrying her necessities in her purse.

She fixed the damage to her face as best she could and reapplied clear gloss to her parched lips. A large glass of water sounded like heaven right now, after she'd cried herself dry.

Finally ready to go back out in public, she had a sudden urge to cry again. "Are you kidding me?" she said aloud to her reflection in the mirror. Her emotions were all over the place, which was unusual for her. Thankfully, no one had come into the restroom the entire time she'd been there, probably because it was late at night.

She took several deep, cleansing breaths to calm down. There was no way she was going to start crying all over again. If she didn't return soon, Kyle would certainly come looking for her.

Raising her head high and swallowing back her emotions, she exited the ladies' room and walked straight to the waiting area on wobbly legs. There was a flurry of activity happening on the floor and Kyle was seated in a chair, his head bowed and a covered cup of coffee in each hand.

"What's going on?" Ashleigh asked him.

Her words startled him as he raised his head abruptly to look at her.

"Paula." He handed her a cup. "The baby is in distress. They're doing a C-section."

Ashleigh's legs refused to hold her. She carefully lowered herself into the chair next to Kyle, careful not to jiggle the coffee too much that it would splash out of the hole in the plastic lid.

She was about to automatically place her hand on

his knee, but she stopped. "Are they going to be all right?" she asked. "What did Rosy say?"

"She didn't have time to say anything—she sent Jenny over," he said, referring to the floor's ward clerk.

"We should know in a few minutes," Ashleigh said unnecessarily. They were both doctors and knew how quickly a Cesarean was performed. The closing of the incision was what took the most time. "I hope the baby won't have to go to the NICU."

Kyle looked at her. "Me, too."

She held her emotions in check. If she thought of the baby as her niece or nephew, then she might get emotionally involved and make a grievous error.

"Did Stephanie go to Delivery with Paula?" Ashleigh wondered if Paula's labor coach was up to witnessing the surgical birth. The hospital's labor rooms were set up for uncomplicated deliveries. That way, women didn't have to be moved down the hall. A C-section, however, was a complication that necessitated moving to the delivery room.

"She was right next to Paula's gurney going down the hall," he said. "How are you doing?"

She shrugged, adopting nonchalance. "I'm fine."

"I hate waiting."

"Me, too," she agreed.

She stood and didn't look at Kyle, unable to stand another minute of tension-filled conversation with him. "I should go wash up and be ready to check out the newest member of the Jennings family."

His heated gaze nearly burned a hole through her as she left him.

"IT'S A GIRL!"

Paula's friend, Stephanie, had practically run down the hall from the delivery room to tell Kyle the good news.

"Are they both okay?" He was unused to not being in the thick of the action like in the E.R.

Stephanie nodded vigorously, her dark ponytail bobbing with the movement of her head. "The baby looks perfect, but Ashleigh's checking her out."

"What about Paula?" he asked.

"They're stitching her up right now." She lowered her voice. "I need a break. You can go in if you want. Ashleigh and Dr. Bausch said it was okay.

"You're going to wait to go back in?" He didn't want to abandon her.

She nodded. "In a little while. I'll get some coffee. It's been a long night."

That it had.

"I'll see you later then." He waved and walked quickly down the hall to meet his newest niece.

He stopped to wash up before entering the delivery room and stood at the doorway a moment to watch the activity going on. Paula's head was hidden by a vertical drape while Rosy concentrated on suturing her, assisted on the other side of the table by a nurse.

In the far corner, Ashleigh had her back to him as she stood in front of an exam table and listened through her stethoscope to their niece's heart and lungs.

Kyle chose to speak to Paula first and made his way to the head of her bed. "Hey there," he greeted her, kissing her forehead and pulling a nearby rolling stool closer so he could sit level with her head. "How's it going, Mom?" He adjusted the IV stand slightly so he wouldn't knock it over.

She smiled that serene smile he'd seen many times over the years right after a woman gave birth. "I have a daughter." She spoke softly. "I can't believe it."

He chuckled. "Amazing. Congratulations."

"How is she?" Paula asked. "They haven't told me anything yet."

"She seems fine from here." There were no signs of concern in the baby's caregivers. He rose. "I'll go check on her."

Exhaustion was evident in Paula's heavy-lidded eyes. "Wait." She reached out for him and he turned back to hear her say, "Her name is Cora."

He smiled. His and Scott's grandmother's name.

He crossed the room, coming up behind Ashleigh. As he reached out to put a hand at her back, he hesitated at the last minute. She was intense as she examined Cora, very professional. She didn't speak to the infant as he'd imagined she might have, nor touch her in a soothing way. *Clinical* was the description that came to mind.

Was she shielding herself? Unwilling to become emotionally attached to her niece because she would be leaving her soon? Or did it have more to do with the negative pregnancy test?

"How is she?" Kyle asked.

She didn't answer, merely continued the exam.

"Ashleigh?"

Still she didn't notice he was there. He came around on the opposite side of the table and reached out to grasp her wrist to get her attention.

Startled, Ashleigh's head jerked up to look at him before returning to her patient. "What?"

"I asked how she's doing." He clenched his jaw as his patience grew thin.

"So far, so good," she said. "Heart and lungs sound good and her APGAR scores were nine and ten. Her weight is six pounds, five ounces, and she appears to be closer to thirty-six weeks than thirty-four plus."

"Her name is Cora," he said quietly.

"What?" She spoke brusquely, as if annoyed.

"I said her name is Cora."

Her throat worked as she swallowed. "After your grandmother?"

He nodded.

She sniffed and her few seconds of emotion were gone as suddenly as they'd appeared. She directed her attention to the nurse waiting to take Cora to Paula. "I'd like her to spend the night in the nursery as a precaution, rather than rooming in. No need for NICU, though."

Ashleigh turned from the exam table, allowing the nurse to take Cora.

She hadn't even picked up her niece to hold her and coo.

Ashleigh left the delivery room and he assumed she was heading to the nurses' station to write orders.

Figuring she'd be back in to let Paula know how Cora was doing, Kyle followed Cora and the nurse over to Paula, who was now sutured and anxious to see her daughter, wrapped in a plaid blanket with a pink stocking cap on her head.

"She's beautiful," Paula said as her baby girl was placed into the crook of her arm. "Where's Ashleigh?" She craned her neck to peer around the room, but she was flat on her back and unable to see much.

"She had paperwork to do." He kept his observations of Ashleigh's detached behavior to himself. "I'm sure she'll be back in a few minutes."

"I can't wait for Scott to see his daughter." A tear ran down Paula's cheek and she brushed it away.

"Want me to see if he's available to video chat with you?" Kyle asked.

"That would be great," she said. "He knew my water broke and he was ready to be here by video when I was close to delivery. But then everything happened so fast when Cora went into distress." She broke down and began sobbing. "I feel bad that he wasn't here for her birth."

"I know," Kyle sympathized. "Let's get you settled in your room and I'll get in touch with Scott."

He left the delivery room to search for Ashleigh, but she wasn't at the nurses' station. "Have you seen Dr. Wilson?" he asked the young male nurse behind the desk.

"She left," he said.

Left? "Did she say where she was headed?" Kyle reined in his anger at the fact that she hadn't come back in to see her sister. "Maybe she went to the nursery?" he suggested.

"I honestly don't know."

Kyle went down the hall to the nursery and asked the same question of the R.N. on duty.

"She was here and said she'd be back in the morning."

"She went home?" He was incredulous.

The R.N. replied, "That's what she said."

"Thanks." Kyle was sullen as he walked away. He didn't have time to go after her. Right now his job was to fill the gap that his brother's absence had caused.

Because Paula's sister sure wasn't concerned about it.

By the time he reached Scott and then made his way to the room on Maternity where Paula had been taken, he was surprised—no, shocked—to hear

Ashleigh at her bedside with the curtain around the bed closed.

He gave them a few minutes of privacy, but he couldn't help overhearing. He wasn't happy with what he heard.

Ashleigh spoke to Paula like a doctor to the parent of her patient, rather than sister to sister. Once again, she was clinical, showing no emotion. "I'd like your baby to spend the night in the nursery. The staff can monitor her and you can get some rest." She didn't even call the baby by name.

She could have been speaking to any stranger on the street. He flexed his fingers, which had been tightly fisted, ready to pull back the curtain to make his presence known, when he was paged over the loudspeaker.

"Dr. Jennings, please call extension twenty-one. Dr. Jennings, extension twenty-one."

That was E.R. Someone must have figured out he was in the building. He hurried down the hall, deciding he could make it down to the emergency room faster than if he stopped to call.

What he wanted to say to Ashleigh could wait.

A LITTLE WHILE LATER, Ashleigh was driving to Paula's. She was glad now that she'd insisted both she and Kyle take separate cars to the hospital from his apartment.

Exhausted beyond belief and keeping a weakening hold on her emotions, she had barely escaped the hospital with her dignity intact. Now she was able to be alone with her thoughts and had no need to put on an act, which she would have had to do if Kyle had been driving her home.

Examining her niece had been excruciating. The child was beautiful and healthy. Everything Ashleigh had ever wanted. Now her sister had three children and Ashleigh still had nothing. Not even the possibility of being pregnant with Kyle's child.

Her phone buzzed in her purse. At the next stop sign she withdrew it to see who it was.

Kyle. He'd sent a text message.

He probably wanted to know where she was. She tossed the phone into her purse and continued driving the deserted roads. She'd get back to him when she reached Paula's.

The sky was beginning to lighten when she pulled into Paula's driveway. She dragged her exhausted body into the house and stripped off her clothes, not caring about anything but the relief of sleep.

She wanted the oblivion of unconsciousness for as long as it took for her to get over the emotional pain grinding her into pitiful pieces.

CHAPTER NINETEEN

ASHLEIGH HAD TOSSED and turned from the moment she hit the sheets, so she was surprised to be jolted awake by the ringing phone. The time was almost noon. She reached for her cell phone, but the sound wasn't coming from it.

Paula's house phone was ringing.

She hauled herself out of bed to get it. The answering machine beat her to it.

Kyle's voice penetrated her sleep-deprived brain as she came down the stairs. "Ashleigh, are you there?" He paused. His tone became harsher. "Ashleigh? Come on, pick up. I've been calling your cell and you're not answering." Another pause. "If you don't pick up, I'll have to come over—"

She grabbed for the extension. "I'm here."

"Is there a problem?" he asked.

"No, I'm just pretty tired," she replied. "Has something happened?"

"Happened?" he echoed. "You disappeared from the hospital last night. You barely spoke to your sister after you examined Cora."

"Oh." He'd called to berate her for not doing her

duty as a physician, as well as not being a good sister. Why had she hoped he might be concerned about her or their personal situation? "Are you at the hospital?" She was hoping to deflect his criticism.

"Yeah, I slept here. I'm filling in this morning." His self-righteous attitude was unusual. Bunking at the hospital when he was on duty was the norm. "Aunt Viv and the kids have already been here and gone after seeing Paula and Cora."

"Okay. So is something else wrong?"

"Are you kidding?" He spoke so loudly that Ashleigh had to pull the phone away from her ear. "You're doing it again, Ashleigh. You're running away when things don't go the way you expected."

She wasn't alert enough to have this conversation. "I can't do this right now." She disconnected. A little more anger from him at this point wouldn't make much difference in the end.

She padded back upstairs to find that her cell phone had several missed calls and voice messages from Kyle, as well as a missed call and a voice message from Rosy. She also had two text messages from Kyle and one from the doctor who was coming to replace her in the pediatric practice.

As soon as Dr. Samantha Collins took over, Ashleigh would be free to go back to Richmond. She waited for the relief to wash over her, but it didn't come.

She replied to Samantha's text first.

Can't wait to see u, Sam. Meet at office tomorrow morning? Is 8 too early?

She hit Send and then listened to the message from Rosy.

"Ashleigh, please call me back as soon as possible. Either page me at the hospital or call my cell. I need to speak with you."

Adrenaline shot through her. Was there something wrong with Paula? Complications after the C-section? Ashleigh's hands shook as she pulled up Rosy's cell number and waited for a connection. The phone rang three times before Rosy came on the line.

"Ashleigh." There was relief in Rosy's voice. "Are you okay?"

"Why is everyone asking me that?" Ashleigh wanted to know. "Of course I'm fine, why wouldn't I be?"

"We're concerned," Rosy said.

"We?" Ashleigh asked. "As in you and Kyle?"

Pause. "Yes," Rosy admitted.

"You've been talking about me behind my back?" Ashleigh's temper flared. How dare they?

"Like I said, we're concerned about you." Rosy's gentle tone annoyed Ashleigh even more. "I know you're upset about the negative pregnancy test. Can we get together to talk?"

"There's nothing to talk about," Ashleigh stated. "I'm not pregnant. Period."

"But you still might be," Rosy said. "That's what

I wanted to talk to you about. The test might have been done too early to detect elevated hCG levels, even in a blood test."

Ashleigh didn't know what to say. She already knew the test could have been premature, but she couldn't get her hopes up. Couldn't bear to be disappointed again. Her temples pounded.

When Ashleigh remained silent, Rosy said, "I'd like you to have another blood test in a few days."

Ashleigh's mouth went dry, making her words difficult to form. "I'll think about it. Thanks, Rosy." She disconnected before Rosy could say anything more.

There was nothing to think about. She knew her body and from the way she'd been acting and snapping at people the past twelve hours, Ashleigh would swear she was experiencing a definite case of PMS. A clear sign that she wasn't carrying Kyle's child.

ASHLEIGH SHOWERED AND DRESSED, unwilling to deal with anyone else who thought there was something wrong with her.

Of course there was something wrong. She was seriously flawed. She couldn't do the one thing that would make her life perfect. Give Kyle a family.

When she entered the hospital's nursery later that afternoon, the distinctive high-pitched sound of a crying newborn stopped her. A nurse was leaning over the child's bassinet. "He's not happy about having blood taken, Dr. Wilson," the young woman told

Ashleigh. "Let me take him back to his mother and then I'll brief you on your patient."

The nurse guided the bassinet and wailing baby out the doorway and down the hall.

Ashleigh read the placards on the two bassinets left in the nursery and stepped to the one holding her niece.

She was sleeping soundly, oblivious to her aunt's anxiety. "Just wait." Ashleigh spoke more to herself than to the baby. "Before you know it, life will disappoint you and you'll start making decisions no one agrees with."

She pulled out her stethoscope and unwrapped the blanket swaddling the baby. She listened to the child's heart and lungs, pleased to find nothing out of the ordinary. The little girl stretched and scrunched her face when Ashleigh inspected her umbilical cord, as if annoyed at being disturbed, before relaxing back into sleep.

"She had a good night according to the night staff." The nurse had returned, silent in her rubber-soled shoes. "I'll get her chart for you."

"Thank you." Ashleigh wrapped the infant securely in the standard plaid hospital receiving blanket. She stared at her a moment, unable to ignore how much she looked like her brothers with her dark hair and pouty lower lip.

"Have they named her yet?" Again, the nurse came up on her soundlessly.

"What?" Ashleigh said automatically. "Oh, yes. Her name is Cora."

The nurse smiled. "How pretty. And not a name you hear all the time. Is it a family name?"

"It's her paternal grandmother's name," Ashleigh answered.

"How special." The nurse switched suddenly to business and handed over Cora's chart.

Her vitals had remained stable, no change that would warrant additional monitoring in the nursery. Blood tests revealed a slightly elevated bilirubin— not unexpected with a preemie. They'd have to keep monitoring it because it would probably continue to rise over the next several days.

"She's ready to room-in with her mother now," she told the nurse as Ashleigh wrote on the chart. "I'd also like to have a monitored car seat session done before I discharge her. There's no hurry, though, since her mother had a C-section and will be staying a few extra days."

"Would you like me to take her to her mother?" the nurse asked. "Or are you headed that way?"

Ashleigh ought to go see her sister since everyone thought she'd been horrible for being more doctor than sister. Last night Kyle had been right beside her while she'd examined the newborn. She'd briefed him and then she'd updated Paula, too. Everyone knew the baby was doing well. What more did they want?

"I'll take her," Ashleigh said. "I have no other patients to see on this floor." She double-checked what room Paula was in and headed down the hall in the direction of Maternity.

She stopped right before the doorway of Paula's room when she heard voices. Theresa and Tom were visiting Paula. Ashleigh continued into the room, pushing her charge ahead of her.

"There she is," Theresa cried, ignoring Ashleigh to come over to peer at the baby. "She's beautiful!"

Tom stood behind Theresa, his hand on her shoulder as he, too, looked at the newborn in her bassinet.

"We should go," Theresa said suddenly.

"You don't have to," Paula said.

"You need your rest." Tom had an arm at Theresa's waist. "Ashleigh, it's good to see you."

"You, too." Ashleigh's gaze moved to Theresa, who was giddy with excitement. Her contented smile told Ashleigh everything. She forced herself to smile at Theresa, whose smile grew even bigger.

"Bye," Theresa said when they were almost out the door. Then to Ashleigh, she whispered loudly, "We're taking it slow for now, but I love the house!"

Ashleigh gave her a thumbs-up and couldn't help wishing she could say the same about her relationship with Kyle. Not that they had a relationship anymore.

"How is she?" Paula's anxiety concerning her daughter was obvious, effectively bringing Ashleigh back to the present.

She picked up the baby and laid her in her mother's waiting arms. "She's doing very well." She filled Paula in on the baby's progress. "She can room-in with you now that she's stable."

Paula's eyes were glassy with tears. She peered down at her daughter and the tears spilled down her cheeks and onto the baby's forehead and cheek. Paula kissed them away before looking up at Ashleigh, "Thank you."

A lump formed in Ashleigh's throat and her own eyes welled up at Paula's emotional response to her daughter.

To deflect her reaction, she turned away to pull the chair next to the window closer to Paula's bed. She quickly brushed an errant tear from her own cheek and took a seat. Pretending she was holding herself together as her sister fussed over her newborn daughter would not be easy.

When she was finally sure her voice wouldn't crack, Ashleigh voiced the question everyone had been asking *her.* "How are you doing?"

"Pretty good." Paula's exhaustion was clear in her eyes, while still gazing at her daughter. Then she raised her head to look at Ashleigh. "I wasn't expecting a C-section. I'm sure that will slow me down."

"Knowing you, it won't keep you down long," Ashleigh said.

Paula cocked her head. "What do you mean?"

Ashleigh said lightheartedly, "You make everything look easy."

"You're kidding, right?" Paula wasn't smiling.

Ashleigh squinted at her. "No, I'm not kidding.

Look at your life. You have a great family. A wonderful, loving husband, two terrific boys, and now you top it off with a beautiful daughter. How much more perfect could it be?"

"Do you actually expect me to believe you think my life has been easy?" Paula asked. "Coming from you, that's quite a joke."

"What do you mean?"

Paula laid the baby on her legs and counted off on her fingers. "You were a straight-A student and I was up all night studying to get B's. You were *captain* of the cheerleading squad and I couldn't get past the first round of tryouts because I couldn't do a proper backflip."

"That was high school." Ashleigh was surprised at Paula's mixed-up view of how easy she thought Ashleigh had it.

"Then there was college," Paula said. "You were accepted at your first choice of college, dean's list every single semester. You got into your first choice of medical schools, which happened to be where your boyfriend was accepted also." She stared wide-eyed at Ashleigh. "Then there was me. Sure, I got into my first choice of college, but I put my degree on hold when I got pregnant with Mark." She held up a hand. "I know, it was my fault—mine and Scott's—but don't you see? This fall was supposed to be when I went back to finish my degree because the boys will be in school full-time."

Paula was trying not to cry as she spoke, but she wasn't succeeding.

Ashleigh could barely hold back her own emotions. "Paula—"

"I wanted something of my own." Paula's voice broke. "A success I could be proud of. Like you have." She stopped speaking, visibly struggling to stay in control.

"But you have the one thing I can never have." Ashleigh choked on her tears. "You have your family." She swallowed thickly. "I'd give anything to have that."

"Then what's stopping you?" Paula asked. "I've worked hard for what I have. Did you ever consider that because things came too easy for you that you never learned how to work for them? Maybe that's why when things got tough between you and Kyle you ran away rather than working through it. You didn't know how to."

Ashleigh couldn't name one thing she'd wanted and not gotten with very little effort. Except a family.

"I thought I did work at it—I thought *we* worked at it." She pushed the chair back as she rose quickly. She walked to the window, her back turned to Paula. "Am I really so shallow that I'm jealous of your life, your family?" She spun to face her sister. "What's wrong with me?"

"Nothing," Paula replied. "When things got difficult, you gave up and walked away. You left your husband, your family, even your profession, to start a new—perfect—life somewhere else. Ashleigh, you never gave yourself the opportunity to learn how to behave differently. To be less than perfect."

Ashleigh couldn't deny anything Paula was saying. She hadn't looked at it that way before. "Aunt Viv told me I was being unfair to Kyle.... Did she ever tell you about Clint?"

"Clint?"

"He was the love of her life, but he left her when he wasn't the same man physically that he was when they fell in love." Ashleigh explained about the accident and Clint's refusal to even speak to Aunt Viv after he moved away.

"That's so sad," Paula said. "I can't believe we never heard about him."

"I know. Anyway, she compared me to Clint."

"That's pretty harsh," Paula said.

"Harsh but true. I didn't realize it before." She was seeing a lot more clearly now. "You're right, Paula. I need to fight for what I want." Her voice was shaky and her emotions were bared. She asked the question that had plagued her for too long. The question she'd hesitated asking during Paula's high-risk pregnancy. "Why did you take Kyle's side in our divorce?"

The baby began to fuss and Paula put her to her breast before answering. "It wasn't that I took sides. I've always been on your side, Ashleigh. I wanted you to fight for your marriage, for Kyle, for your life. I thought if you realized how much you were losing by giving up—not only Kyle, but everything you had, including your sister—that you'd reconsider. Maybe I went about it the wrong way…."

Ashleigh sat in the chair by the bed and saw her sister in a different light. "But it didn't work out that way. All because of me. I'm the reason we lost two years as sisters. I'm so sorry."

"I never should have turned my back on you. *I'm* so sorry." Paula reached out with her free hand to take Ashleigh's. "I've missed you."

"I've missed you more."

"I know how difficult it was for you to come back to help me. You didn't have to." A tear ran down Paula's cheek. "I know I never said it, but I really do appreciate it."

"No matter what was going on between us, you have to know I'd always be there for you." Ashleigh squeezed Paula's hand. "We're family. Always and forever."

Paula was optimistic about her relationship with her sister for the first time in years.

"I'm so sorry for everything." Ashleigh rose to reach for a tissue on the table next to Paula's bed. She gently blotted away the moisture under her eyes. "I was extremely confused back then." She let out a self-deprecating laugh. "I still am."

"It's not too late to get what you want," Paula told her.

"If only that were true." Ashleigh proceeded to tell her about the pregnancy scare and the negative test.

"I can't believe it." Paula was incredulous. "You two have been so at odds whenever I've seen you. You're back together? I knew something was different, but I didn't know what." Paula's mood brightened.

"I wouldn't say that we're back together," Ashleigh said. "We had it out and I told him it's over. He's been pretty cool to me since then. I can't do anything right in his opinion, including being a doctor."

"Maybe he's as upset about everything as you are and he doesn't know how to express it." Paula knew she was digging, but she was determined to be optimistic.

Ashleigh didn't say anything, merely shrugged as if she didn't care. Paula knew otherwise.

She switched Cora to the other breast, running a fingertip over her little one's temple as she latched on. She actually had a daughter. How could she ever have doubted that she wanted this child?

"So what do you want?" Paula asked Ashleigh. "Do you want to go back to Richmond, back to the life you've made for yourself there?"

Ashleigh didn't meet her eyes, didn't answer.

Paula continued. "Or do you want to work it out with Kyle, here?"

"That would never work." Ashleigh spoke quickly, shaking her head vehemently.

"Why not?"

"Because I can't give him a family," she said. "And that's what he wants more than anything."

Paula couldn't believe her sister. "You're kidding, right?"

Ashleigh cocked her head. "No, I'm serious."

"Don't you know he loves you no matter what?"

Ashleigh's shoulders drooped. "I know he loves me and I love him. But that doesn't mean I can make him happy. It's not going to work out with us. If he'd wanted me to stay, both now and two years ago, then he would have said so. All he ever did was research into how we could have a successful pregnancy. He just kept trying to fix me."

Paula would have loved to have extended the conversation, but a nurse came in to check her incision and Ashleigh's phone began to vibrate.

"I need to take this." Ashleigh rose, then squeezed Paula's hand. "I'll be back later. Take care of yourself and your little girl—Cora," she corrected, before leaving Paula's room.

"HELLO." ASHLEIGH MODERATED her voice when she answered her cell phone while hurrying down the hallway to find a quiet place to speak to Samantha.

"Hi, Ash," her friend and colleague greeted her.

"How are you, Sam?" Ashleigh was almost hoping Sam was about to tell her she would be delayed in coming to Grand Oaks. That would give Ashleigh a few extra days before leaving town. She'd enjoyed practicing medicine again, once she'd gotten over her initial anxiety. Even being around Kyle had been incredible, except when they disagreed.

Not that she would have to worry about that anymore.

The reality was that she needed to get back to Richmond before her boss started complaining again. Having someone take over her pediatric practice was the single thing keeping her here now that Paula had delivered her baby.

No matter how much Paula might try to convince her otherwise.

Sam and Ashleigh chatted a few minutes before Sam said, "I'm getting settled in the quaint hotel you recommended and wondered if you wanted to meet for dinner."

"That sounds great." Ashleigh had no other plans. "Oh, wait, I can't." She'd forgotten about picking up the boys from Aunt Viv's. "Let me get back to you." She could ask Kyle to take them, but she didn't know if he was working.

Ashleigh ended the call and hesitated before punching Kyle's number. She wasn't in the mood to hear him berate her for whatever it was he thought she did or didn't do this time.

She took the coward's way out and texted him. He responded almost immediately, but not with the answer she expected.

Sorry, I can't. Maybe Aunt Viv can keep them longer?

He couldn't? He had plans? He would have said he was working, if that were the case, right?

Her chest tightened and she struggled to breathe. She didn't like where her mind was going. He discovered she wasn't pregnant and he'd moved on? Already?

Did he have someone waiting in the wings?

Undoubtedly someone who didn't possess her flaws.

KYLE HAD RECEIVED Ashleigh's text while he sat at a table in the break room after spending the morning on duty in the E.R. He took a bite of his apple and wondered what she had to do on a Sunday night that she needed someone to watch the boys.

Anything family-related probably would have included the boys.

His chair scraped the linoleum floor as he stood, then tossed the apple core in the trash. He had a few minutes, so he ought to go see how Paula and Cora were doing. His sister-in-law might even know what Ashleigh was up to.

"Hey," he said to Paula when he arrived at her doorway.

She greeted him with a huge grin, a proud mama with her newest offspring in her arms.

He came over to get a better look at Cora and couldn't help but be in a better mood.

"She's perfect," he told Paula.

"Yes, she is," Paula agreed. "And she's so perfect that she can stay in my room with me."

"That's great!" Relief washed over him after all Paula and Cora had been through. "Did Ashleigh come in to see her today?"

"She was just in here with me." Paula remained cheerful, unusual for when the subject of Ashleigh came up.

"Go on," he prodded, tilting his head toward her and narrowing his eyes.

Paula had a silly grin on her face. "We made real progress this morning. I think we're close to a mutual understanding."

"Really?" He had a hard time believing that after the way Ashleigh had been so cool toward him.

Or maybe it was only Kyle she had a problem with.

"Yeah," Paula said. "She asked me why I didn't side with her during the divorce."

"What did you tell her?"

"The truth. I wanted her to fight for her life, her marriage, her family. I never thought she'd give up."

"Me, either." He'd never imagined them divorced and to this day it still didn't compute.

"She's really hurt that everyone was against her. She had no one left to confide in or just talk to."

He never should have allowed Ashleigh to leave. He should have fought harder, but at the time he was grieving for their lost children and not thinking straight.

"We also had differing views of the other one's life," Paula continued, "and I know for me I see her differently now."

"How's that?"

"Turns out we're both jealous of what the other one has or has accomplished."

Kyle's eyes widened. "But you're both successful in different ways."

Paula continued, nodding her head. "Believe me, I was astonished to find out she assumed I was living the easy, perfect life here while she had the career and everything else I thought I wanted."

"Do you think Ashleigh really wants a family?" he asked.

"More than anything, from the way she spoke," Paula said. "But you know that, don't you?"

"She always said she wanted a family for me. I guess I just began to doubt whether or not it mattered that much to her."

This time Paula's eyes widened. "Kyle, of course she cared. She was devastated each time she miscarried—over and over again."

He held up a hand. "No, I knew that."

"She thinks she failed you," Paula said. "Life had always come easy for her, until she tried to have a baby. And I think that just broke her, Kyle."

Everything made so much more sense. He took a breath and tried to vocalize his thoughts clearly. "How can she think she failed me? This is all my fault. I always told her she was perfect, that we were perfect together. But when things unraveled, I didn't do enough to help her through it."

Paula didn't comment, merely waited for him to continue.

"There are other ways to make a family…if that's what she wants—we want. Truth is, children or no children, I just want to be with Ashleigh no matter what." He truly believed it. His mouth went dry. He knew in his heart he didn't want to live without her.

Paula didn't say anything for a moment. "You know how she feels about adoption," she said quietly. "Whether it's fair or not, she's not going to change her mind. She's afraid she'd be devastated if an adoption fell through."

"I know, but we could use a surrogate or even become foster parents."

"Have you mentioned that to her?"

"Well—"

Her mouth twisted into a scowl. "That's what I thought," Paula scolded.

"You're right," he said with conviction. "There's a lot we haven't talked about."

"You have to talk to her," Paula said. "You can't wait for her to come to you. She thinks she failed you. That you don't want her if she can't give you children."

"But she didn't fail me." He wanted her more than air to breathe and had never considered their miscarriages as her failure. "I want her whether we have children or not."

"Then tell her that—show her. And then ask her what she wants."

Paula's advice sounded a lot like the advice Stan gave him last night. Maybe they had a point.

"What if she doesn't want to talk to me?" he asked. "She told me we were through. She doesn't want to try again."

"How much do you want her in your life?" Paula asked.

Kyle didn't hesitate. "More than anything."

"With or without children?"

"Absolutely."

"Then tell her that—tell her what you've just told me and don't let her walk away from you." Paula was adamant. She looked him straight in the eye. "You're running out of time."

CHAPTER TWENTY

WEDNESDAY MORNING DAWNED dark and cloudy, as if the weather had become the barometer of Ashleigh's life.

She'd showered and dressed, done everything she needed to do, and now she sat at Paula's kitchen table sipping coffee, reading the *Washington Post* on her laptop and drumming her fingers.

Sunday night she'd met with Sam to discuss the pediatric practice over dinner. Sam was so enthusiastic that Ashleigh experienced a touch of jealousy.

Was she having second thoughts about giving up medicine once again?

Of course not. This was the right thing to do. It was the only thing for her to do.

Being in the same town with Kyle would be impossible. She'd spent the past three days dodging his calls and messages, but they both knew love wasn't enough to make their marriage work.

Now he was free and so was she.

Her mother had finally arrived home Sunday afternoon, so Ashleigh had left her in charge of Mark and Ryan, while she took care of personal business out of town.

Drinking down the last of her coffee, she rose from the table, rinsed the cup and put it in the dishwasher. Then she powered down her laptop, zipped it into its protective sleeve and slid it into her briefcase that sat next to the front door.

Her car was already loaded and once she made sure Paula got home okay and was settled, Ashleigh would be on her way to Richmond. Their mom was anxious to help out and Emma would be available when needed, but Paula was recovering nicely.

After all, Ashleigh would only be two hours away. Now that she and Paula had reconciled, Ashleigh had a reason to come back to visit. She and Paula had spent several hours on the phone and in person over the past few days, talking and laughing and getting back to being sisters again.

Even if she and Kyle hadn't worked out, at least she had her sister back.

Ashleigh took a last turn through the house, making sure everything was in order for Paula and Cora's arrival home. Nothing left to do but drive to the hospital.

Yesterday afternoon she'd installed Cora's car seat in Paula's van, which wasn't an easy proposition. No wonder they said so many people didn't install them properly. She'd barely made it to the police station in time to have it checked and she was pleased when they gave her the okay.

Sadly, it wasn't a skill she'd ever need again.

Fifteen minutes later, she was standing at the

doorway of Paula's hospital room. "Ready to go?" Ashleigh asked.

Paula's grin was huge as she sat on the edge of the bed in the clothes Ashleigh had brought her Monday morning. She held her daughter, who was wearing the cute pink outfit Aunt Ashleigh had bought her.

"Is the car seat installed?" Paula asked.

"Perfectly," Ashleigh told her. "At least according to the Grand Oaks Police Department."

"Very impressive." Paula grinned.

"I have some skills." Ashleigh laughed, wishing she had more time to spend with her sister. If her boss hadn't pressured her into coming back to Richmond for a meeting later today, she would have spent a few more days with Paula and her family.

After going over discharge instructions with the nurse and being pushed to the main entrance of the hospital in a wheelchair, Paula and Cora were ready and waiting by the time Ashleigh pulled the minivan into the circular driveway in front of the hospital.

Ashleigh snapped Cora's infant carrier into the car seat base so Paula didn't have to do more than get herself buckled in.

"Are you sure she's secure?" Paula asked.

"Yes, Paula, she's fine." Ashleigh didn't tell her she'd practiced last night with one of Ryan's stuffed bears. She didn't want to appear incompetent today. Even though it had been Paula who had buckled Cora in before leaving her hospital room, Ashleigh had wanted to be prepared. "I even bought one of those mirror things for her seat. That way you can see her when you're driving."

The mirror was lined up with the rearview mirror, so Ashleigh had a good view of her niece, but Paula appeared satisfied her daughter was safe.

They arrived at Paula's a few minutes later. Kyle's truck was parked at the curb. "I wonder why he's here." Ashleigh hoped she sounded casual even though her heart pounded loudly in her chest.

"Oh, I forgot to tell you he texted me while you were getting the car, to find out when I'd be home," Paula said. "He decided to meet us at my house since we were leaving the hospital. He has a present I'm guessing is for Cora, but he wouldn't say."

Ashleigh pulled into the driveway, her legs wobbly as she went around to help Paula out of the van and then Cora. As they turned to walk to the front door, it opened and there stood Scott, with Kyle right behind him.

The next few minutes were a blur. Much kissing and hugging were done by Paula and Scott as Ashleigh and Kyle looked on. Tears were plentiful and even Ashleigh became misty.

"Kyle drove to Norfolk to pick me up," Scott explained to Paula after they were settled with Cora on the couch. "The sub docked earlier than we'd planned and I was able to get leave."

Ashleigh was the outsider as they all chatted, Kyle included. Watching her sister with her husband and new baby was as painful as a knife stabbing

Ashleigh's chest. She didn't want to be jealous, but there it was.

The giant green monster was front and center, and definitely not going away.

She excused herself and went to the kitchen. Pulling her sister's van keys from her jeans pocket, she placed them next to a note she wrote to Paula.

I'm sorry for leaving without saying goodbye. My boss is adamant I get back for a meeting and I didn't want to intrude on your homecoming. Will call you soon. Love you, Ash.

She slipped out the back door without anyone noticing and started her journey back to her apartment in Richmond to resume the life she'd made there.

"CAN I GET you guys anything?" Kyle asked Scott and Paula.

"Water would be great," Paula said, and Scott agreed.

He wanted to give them a few minutes alone, but most of all he was anxious to speak to Ashleigh. She'd dodged his calls and had been missing in action the past few days. She had to be calmed down enough by now to rationally discuss their future.

When he entered the kitchen, where he expected to find her, she wasn't there.

"Paula?" Kyle shouted. He picked up the note

and headed back to the living room. "Did you know Ashleigh was leaving?"

"She's gone?" Scott said.

Kyle was numb. "Appears so." He couldn't decide if he was more hurt or angry that she'd left without saying goodbye.

Or that she left at all.

"I knew she was leaving today," Paula admitted. "I thought she'd stick around longer. At least to say goodbye."

"She did," Kyle spit. "In a note." To her sister. Nothing to him.

He wasn't sure why he was surprised. He'd known all along she'd leave town at her first opportunity.

"Where are you going?" Paula asked when he put his hand on the doorknob.

"I'm going after her," Kyle said through gritted teeth.

"You two never talked?" Her eyes widened in surprise.

"She's been avoiding me since Sunday." They needed to work things out, once and for all. "This has got to stop."

Paula didn't say a word, simply stared at him expectantly until he left her house.

Why hadn't he pushed Ashleigh harder to discuss a reconciliation?

THE DRIVE TO RICHMOND wasn't as simple as it should have been. Kyle encountered a thunderstorm that matched his mood, as well as traffic on 95, adding another twenty minutes or more to the trip.

Late in the afternoon, Kyle finally arrived at Ashleigh's apartment to discover she wasn't home. He returned to his truck and called her cell, but she didn't answer. He declined to leave a message.

He considered texting her, but figured she wouldn't reply to that, either.

Ashleigh's apartment building was one of several sixties-style buildings all in a row with tan brick facades. Traffic was heavy on the main road and three stoplights could be seen from where Kyle was parked. So different from the small, quiet town where they'd both been raised.

Kyle had never been here before. Had never been privy to any part of the new life Ashleigh had forged in Richmond.

Was she truly happy here? Happier here than in Grand Oaks with her family? With him?

Of course she was. He'd let her down. He hadn't given her what she needed—the freedom to accept her own limitations.

He leaned his head back on the seat and closed his eyes, resting until she pulled into the apartment complex's parking lot. He jolted awake when a closing car door slammed nearby.

It wasn't Ashleigh, but her car was now in the lot. She must not have noticed his truck when she'd arrived.

He made a quick decision and started the engine.

He pulled out of the parking lot in the direction of the little shop he'd seen upon his arrival.

Ten minutes later he was back at Ashleigh's door. He lifted his hand to knock, said a little prayer that she would at least listen to him and rapped on the door.

The light through the peephole disappeared and he knew she was there. The lock clicked and she slowly opened the door.

"Hi," he greeted her, noting her eyes were red as if she'd been crying.

"Hi," she whispered.

"Can I come in?" *Please don't send me away.*

The door opened wider, but she didn't say anything. He handed her the bag he'd hidden behind his back. "For you."

Her lips pursed and her eyes narrowed as she took the bag and peered into it.

"Butter pecan?" She removed the ice cream from the bag.

"I wanted bubble gum like we ate on our first date, but the store didn't have any." He was actually more nervous in this moment than he had been their first date. "I chose butter pecan since your taste has matured over the years." He swallowed his nerves. "And I'm hoping I've matured enough for you to take a chance on me."

He didn't know what to expect after blurting that out. She hugged the ice cream to her, lowered herself to the nearest chair, put her head down and began to cry.

His heart broke at her overwhelming emotion. "Hey, it's only ice cream." He knelt in front of her and took her hand.

"I saw your truck out there when I got here," she said. "You've never come here before."

"I know."

"You never came after me, Kyle." She sobbed. "You didn't even try to stop our divorce."

"I was a fool. I thought I was doing what you wanted by letting you go."

She shook her head slowly. "You know it won't work," she sobbed. "Starting over will get us to the same place."

"I disagree," he said. "Give us a chance, Ash."

"But you want a family and I can't give that to you."

"Are you telling me you never want to have a family?" He turned the tables.

"Of course I want one," she said.

"Then let's sit down and figure out how to make that happen. If I learned one thing from months of therapy, it's that you can't get what you want out of life if you're not actively pursuing it." He frowned. "I think I forgot that over the past few weeks."

"You saw a therapist?"

He nodded. "A grief counselor. She made me realize that I'd spent so much time looking for answers that I never allowed myself to grieve. I never gave you the chance to grieve, either." He kissed the back of Ashleigh's hand. "I'm so sorry that I didn't give you the support you needed. I was only concerned about fixing the problem."

She squeezed his hand. "Kyle, I ignored my grief, too, and never faced the cold, hard truth about my infertility. Instead, I started over—left my entire life behind—when I couldn't make things turn out like I thought they should."

"We both did what we believed was right at the time," he said. "Now we have a chance to start over."

Ashleigh sighed. "I flew up to Rhode Island Monday to talk to that specialist you know up there."

His eyes widened. "You went to see Lou Myers?" He hadn't a clue.

Sadness was reflected in her eyes. "Yes, and he confirmed what I already knew. There's nothing new to try. I have to accept it's not going to happen for me."

She'd been proactive by going to Rhode Island. That was a major milestone for her. "What if I say the same thing?" he asked. "What if I say I'm giving up on having children?"

"That's crazy," she said. "There's no reason for you to do that."

He squeezed her hand. "But there *is* a reason, Ashleigh. I'm in love with you, sweetheart, and that's the bottom line. I don't want to live without you. Kids or no kids, it doesn't matter. As long as you're in my life. If we're together, then nothing else matters."

She didn't look as if she believed him. "But you could find any number of women to give you the family you deserve."

"Those women aren't you," he said. "You're the only woman I've ever wanted." He didn't know how to convince her. He'd been so stupid, not telling her this before. "I know I should have said that a long time ago," he said. "But I truly thought you knew that's how I felt. Then you left and I just surrendered to the fact that I'd never be happy again."

"Really?"

"Really. Let me prove how much I love you. Start over with me, Ash." He leaned in to kiss her, sealing the promise.

"Um," Ashleigh mumbled, when he removed his mouth from hers. "I kind of gave notice to my boss this afternoon."

"You did?" Rhode Island *and* she quit her job?

"I had a lot of time to think on the drive here." Her lips twitched. "I was thinking I'd like to continue practicing medicine. There's nearly enough work for two doctors in the practice back home, and maybe Stan will only want to come back part-time."

"You were already planning on moving back to Grand Oaks?" He couldn't believe it.

A hint of a smile formed on those luscious lips of hers. He kissed her again.

"I want to be closer to Paula and her family. We've lost two years and I don't want to lose any more time."

"Oh." No mention of wanting to be with him.

"But most of all, I want to be closer to you. I knew we'd never have a chance to work things out if I didn't come back." She paused. "I do love you, Kyle."

He couldn't breathe, unable to believe what he was hearing. "I love you, too." Maybe there were no other options when it came to having a family. It didn't matter. All he wanted was Ashleigh. She was enough family for him.

He picked her up and carried her to the freezer—he didn't want the ice cream to melt. "Where's your bedroom?"

"This isn't at all like our first date." She giggled when he dropped her onto her back on the bed.

"Just like when choosing ice cream flavors, tastes mature over the years."

EPILOGUE

Less than a year later

"I WISH YOU'D TELL ME where we're going," Ashleigh told Kyle as they bumped along on the road leading out of town. "I can't believe you practically kidnapped me from the office."

Stan had decided to stay on part-time after he made a full recovery from his heart surgery, which gave Ashleigh a little freedom and time off.

"Keep your blindfold on and you'll know soon enough." Keeping one eye on the road, he reached over to the passenger seat to take Ashleigh's hand. The glint from her diamond-encrusted wedding band made him smile. "And you came willingly."

She chuckled. "You tricked me."

"Are you saying you *didn't* want me to kiss you until you melted into a puddle?" He couldn't remember ever being this happy. He squeezed her fingers that he'd laced through his.

"You whisked me out of my office blindfolded and with my hands tied behind my back!" Her outrage was comedic, but she'd forgive him as soon as they arrived at their destination.

"By the way," he said. "Edna Thornton called. She heard the lawsuit was finally thrown out and now she wants to make a large donation." After several dead ends, Tom's investigator finally found someone who would testify that the driver didn't always wear his medical-alert bracelet. When the guy found out, he dropped the lawsuit immediately.

"You're changing the subject," Ashleigh said. "Did you tell her you had other donations?"

"I didn't want her to change her mind. We can use all the financial help we can get. I was polite and thanked her." He squeezed Ashleigh's hand. "Thanks to you, too." She was the one who'd come up with several other possible donation sources and he'd moved ahead in helping children in need.

"Are we there yet?" Ashleigh squirmed in her seat.

"Almost," he cooed, withdrawing his hand from hers to enable him to turn into Aunt Vivian's long driveway. There were at least a dozen other cars parked off to the side, which was why the blindfold had been a necessity.

He parked and turned off the engine.

"Can I take this off now?" she asked.

"Not yet." He'd freed her hands earlier on the promise she wouldn't remove the blindfold until he told her to.

He got out of the truck, quietly sent Harry and Isabel away so the dogs wouldn't ruin the surprise and jogged around to Ashleigh's side to open her door. He took her hand and helped her out.

"Are we on a farm?" Her nose was in the air as she sniffed.

"You're getting warm," he said.

"Are we going horseback riding?"

"In those clothes?" He gestured, as if she could see, to her black dress pants and white blouse.

"Maybe you brought me a change of clothes?"

"That would have been a good idea, but no." He laughed.

They were at the front door and Kyle knocked loudly.

Aunt Vivian answered almost immediately. "I'm glad you could make it," as if they were the only ones at the house.

At the sound of her aunt's voice, Ashleigh ripped off her blindfold.

"Hey!" Kyle said.

Ashleigh's intake of breath was enough to make him know for sure she hadn't figured out that she was coming to a surprise baby shower.

"SURPRISE!" THE WOMEN in the full room yelled in unison, followed by excited chatter among themselves.

"What's going on?" Ashleigh knew full well what the answer was.

She looked around at who was gathered in Aunt Viv's living room, some with drinks, others with small plates of food. All focused on Ashleigh as they laughed or smiled. The energy in the room was invigorating.

Besides Aunt Viv, there was Ashleigh's mother, as well as Kyle's mother all the way from Arizona. Rosy Bausch and newly engaged Theresa had their heads together in conversation, while Cammie was perched on the ottoman near them. Paula was laughing and her darling little girl, Cora, sat on the floor next to her as she played with some colorful toys. There were a couple of women from the hospital and a few newer friends from Richmond, all gathered for one reason.

She and Kyle were expecting twins.

It still didn't seem real, but in about two months the woman sitting on the sofa near Paula—Denise—would be giving birth to their biological children. A boy and a girl. How perfect was that?

Ashleigh returned her attention to the person who'd made it happen. Her sister, Paula. She'd put them in touch with a friend of hers, a military wife who had been a surrogate once before and whose husband was deployed.

The babies would be their biological children, using Ashleigh's eggs and Kyle's sperm by in vitro fertilization. A true miracle, thanks to the advice Kyle's Rhode Island colleague had given her.

She'd even looked into adoption in case the in vitro didn't take, after she realized Kyle had been right about only needing each other to be happy. Anything else would be a bonus. Together they could handle anything.

Ashleigh walked over to Denise. "How are you doing?" The pregnancy had happened so fast and on the first try.

Meant to be, as Kyle referred to it.

Denise patted her large belly. "We're all hanging in there," she said with a laugh.

"I wish they'd get here," Paula said. "Cora is growing up too quickly and I can't wait to hold my tiny niece and nephew." Paula had begun classes last fall and Ashleigh had helped to watch Cora and her brothers. They'd decided that when the twins were born, Ashleigh could cut back her hours and Paula could babysit when she wasn't in class. Their mother was anxious to help out, too.

Kyle came up behind Ashleigh and kissed the nape of her neck, making her smile.

"Hey, Denise." He greeted their surrogate, then whispered in Ashleigh's ear, "Scott and I are taking the boys to laser tag."

Ashleigh turned to see Scott at the front door. She waved to her brother-in-law, who had recently returned from another deployment. "Have a great time." Then she pointed at Denise and raised her eyebrows at Kyle, "Take advantage of your freedom now because that will end the minute our babies are born."

He laughed and kissed her again, this time on the lips. "I can't wait." He made his way to the front

door. Their love could withstand anything if she allowed it to.

She turned back to join the party and was overwhelmed by the cocoon of love and support she'd
been given. Her homecoming had been pretty rocky
at first, but, in the end, everything turned out to be
pretty darn perfect.

Why hadn't she considered the surrogacy option
before? She'd asked that question repeatedly over
the past months and kept coming up with the same
answer.

Probably because she'd been desperately trying to
deny that she wasn't perfect.

Turns out, imperfect was okay.

Kyle turned at the door to flash her a smile. More
than okay, she amended.

* * * * *

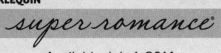

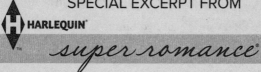
Cop by Her Side

By Janice Kay Johnson

Jane felt a weird twist in her chest when she saw the displayed
name on her cell phone. Clay Renner. Somehow, despite the
disastrous end to their brief relationship, she'd never deleted
his phone number from her address book. Why would *he* be
calling in the middle of the afternoon?

"Vahalik."

"Jane, Clay Renner here."

As always, she reacted to his voice in a way that aggravated
her. It was so blasted *male*.

"Sergeant," she said stiffly.

"This is about your sister." He hesitated. "We've found
Melissa's vehicle located in a ditch. She suffered a head injury,
Jane. She's in ICU. But I'm focusing on another problem.

The girl, Brianna, is missing."

Of all the things she'd expected him to say, this didn't even come close.

"*What?*" she whispered. "Did anyone see the accident?"

"Unfortunately, no. Some hikers came along afterward."

"If another car caused the accident and the driver freaked…?" Even in shock, she knew that was stupid.

"A logical assumption, except that we've been unable to locate Brianna. We still haven't given up hope that your sister dropped her off somewhere, but at this point—"

"You have no idea where she is." Ouch. She sounded so harsh.

"Thanks for the vote of confidence, Lieutenant."

She closed her eyes. As angry as she still was at him, she knew he was a smart cop and a strong man. He didn't need her attitude. "I'm sorry. I didn't mean…"

"We're organizing a search."

She swallowed, trying to think past her panic. "I'll come help search."

"All right," Clay said. He told her where the SUV had gone off the road. "You okay to drive?"

"Of course I am!"

"Then I'll look for you."

Those were the most reassuring words he'd said during the entire conversation. And as Jane disconnected, she didn't want to think about how much she wanted *his* reassurance.

Will this case bring Clay and Jane together?
Find out what happens in COP BY HER SIDE
by Janice Kay Johnson, available July 2014 from
Harlequin® Superromance®.
And look for the other books in
***The Mysteries of Angel Butte* series.**

LARGER-PRINT BOOKS!
GET 2 FREE LARGER-PRINT NOVELS PLUS 2 FREE GIFTS!

HARLEQUIN
super romance

More Story...More Romance

YES! Please send me 2 FREE LARGER-PRINT Harlequin® Superromance® novels and my 2 FREE gifts (gifts are worth about $10). After receiving them, if I don't wish to receive any more books, I can return the shipping statement marked "cancel." If I don't cancel, I will receive 6 brand-new novels every month and be billed just $5.69 per book in the U.S. or $5.99 per book in Canada. That's a savings of at least 16% off the cover price! It's quite a bargain! Shipping and handling is just 50¢ per book in the U.S. or 75¢ per book in Canada.* I understand that accepting the 2 free books and gifts places me under no obligation to buy anything. I can always return a shipment and cancel at any time. Even if I never buy another book, the two free books and gifts are mine to keep forever.

139/339 HDN F46Y

Name _____ (PLEASE PRINT) _____

Address _____ Apt. # _____

City _____ State/Prov. _____ Zip/Postal Code _____

Signature (if under 18, a parent or guardian must sign)

Mail to the **Harlequin® Reader Service:**
IN U.S.A.: P.O. Box 1867, Buffalo, NY 14240-1867
IN CANADA: P.O. Box 609, Fort Erie, Ontario L2A 5X3
**Are you a current subscriber to Harlequin Superromance books
and want to receive the larger-print edition?
Call 1-800-873-8635 today or visit www.ReaderService.com.**

* Terms and prices subject to change without notice. Prices do not include applicable taxes. Sales tax applicable in N.Y. Canadian residents will be charged applicable taxes. Offer not valid in Quebec. This offer is limited to one order per household. Not valid for current subscribers to Harlequin Superromance Larger-Print books. All orders subject to credit approval. Credit or debit balances in a customer's account(s) may be offset by any other outstanding balance owed by or to the customer. Please allow 4 to 6 weeks for delivery. Offer available while quantities last.

Your Privacy—The Harlequin® Reader Service is committed to protecting your privacy. Our Privacy Policy is available online at www.ReaderService.com or upon request from the Harlequin Reader Service.

We make a portion of our mailing list available to reputable third parties that offer products we believe may interest you. If you prefer that we not exchange your name with third parties, or if you wish to clarify or modify your communication preferences, please visit us at www.ReaderService.com/consumerschoice or write to us at Harlequin Reader Service Preference Service, P.O. Box 9062, Buffalo, NY 14269. Include your complete name and address.

HSRLP13R